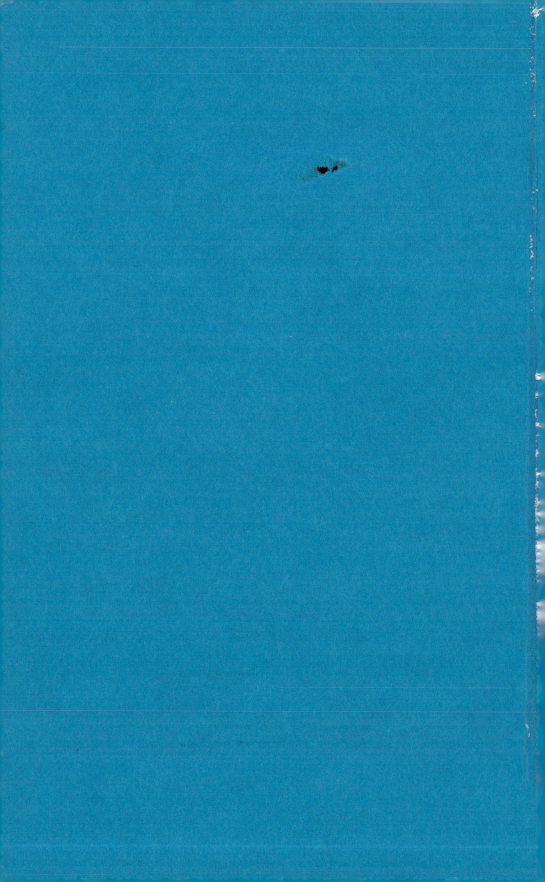

SMOKE OVER MALIBU

Also by Tim Walker

Completion

TIM WALKER

SMOKE OVER MALIBU

WILLIAM HEINEMANN: LONDON

1 3 5 7 9 10 8 6 4 2

William Heinemann
20 Vauxhall Bridge Road
London SW1V 2SA

William Heinemann is part of the Penguin Random House group of companies
whose addresses can be found at global.penguinrandomhouse.com.

Copyright © Tim Walker 2017

First published by William Heinemann in 2017

www.penguin.co.uk

A CIP catalogue record for this book is available from the British Library.

ISBN 9780434022571

Set in 13/15.5 pt Fournier MT
Typeset by Jouve (UK), Milton Keynes
Printed and bound by Clays Ltd, St Ives plc

Penguin Random House is committed to a sustainable future
for our business, our readers and our planet. This book is made
from Forest Stewardship Council® certified paper.

To Bea

[Hollywood's] conception of what makes a good picture is still as juvenile as its treatment of writing talent is insulting and degrading.

> — Raymond Chandler, from 'Writers in Hollywood' (1945)

Whenever a friend succeeds, a little something in me dies.

> — Gore Vidal

The dead guy's place was in the Canyons, at the end of one of those bronchial cul-de-sacs above Franklin that I can still never find without the GPS. The homes petered out into parched scrub and eucalyptus at the top of the street, where the bungalow I was hunting squatted alone on a knoll like a kid left out of a game. As I parked the truck in the turnaround, the sound startled a gang of mule deer who'd been grazing on the slope across from the house. They hurried away through the undergrowth, into the hills beneath the Hollywood sign. I killed the engine and stared after them awhile, still only half-awake. It was eight-fifteen a.m.

I could tell you about the weather, but this is Los Angeles – you already know about the weather. So I'll tell you about the bungalow: it was a 1940s Craftsman in avocado, with white trim, leaded windows and a long porch at the top of a steep flight of wooden steps. Cleo Habibi idled in the porch-swing at the summit, flaunting her West Coast dentistry as I clambered to meet her.

'Hey, Lucky.'

Cleo had on her sale-day ensemble: blue jeans to signify the weekend; a grey blazer that says she's all business. She was hugging her tablet computer. As I reached the top step, she raised a long, black Audrey Hepburn eyebrow and waited for me to catch my breath. I'd achieved consciousness on the couch an hour beforehand, with just enough time to choose between a shower, a shave or a pot of coffee. I chose the coffee.

'Man, you look rough,' she said. 'Need a lie-down?'

'Very funny. Who's the stiff?'

'Name's Marty Kann. Seventy-four. Production designer, retired. Massive stroke. Survived his darling wife Pam by a mere eighteen months.'

'That's sweet.'

'Ain't it.'

'Spawn?'

'One. Marty Jr. Lives in Reno.'

'Well, somebody has to.'

She handed me the tablet, and I scanned the items she'd marked for my attention: a Spanish Revival-style tile table; two Bill Curry Stemlite lamps; some vintage movie merch. A respectable inventory.

'We just dug out a couple Native American baskets,' she said. 'Could be authentic; could be from one of those gift shops down at the pueblo. But you should take a look. Mrs Kann was a set decorator. These two had taste.'

'Sure. Thanks, Cleo.'

Cleo Habibi will as happily unload the home of a dead parking valet as a dead movie star. But whether it's some Holmby Hills pile or a *casita* in Highland Park, her commission is a flat 30 per cent, and she is a sucker for nothing – except, on occasion, an English accent. Hence our arrangement: I get a tip-off and first refusal on any promising Californian *objets*; she gets a good price and half an hour of my scintillating conversation. She's single with forty in the headlights, just like yours truly. We all get our kicks where we can.

'You want to wait for your partner?'

'Nah, he'll be a while. You know Raúl.'

'Okay,' she said. 'Then let's get started.'

Estate sales are installation art, each bereft home a retrospective, curated by Cleo's assistant Yolanda and her menopausal minions. They clean, they catalogue, they value, they display. Every Habibi Estates home has the same odour, a blend of industrial-cleaning products disguising the olfactory traces of the departed: their cologne, their last cooked meal, their valedictory bowel movement.

The house was bigger inside than out. The handsome, high-ceilinged sitting room had a view through to the galley kitchen and a Danish drop-leaf table set for six. A side corridor led to the bathroom, two bedrooms and a study. Beyond the dining room, sliding glass doors gave out onto a patio and a once-prim back garden, now browning with neglect.

Cleo was right – these two had taste. The decor may have been dated, but it was composed with an artist's eye. Each room had its own distinct, detailed vibe like the different rides at Disneyland: the sitting room was an Alpine ski lodge, the kitchen a kitschy roadside diner. The bathroom had hinoki panelling and a bamboo feature, as if transplanted whole from a Japanese tea house.

'Nice place,' I said.

Cleo folded her arms. 'We did *not* find it this way.'

'No?'

'Not at all. Those eighteen months Marty was alone? He did a good job burying all this in garbage. Looked like a flophouse. Smelled like a bar.'

'Huh. So you tampered with the evidence.'

'My guess? Guy drank himself to death.'

'Loneliness,' I replied. 'It's a killer.'

She frowned and looked at the floor, and I figured I'd said the wrong thing. I changed the subject: 'Let's start in the kitchen.'

Hollywood can be barren ground for an antique picker; almost no one stays in the neighbourhood long enough to gather a trove of lasting value. But the Kanns had found their homestead and settled. I could tell as much by the microwave oven built into the turquoise kitchen surround; it was the size of a minivan, manufactured no later than the mid-'80s. Old people rarely redecorate, so by the time they finally expire, their properties are amber-clad mosquitoes, deep-storing the DNA of at least two decades previously. I browsed the spines of Pam Kann's cookbooks: Julia Child, *Wok Cooking Made Easy*, *The Essential Salad Compendium*.

The Kanns liked to travel. In one of the kitchen cabinets was a selection of souvenir coffee mugs. The Dr Pepper Museum in Waco, Texas. The John A. Roebling Suspension Bridge in Cincinnati, Ohio. In the open cupboard below, I found the first item worth my time.

'Hey, Cleo, you know what this is?'

I took a stout ceramic figure from the cupboard and set him on the Formica countertop between two stacks of matching crockery. He was ten inches tall and almost as wide, wearing red tails, a green waistcoat, riding boots and a top hat, with a bullwhip coiled at his waist.

'I have a feeling you're going to tell me.'

'You ever see *Dumbo*?'

'The flying elephant? When I was a kid, I guess.'

'This is the Ringmaster, from the circus. The bad guy. Remember?'

Cleo shrugged. 'Nope.'

I lifted the Ringmaster's head and shoulders free of his body.

'He's a cookie jar, see?'

'He's ugly as shit.'

I smirked and studied the jar. The glaze was mostly in fine condition, though I could see a fingernail chip on the lid's inside rim and a hairline crack on the base. He *was* ugly, but I didn't much care: I still get that first-kiss thrill anytime I find a piece with a history, lurking in a cupboard or a loft. I wondered whether the Kanns were accidental collectors, or connoisseurs.

'See that?' I pointed to the maker's mark. 'Kirby Balboa pottery, Newport Beach. Licensed by Disney to make official ceramic merchandise. *Dumbo* was, what . . . nineteen-forty? 'Forty-one?'

'Beats me.'

'Well, he doesn't look too bad for seventy-something. I'll give you two-fifty.'

'Two hundred and fifty bucks? For *that* thing?'

'He's worth more. Cookie jars are a hot market.'

'Wow. Okay, sold.'

'And I could've had him for twenty. Aren't you glad I'm so honest?'

'Honest as a bus-bench lawyer,' said Cleo, who then turned and yelled over her shoulder: 'Yolanda. YOLANDA!'

Her assistant shuffled into the kitchen wearing a Habibi Estates-branded polo and Marigolds, holding what looked like the dust filter from a vacuum cleaner.

'Would you please bubble-wrap this monstrosity for Lucky?'

Yolanda nodded quickly.

'*Thaaaank* you.'

Cleo carried a sheet of red spot stickers, and she slapped one on every piece I picked. In the sitting room was the Spanish Revival-style side table, with six decorative tiles inlaid in walnut, depicting a Conestoga wagon crossing the Sierra, its Stetsoned guide clip-clopping ahead. Minimal wear and tear. Red spot. A rare and elegant Kem Weber Airline chair faced the hearth, re-upholstered but otherwise in excellent nick: a mid-century piece worthy of a museum exhibit.

'You said he was a production designer?'

'That's right. And she was a set decorator.'

'Huh. Makes sense.'

Someone had arrayed a selection of empty picture frames on the mantelpiece. A plastic Christmas spruce stood tilting towards the hearth, adorned with baubles as if it were mid-December. The tree was $15, the decorations $40 for the set.

At the back of the wardrobe in the master bedroom, behind a thicket of wooden shoe trees, I found a gym bag containing tinned food, chlorine tabs, a first-aid kit, a torch and extra batteries: the Kanns were earthquake-ready, just in case The Big One struck. That noodle soup won't save you now, I thought to myself. I disregarded the clothes and demanded red spots for the Stemlite reading lamps and the Navajo Dazzler rug at the foot of the queen-size bed.

'These are the baskets I was talking about,' Cleo said. 'What do you think?'

Yolanda and her subordinates had filled two coiled juncus baskets with old sunglasses and scents and arranged them side by side on top of the dresser.

'They look like tat,' I said. 'But I'll take them, see what the boss thinks.'

Cleo emptied the baskets onto the bedspread so I could take a closer look at the weave. I couldn't say for sure – I just work here – but I had a feeling they were Mission Indian-made, maybe even nineteenth century. That meant a three-figure price tag. I decided I'd been generous to warn Cleo of the cookie jar's worth.

'I'll give you fifty for the pair,' I said.

'Fifty dollars? You've got to be kidding.'

'Fine,' I replied, and I knelt to roll up the rug. This is how we flirt.

'Eighty.'

'Come on, Cleo. I'm giving you good money for the Weber chair.'

'Okay. Seventy.'

'You're haggling for the sake of ten dollars?'

'Screw you. A hundred.'

'Alright, alright. Seventy.'

The second bedroom still bore the unmistakable traces of a teenage Marty Jr: racks of redundant CDs, ranks of plastic action figures and an old games console coated in the accumulated grease of a dozen kids' fingertips. Peeling bubble-gum stickers papered the chest of drawers. The walls were a map of questionable pop-cultural landmarks, and I tutted as my eye passed over posters for *Deadbolt* and *Axeman*, both tawdry comic-book blockbusters from the early aughts.

'What?'

'All this superhero crap,' I said.

Cleo chuckled to herself. 'So British.'

Americans still think I sound English; to the English, I'm beginning to sound American. Plummy accent, apple-pie vocab.

Marty Kann's study was snug and neat, the latter of which was likely Yolanda's doing. Facing the desk was a nearly-new Herman Miller chair with added lumbar support, the essential accessory of the sedentary, 21st-century creative. The shelves bore art books, pulp novels, ancient VHS tapes and a smattering of studio ephemera. On the walls, among the empty hooks where favoured pictures had already been removed, were framed set photos from films on which I supposed he'd earned production credits: some sci-fi, some fantasy, a couple of corny thrillers and an old Kurt Russell movie I'd never seen.

I was a writer in another life, so I have a thing for desks, and Marty did not disappoint. He'd spent at least the last few years of his career behind a single-pedestal, brushed-steel tanker desk, a weighty, purposeful worktop for a man who means it. A Boston sharpener was clamped to one edge, handy for whittling Blackwings. He'd fitted locking castors to the legs, and I could see the ruts in the shagpile where he'd moved it to the far wall to escape the diverting view from his window – a patch of lawn, a lemon tree. I examined the manufacturer's brand beneath the keyhole on the pencil drawer: McDowell & Craig, Norwalk, CA.

'We couldn't find the key,' said Cleo. 'But the drawer's unlocked.'

'Not a problem,' I said, brushing my palm across the metal desktop. 'We can get the lock changed. With a spit and polish, this'll fetch eight hundred. Will you take four-fifty?'

'Six?'

'Five-fifty.'

We shook on it, and Cleo tapped the details into her tablet. Beside the desk were two packing boxes filled with Marty's pencils and unused sketchbooks; two more with old, rolled drawings. Most of his work had gone to his son or to a studio archive, said Cleo. I offered her fifty clams for what remained, assuming there'd be something in there to frame up and flog to a film buff. A final box held reams of blank stationery, some of it personalised. I admire a guy who still composes his correspondence in longhand. But really, who was going to buy a dead man's letterhead?

I've now and then found major pottery nestling in the grasses of old Hancock Park mansions, but the Kanns' yard was unremarkable. The planting beds were stripped, the water feature stagnant. I gave the wicker furniture a once-over. Cleo shaded her eyes and watched scrub jays flitting through the bougainvillea.

The back entrance to the garage was down a set of cement steps to the side of the house. The space had been converted into an artist's studio. Inside, one of Cleo's employees was arranging easels and oil paints. Canvases leaned in a stack against the wall, the top one smeared with depressive, expressionist stripes of grey, green and taupe.

'Who was the painter?'

Cleo shrugged again. 'I guess Marty,' she replied.

'Not a fan?'

'I don't really go for that abstract stuff.'

'Tell you what,' I said, inspecting another canvas and finding more of the same, 'I think you were right about the drinking.'

I turned to find Cleo holding an old, red firefighter's helmet, partially blackened by fire damage, with the words 'Engine 13' on the front.

'Recognise this?' she said. 'It's the guy's helmet from *Axeman*. Guess Marty or Pam must've worked on that movie. Did you see it?'

I scoffed: 'What do you think?'

'I take it you're not interested,' she replied, and put the helmet back on its shelf. 'Your loss. Some geek is gonna love it.'

10

On another shelf I noticed two leather baseball gloves – one child-sized, one adult – and was momentarily bummed out by the thought that Marty and Marty Jr would never play catch again. A dusty diner neon hung high on the wall, refugee from the scenery of some rock-and-roll period piece: 'Burgers Fries Shakes'. It looked fixable. Red spot. A pair of small pet crates had been stacked next to packing boxes bearing the Habibi Estates logo, which were stuffed with *Life* magazines, copies of *Reader's Digest* and Marty Jr's old comic books.

'They had cats?'

Another shrug. To take too great an interest in the emotional lives of an estate's late owners – their work, their relationships, their pets – would be to confront the melancholy realities of her business. I could hardly blame Cleo for keeping her distance. She flicked a switch, and the rusty garage door heaved itself open with a scream.

2

A courier's note poked from the Kanns' mailbox, saying *Sorry We Missed You*. It had started to yellow and curl in the heat. Two senior señoras were already in line at the foot of the porch steps, waiting for the sale to commence at ten a.m. Cleo's most committed regulars, they glared at me as I emerged from the garage, terminally resentful of the VIP privileges I was afforded by Habibi Estates. I waved to them, teasing. 'Hello, ladies.'

Across the street, Raúl Gupta was lounging against the truck, eating a breakfast burrito. Specks of scrambled egg garnished his moustache. He was resting both elbows on the bonnet behind him, which merely accentuated the proud thrust of his pot belly. We both have our stomachs, Raúl and I, but mine is the understated paunch of a slender six-footer, concealed for the most part by dark sweaters or fitted shirts. Raúl's, by contrast, busies itself beneath his too-small logo Ts like a raccoon rummaging through a handbag. Mine is a symptom of age and laziness, his is a fundamental feature. He made a little bow as I approached.

'My liege,' he said, doffing his Ray-Bans.

A lot of people in LA rise early for conference calls to New York and London, but Raúl seems to live on Hawaii time. Ever since his Camry had a falling-out with a fire hydrant, he's also missing a car — and the cul-de-sac was an uphill walk from the closest bus stop. Add to that the leash around his wrist, which was attached to his obstinate French bulldog, and you have a tasting menu of the excuses I was about to hear for his being almost a full hour late.

'I bought you breakfast,' he said, and produced a second foil-wrapped burrito from his back pocket, distorted by the curve of his buttock.

'Thanks,' I replied. 'I'll eat after.'

The dog sat blinking on the bench seat of the truck as we shouldered the tools of our trade: moving blankets, shrink-wrap, a stair-climbing dolly. We worked through the house methodically, Cleo trailing behind, crossing each item off her inventory. The line of impatient shoppers snaked along the block by the time we clanged down the steps with the tanker desk strapped to the dolly, both of us clinging on like cattle wranglers.

To look at us you'd think Raúl was the one out of shape, but after we'd hefted the desk into the truck, it's me who was wheezing, sweaty as a Coke from the freezer cabinet. I let Raúl secure our haul, while I wrote out a cheque to Habibi Estates and Cleo addressed the queue from the porch balustrade: 'Ladies, no large handbags near the jewellery! Gentlemen, no fighting over the Frank Sinatra records . . .'

Raúl hopped from the tailgate to the tarmac. 'Gimme a minute,' he said, and he jogged back towards the garage. I pondered the people in line. The two old maids vied for pole position: eternal rivals bonded by a mutual respect, the McEnroe and Borg of weekend antiquing. Behind them, a heavyset Latino gentleman with untidy facial hair; a pair of old hippies, or else ageing studio execs in mufti; a woman dragging a toddler in a tutu, perchance lost en route to a child beauty pageant; a speckling of hipsters, one straight-facedly sporting a fedora.

Once they were inside, the competition could be fierce. Cleo's customers were not above switching price tags. Some would secrete costlier items around the house and return to buy them for half-price after the midday markdown.

I watched as a station wagon pulled up and spewed out three generations of suburban soccer mom. They joined the line behind a guy with a mobility walker, whom I fancied wouldn't even make it as far as the front door. Many of Cleo's most loyal customers were only a few bridge hands from the grave, but as their health faded, the urge to hoard burned ever brighter. Good news for Cleo: when they shuffled off a year or two hence, she could sell the same old rubbish all over again.

As the shoppers finally climbed the steps to the bungalow, Raúl returned from the garage with his arms full. Under his left was one of the pet crates; under his right, one of the packing boxes filled with magazines.

'Is he *still* not house-trained?' I said.

'C'mon, Lucky,' said Raúl. 'Give the kid a break.'

Rather than teach his pet to defecate outdoors, Raúl had papered his floors with newsprint, and then repeatedly failed to admonish the animal when it crapped all over the condo. Now the wretched creature would only perform a bowel movement if it was hunkered down on a copy of *California Sunday*. Hence the magazines. The little dog stared inscrutably at us both.

'Does he actually do anything except eat, sleep and shit?'

'He has *mucho* skills,' said Raúl. 'He is a crime deterrent. He is a fantastic listener. And he sucks in women like a goddam shoestore.'

'Really? Because to me, he reads kind of gay.'

Raúl ignored that and held out the crate for the dog to nose. 'Look what I got, buddy. Now you can travel *anywhere*. The world is your oyster!'

'Isn't that like sleeping in a dead person's bed? What if it's haunted by a cat?'

Cleo strolled to us across the turnaround. I held out the cheque, which she folded into her blazer pocket.

'Pleasure as always,' she said. 'So I'll see you soon?'

'As long as people keep dying,' I replied.

She noticed the dog, still mute and inert in the driving seat.

'*AAAwww!* Is that a French bulldog? Is he *yours*, Raúl? What's his name?'

'Burgers,' said Raúl.

Cleo paused and pursed her lips.

'Burgers? Why'd you call him *Burgers*?'

'Because imagine me standing in the middle of a park with my empty dog leash, yelling *"Burgers! Burgers!"* . . .'

She considered the image in silence for a second, and then tipped her head back and laughed, grabbing Raúl's arm to keep her balance. Raúl nodded triumphantly at her amusement. 'And *that*,' he said, 'is why I called him Burgers.'

Cleo recovered and sighed and dried her dark eyes delicately so as not to smudge her mascara. She bent over to ruffle the dog's ears.

'Aaawww, Burgers,' she said. 'You are so *cute*!'

Raúl just gave me a long look, steady and smug, as if to say: *See?*

The truck is a customised Dodge cube, circa 1985, with bouncy suspension, duff a/c and half a million miles on the clock. It has the words 'Bart's Olde California' and a phone number stencilled along the side. Bart has added some other personal touches over the years, like the ladder rack and the running board. The faulty mechanical tail-lift is long gone, and in its place Bart has jerry-rigged a retractable stepladder to save his AARP knees from hopping on and off the tailgate.

He ought to have traded the vehicle in years ago but, being an antique dealer, he's disinclined to replace anything that still functions.

The cab smells like the '80s: cigs, stale Nescafé, synthetic fibres. Hell, it even sounds like the '80s. The radio's bust and can only find KCRW for seconds at a time, but there's a cassette player and a handful of Bart's old tapes in the glove compartment with the paperwork and the peppermint Altoids. We've a choice of *Graceland*, *After the Gold Rush*, *Running on Empty* or – Raúl's favourite – the original Broadway cast recording of *Les Misérables*. The lyrics to 'I Dreamed a Dream' are baked into my subconscious, like the unwanted raisins in an oatmeal cookie.

I fought hard with the stick and the wheel to squeeze out of the turnaround, now that the truck was heavy with furniture and the shoppers' parked cars had congested the kerbs. Cleo stood in the door of the garage, smiling wryly at my efforts. Looming at her shoulder, as uncomfortably close as a tailgating lorry, was the heavyset guy with the scruffy facial hair. He was holding the *Axeman* helmet, and he watched with narrowed eyes as we rolled away.

'Hey,' said Raúl. 'Was that Paul Giamatti?'

'Paul Giamatti the *actor*? Where?'

'In the garage. That fat guy. Looked like Paul Giamatti.'

'What? That guy looked nothing like Paul Giamatti.'

'He was like a Latino Paul Giamatti.'

'Well, then he wasn't Paul Giamatti.'

'But he *looked* like Paul Giamatti, is what I'm saying.'

'Sure. If Paul Giamatti were ten years older, a foot taller, twenty pounds heavier and had another guy's face.'

'Hey, Giamatti is extremely versatile.'

I had only consumed half of my warped breakfast burrito; the remainder sat wrapped in one of the cup holders. I could sense Raúl sizing it up. Burgers perched on his lap, peering over the dashboard.

'You can eat that if you want,' I said.

'Really?'

'Yeah, I'm done.'

'You hear that, Burgers?'

Raúl had torn some pages from one of Marty Kann's old subscriptions and laid them in the base of the pet crate, which sat between us on the bench seat. Now he slid the burrito from its foil wrapping and put it inside, tugging a morsel of chorizo from the tortilla and offering it to the dog. Burgers sniffed it, licked it, and then allowed himself to be led into the crate by the nose. Raúl closed the cage door behind him. I could hear Burgers masticating over the rattle of the engine.

'So I put your name on the guest list for *Blowing Up* at the Lo-Ball,' said Raúl.

'Huh,' I replied, trying to sound grateful but non-committal.

'Plus one,' he said. 'Bring a lady.'

'Huh,' I said again, eyes on the road. 'So what is it, like an open-mic night?'

'An *open-mic night*? Who do you think I am? It's *Blowing Up*! It's one of the city's top comedy nights. Read *LA Weekly* once in a while, asshole.'

In the two years we'd worked together, I'd avoided ever seeing Raúl's stand-up act — mostly out of fear: fear he'd be bad; fear he'd be good. The fear is laced with envy, that he possesses the *cojones* to stand alone before a crowd and invite their judgement. The Lo-Ball was high stakes — his biggest gig to date — and he was uncharacteristically anxious. I'd yet to decide whether I could bear to attend.

'Are they paying you?'

'Headliner gets a share of the door. I get free drinks. But if I do good, Verne says he'll make me a regular.'

We paused at a Stop sign on Beachwood. I pulled my e-cigarette from my jeans pocket and puffed on it. E-cigarettes are to cigarettes what *The Godfather Part III* is to *The Godfather Part II*, but you can only hock so much phlegm before you start to get spooked by the prospect of lung cancer.

'That shit'll kill you,' said Raúl.

'No, it won't. That's the whole point.'

'Is it FDA-approved? I don't think so.'

'Jesus, Raúl. It's lighter than a Marlboro Light.'

'Whatever you say, Sir Lucky. I just think: if you're gonna quit, then quit.'

This 'Sir Lucky' nonsense? I am the second son of a minor English aristocrat and his American trophy wife. Pater's proper title is Alistair Kluge, Viscount Wonersh, which makes me the Hon. Lucius Kluge: Honourable, Lucky, Clever. Are any of those adjectives accurate? Everything's relative.

Raúl Gupta is how this fish-out-of-water comedy becomes a buddy flick. Part Chicano, part Gujarati, all Angeleno: Eastern flavours swaddled in SoCal culture, like a Korean taco. At law school he played percussion for a post-post-punk band, which gave him an appetite for the limelight that, at twenty-nine, remains unsatisfied.

'So tell me a joke,' I said. 'What should I expect from your act?'

'I cover a lot of topics,' Raúl replied. 'Dating, dog ownership, coffee culture, Asian-American enterprise, my parents. But I can't just do you a bit in the frickin' truck. Besides, the element of surprise is a crucial tool in a comic's arsenal.'

I inhaled another hit of liquid nicotine. 'Did you compose that mantra yourself, or do they teach it in Comedy 101?'

He turned to look at me, less than impressed. 'Do you act like a douchebag on purpose?' he said. 'Or does it come naturally?'

I grinned: I do it on purpose. I swung the truck onto Franklin, squinting as the mid-morning sun cut through the cab like a reprimand.

3

Bart's Olde California is in Los Feliz, at the intersection of Hollywood and Hipster. Around here, gentrification can be swift and merciless; the Korean nail bar next-door recently became a vegan café. So far, the store has stayed afloat on the rising rents, but not even Bart has sandbags enough to stem the flood of design boutiques and gourmet burger joints. In the car park out back, I eased the truck into the space next to my jeep – a '74 Bronco: one of the last good years. Thanks to that breakfast burrito, the cab now stank of dog poop. I left Raúl to clean up and went inside.

The store takes up 3,500 square feet of prime Los Angeles real estate, approximately 3,450 of which are occupied by antiques. If you walked in off the street by chance, you'd think Norma Desmond and Charles Foster Kane were having a garage sale. Furniture fills the floors and art the walls, illuminated with mixed efficiency by lighting features from every era since the birth of the electric bulb, which is just barely younger than the state of California. Whether it's Spanish Revival, Mission or Monterey, if it has a place in the history of the Golden State, then it falls within our purview.

A groovy mid-century boomerang table is stacked atop a Colonial chest. Art Deco kitchen cabinets are clogged with hand-painted Catalina plates. A high-backed wooden Windsor chair sits alongside an Eames recliner, like a college kid and his grandfather watching *Monday Night Football* in the man-cave. One wall is smothered in old signage; the neons have to be lit on rotation to keep a lid on the electricity bills. Customers are greeted at the door by our mascot, Oscar: a life-sized fibreglass ostrich whom Bart claims once graced the grounds of Lucille Ball's Beverly Hills estate. He's about the only thing in the store that's not for sale.

Passing trade can be put off by our prices – but hey, we're an antiques emporium, not a junk shop. And business is sufficiently brisk, because everybody likes to mix their Ikea clutter with something singular: a Gucci belt to hold up their Gap slacks. Besides, people here are positively awestruck by anything remotely old. The framed 1899 Bison Brewing Co. lithograph that hangs on the wall behind the cash register would be one of the youngest items in my father's house; to Californians it might as well be a cave painting. For most Angelenos, our selection of 1920s Gladding McBean lamps with hand-stained glass shades are as ancient as two pieces of flint struck together to make a spark.

People once came to Southern California for their health, believing the blue skies and the sultry Santa Anas could cure their tuberculosis, their pneumonia, their conscience, their insomnia. But really, they were just coming here to die. And if our catalogue is anything to go by, they kept right on coming.

Bart Abernathy's ancestors were forty-niners, which makes him that rare thing, a sixth-generation Californian. He turned seventy a while back and started to stoop, though you'd never guess his age from his glowing umber complexion. He has a wardrobe full of billowing silk Aloha shirts. It's possible they were briefly on-trend in about 1976; I'm too young to recall. Today's was turquoise, with a sea-life pattern: starfish, orcas, octopi. I found him trying single-handedly to move a mahogany dresser into a new spot.

'Seriously, Bart. You've got to stop doing the heavy lifting,' I said. 'You're going to give yourself another hernia.'

'Well, if it isn't the Lone Ranger,' Bart replied, plucking a handkerchief from his trouser pocket to mop his brow. 'Where's Tonto?'

'Out the back. We picked some great pieces at Cleo's sale.'

'Oh, yeah?'

'Mid-century, mostly. An Airline chair – haven't seen one of those in a while. And some juncus baskets that I want you to check out.'

'Well, that's just great. Good job, Lucky. Now, lend me a hand.'

I wouldn't go so far as to call Bart a mentor, much as he'd like me to. But I enjoy earning his approval, and he enjoys bestowing it. Together, we shoved the dresser up against the wall next to a display case filled with old bowie knives. Bart took a moment to compose himself after all the exertion, and then retreated to his swivel chair behind the cash register.

The back door swung shut with a bang as Raúl came in, carrying Burgers and cursing to himself. He set the bulldog down and it trotted to the beanbag at Bart's feet, where it keeled over and dozed.

'Hey there, hombre,' said Bart. 'What's the rumpus?'

'It's Sasquatch Pete,' Raúl replied. 'Says we have to move the truck again. Says his delivery guy can't get into the spot. Asshole.'

Sasquatch Pete owns the new café next door. He is the biggest, most irritable vegan east of the 405, and he's always complaining that our truck is too large for the car park. This, by the way, was never a problem for the Koreans.

'Well,' said Bart, 'God forbid Pete should ever go without his tempeh bacon.'

'Let him simmer,' I said. 'I'll move it in a while.'

Bart put on the pair of spectacles that dangled from a string around his neck. He prodded the computer keyboard on the desk by the register, as if assessing its ripeness. 'Raúl,' he said, 'I have an email here from a gentleman in Boulder, who is looking to purchase one of the Juan Camilo watercolours. I hoped you might be able to arrange the logistics before lunch.'

Bart has only recently bowed to the imperatives of the internet, and he still has difficulty achieving anything more complex online than sending an email. So it falls to Raúl to maintain our website and mail-order operation. Frankly, without gentlemen in Boulder, the store might struggle to keep its head above water. But just as Raúl was leaning down to read the email in question, we were interrupted by a flesh-and-blood customer.

When it opens, the front door to the store plays the first six notes of 'The Star-Spangled Banner', not entirely in tune. Raúl glanced over my shoulder as it chimed, and I saw his face drain of indignant thoughts about Sasquatch Pete, to be replaced by something like rapture. I turned to appraise our latest client.

The girl at the door was a genuine bowel-churner: her features astoundingly symmetrical; her long hair a lustrous cappuccino; her buns tight as a cashmere sweater after a hot wash. She was tucked into yoga pants and a pink designer sweatsuit top that looked as fresh as if it had never absorbed a drop. I've spent long enough in LA to be sceptical of such network primetime beauty. These days my tastes tend towards premium cable: I like a crooked tooth or untended eyebrows, women with a complex allure that creeps up on you like Season One of *The Wire*, until you can't help but watch to the end. All the same, I could see why Raúl's jaw had gone slack.

She wafted into the store past Oscar the ostrich, her brown eyes wide and deep, fingering the antiques furtively. Bart spoke first, since Raúl and I were both just staring: 'Can we help you with anything, my dear?'

'Oh *heeeeey*,' she said, cocking her head and unleashing a smile that could choke the life from a less jaded man. 'I'm actually looking for a desk? Or like a table you could use as a desk? But probably like a "desk" desk, y'know? My friend recommended you guys. And I went to CB2 and Design Within Reach or whatever, but I really wanted to find something that had some, like, *character*?'

The girl had the soft, high voice of a cartoon princess, her words cascading over one another and her sentences curving exponentially ceilingward as they neared their conclusion. Bart, scenting the whiff of a major sale, shuffled out from behind the register. 'A desk? How wonderful! For yourself, I presume . . . ?'

She nodded. 'Yeah – for writing? Because I normally do like emails or whatever at the kitchen table or by the pool or on the couch but I have like this new project I'm working on and I really figured it was time, y'know, to have a place to really, like, *write* or whatever?'

A writer, I thought. Another one.

'What's the project,' I asked, 'sitcom or epic poem?'

'Oh, I don't know if I should say,' she replied, suddenly coy. But she couldn't help herself, and she arranged her features into something like seriousness. 'It's a book, actually?' she said. 'Of essays. Like, life-lessons? Kinda for young women? I mean, at first I was thinking I would, like, write it at one of those like writers' retreats in the desert or the mountains or whatever? But then I said to myself, "*No*, I should *so* do this at home," because then I can totally like focus on my life and all the things I've been through, *y'know*?'

'Huh.' I nodded and tried my best not to say anything impolite.

'How wonderful,' Bart said again, and he gestured towards the front of the store. 'Did you happen to notice the Spanish Colonial trestle desk that's displayed in the window? It has some tremendously intricate, carved—'

'Oh I *diiiid*,' she interrupted him, in a tone that I took to mean: *Nice try, Grandpa*. 'I totally did. But really, I'm like looking for something a little more . . . ?'

'Modern!' Raúl spluttered, seizing the moment a little too eagerly to be cool.

'Ex-*actly*,' the girl replied, drawing out the word and dipping it in vocal fry as she angled the warm rays of her attention towards him.

23

'I know just the thing,' he said. 'Follow me.'

He turned abruptly and strode out through the back door. The girl gave me a bashful smile as she edged past and pursued him.

Allowing Raúl to make a sale on his own – especially to an attractive young woman – is a risk. By the time I got out to the car park, he'd yanked open the back of the truck to reveal Marty Kann's tanker desk. It faced outwards from the truckbed, proud as the prow of a battleship, built to cleave the seas of creativity. The girl put her hands to her chest, which, by sheer coincidence, was precisely where Raúl hoped to put his own.

'Omigod you guys, I *loooove* it,' she said. 'It's so . . . like, retro? Like, out of an old movie? I mean, I can *totally* see it in my house with my laptop and my books and like an Anglepoise or whatever? Seriously.'

'It's a fabulous piece,' said Raúl, nodding in agreement. 'That's a . . . Hey, Lucky, who made this desk?'

'McDowell and Craig,' I replied.

'Right,' said Raúl, as if he'd known all along. 'McDowell and Craig. Big designers. Very influential.'

Beautiful people can be spectacularly credulous. That's what happens when the world is always willing to reinforce your self-esteem with half-truths.

'Oh *cooool*,' she cooed. 'And like, how much is it?'

'How much is it, Lucky?'

'Twelve hundred,' I said. 'And it needs a polish.'

'That's a cute accent,' she replied.

I wasn't sure I'd be happy for the tanker desk to leave us so quickly, nor to see it wasted on this particular customer. She didn't strike me as the type to spend her days toiling alone over a blank piece of paper. This was a desk that required commitment.

'It's missing the key to the pencil drawer,' I said, in a vain attempt to dissuade her. 'You'd need to get a new lock fitted. And you might want to lose the castors, too. They're not original.'

Raúl has devoted endless YouTube hours to schooling himself

24

in pick-up artistry. To my knowledge, this has made him no better or worse at manipulating members of the opposite sex, but it has made his pronouncements on the subject all the more insufferable. He tossed me a look that said: *I'll take it from here, my man.* Unable to watch any longer, I went back inside.

When the girl returned from the car park several minutes later, she made directly for the door, stopping beside Oscar only to turn, wave and say, 'Thanks so much, guys; this was *so* amazing?' Bart and I gazed wistfully through the window as she slid into a soft-topped Mini Cooper that was parked at the meter outside. Raúl came in after her, flourishing a scrap of paper like a full bingo card.

'Gentlemen, success!'

He thrust the note under my nose to display the digits she'd scrawled on it, which began with an 818 area code.

'Congratulations,' I said. 'Did she give you her number because she wants to share a milkshake, or because you managed to sell her the desk?'

'Alright, alright. She bought the desk,' he said, rolling his eyes and reaching into his pocket to pull out a folded cheque. '*But . . .* She also said that she *might* come to my show Saturday night.'

I snatched the cheque and made to put it in the cash register, but not before glancing at the girl's swoopy handwriting. 'Hang on,' I said. 'This is for eight hundred dollars. Didn't I say the desk was twelve hundred?'

'Yeah, I gave her a twenty-five per cent discount. For the lock and the polish.'

'Four hundred dollars! Learn some bloody arithmetic, Raúl. We paid Cleo *five hundred and fifty bucks* for that desk!'

'So? That's a two-hundred-fifty-dollar profit.' He tapped his temple with his forefinger. 'Arithmetic, Sir Lucky.'

I suppose the look in my eyes suggested imminent violence, because Bart chose that moment to intervene. Truth is, he'll sometimes cut up to 40 per cent off a price tag, but only when he wants to get rid of a dud piece.

'Now, Lucky, Raúl is correct. At least we made a profit – and a new client.'

'Bart,' I said, 'the rent *just* went up! We can't afford this kind of thing.'

'Well, no. That is true. But let's consider this a teachable moment. Raúl, you know you really ought to get a second opinion from Lucky or myself, if ever you want to offer a discount.'

'Okay,' said Raúl, finally chastened. 'Sorry, boss. Oh – there is one other thing. I said we'd deliver it to her in Calabasas.'

I spontaneously combusted. '*Calabasas?* Christ. Might as well be Bakersfield.'

Calabasas is deep in the Valley, and to get there would mean piloting the truck along at least one highly undesirable freeway.

'Said we'd deliver it tomorrow. Dude, do you still not know who that *was*? That was *Whitney Blair*.'

'Who the hell is Whitney Blair?'

'She's from *Beyond the Hills: The Valley*. The structured reality show?'

'Never heard of it. A reality star? Thought she said she was a writer.'

'Y'know, Lucky, a person *can* do two things at once. Speaking of: she did a sex tape! Check it out . . .'

He took out his smartphone and thumbed at it feverishly until it started to make dirty noises. He turned the screen to me, beaming. There indeed was the girl, Whitney, on all fours on a suede sofa in a non-specific contemporary sitting room: white walls, laminate flooring, tacky art. She was naked but for her lipgloss and buttery make-up, staring past the camera as some ripped dude, his head cropped out of the frame, pistoned her from behind. Her tanned, rigid breasts swung from her chest like church bells – ding, dong – as she moaned and gurned, half in pain, half in ecstasy: the internet's unnerving, ubiquitous sex-face.

'It's *hot*, right? I think I'm in love.'

I could almost hear Raúl's mind go to work on his personal soft-porn fantasy: the furniture mover derives sexual favours from the television star as he delivers her new desk. In fact, he probably derives the favours *on* the desk.

Raúl called the clip a sex tape, but there surely had to be a third person in the room, filming – plus maybe a soundman – which to my mind made it a common or garden porno. I thought about how hard it is to get a stain out of suede.

'I get the picture,' I said, after a few seconds. 'Put it away.'

Raúl flicked off the video as Whitney's yelps began to increase in urgency. Burgers had stirred from the beanbag, perhaps mistaking the smartphone for a puppy in distress. Bart removed his specs and dabbed his brow with his handkerchief. 'My golly,' he said, his voice a little unsteady. 'Is it time for lunch?'

Shaking his head, he sank into the chair behind the register and reached for the Tupperware tub that contained his tuna sandwiches, an old soul being steadily eroded by the tides of the twenty-first century.

4

When I got home, there was another car in my spot. I left the
Bronco parked on the street and strolled up the path at the side
of the house, carrying a bag of limes and a still-cool six-pack of
Tecate.

I live in the one-bedroom guest cottage behind a restored jig-
saw Gothic in Angelino Heights. The big house is venerable as
they come in Southern California, with round-end shingles, high
bay windows and a wide wooden porch with a hand-carved balustrade. The guest cottage is a newer build but blessedly in
keeping. I've a deck at the back in the shadow of Downtown, an
outdoor grill, a patio set and some potted cacti: the dream of the
suburbs, in the heart of the city.

The car in the driveway was a charcoal-grey Audi convertible.
I didn't recognise it, but it was a brand-new model, so that didn't
mean much. My landlord is a retired record exec who got out of
the music biz just before it tanked and now spends most of the
year at his ranch in Ojai or his ski lodge in Jackson Hole. A pair
of women's designer wedges lay discarded in the passenger-seat
footwell, so I guessed it had to belong to one of his daughters,
or his latest girlfriend. I was wrong.

Abigail Musker was sitting with her bare feet up on one of my
patio chairs, close-reading a screenplay on her Kindle. She wore
a sleeveless linen blouse, white denim trousers and crimson toenail
varnish. Her sunglasses were on her head, holding her fair hair
out of her eyes. She didn't hear my approach over the white noise
of the 101 freeway, so I gave her a start when I spoke.

'Abby Musker. What could possibly bring you this far east of West Hollywood?'

Abby looked me up and down, likely considering the significance of the six-pack, the stubble growth and the sweat patches on my shirt.

'Well hey there, Lucky. Where have you been?'

'Just now, or in general?'

She smiled. 'Just now,' she replied. 'Or in general.'

'At work.'

'On a Sunday?'

'You forget: I'm in retail now.'

'Right, of course. That junk store in Los Feliz?'

'It's an antiques emporium.'

'Sure it is.'

Abby is my former agent Todd Carver's former personal assistant. She's petite, unguarded and altogether too nice a person for her industry of choice. Despite the trappings of adulthood, she still seems to me to be no more grown up than the ingénue intern she was when I first encountered her, stalking awkwardly across the lobby of Daring Creative Management like a child who'd borrowed her mother's stilettos.

'How'd you know where I live?'

'You're in the phone book. Very OG.'

'Huh.'

'I love your street,' she said. 'The houses are so *old*.'

'This is a Historic Preservation Zone.'

'Schmancy.'

I brandished the beers in my hand. 'You want something to drink?'

'Got any white wine?'

'Probably.'

I let myself in through the French doors. Fortunately, the evening was sufficiently warm to sit out on the deck, because my place wasn't fit to receive visitors. Half a week's washing-up crowded the sink, a basket of unlaundered underwear occupied the sofa. My cleaning lady only comes once a fortnight, and we were beyond halfway to her next appointment. The fridge rarely contains any real food besides last night's pizza and a handful of hot sauces. But I found a half-empty bottle of Pinot Grigio and poured my guest a glass. I cracked a beer, chopped a lime and forced a slice into the open mouth of the can.

Outside, Abby was gazing at the skyscrapers as they pinkened in the carbonic sunset. A thin layer of Mojave dust coated the patio table, so I swept a patch clear before setting the glass down in front of her. I slid into a spare chair.

'So,' I said. 'New car?'

'That's right. Got a pay bump when I joined CTA.'

I raised my can aloft. 'You left DCM? Cheers to that.'

'Last year. I'm in the TV Lit department. Maybe I could be your agent, you ever want to get back in the game.'

'Can't see Todd letting that happen. Probably has my mugshot taped up behind every receptionist's desk in town.'

'I haven't been Todd's PA in a long time. I pick my own clients.' She sipped her Pinot. 'Have you been writing at all? I'm looking for the next great cable drama. You always liked to write long.'

'Nah,' I replied, and took a deep draft of lager. 'Is that why you came over – to add me to your client roster?'

She paused, pouted. 'Not exactly,' she said. 'It's about Glyn.'

'Ah.'

Glyn Perkins was my writing partner before I quit the industry. We came up together at Oxford, came out to California to make our names – and then it got complicated. But that's another story. Abby sipped her wine.

'I know you guys don't talk much,' she said.

'We don't talk at all. It's been a long time, Abby. Years.'

'I realise that. But see, Lucky: I think he's gone missing.'

I put my drink down and studied her to judge whether she was joking – apparently not.

'Define "gone missing",' I said.

'He usually calls me like once a month. Just to say "Hey", shoot the breeze. I don't work with him anymore, but force of habit, I guess. You know Glyn . . .'

'I used to.'

'Anyhow, last month: no phone call. This month? Still no phone call. So I tried calling *him*: no answer. Sent him an email: no reply. I sent Todd's new PA a memo to ask whether Glyn had gone on vacation, but he said he was probably just crazy with work. The studio's still waiting on a script for *Marshal Eagle 3.*'

I winced. 'They're making a *third* one?'

Abby sighed and said, patiently: 'We all know how you feel about superheroes, Lucky. But the way the industry works is: a movie makes three hundred million domestic, they make a sequel. The sequel makes three hundred million, they make another sequel. Did you know *Marshal Eagle* is huge in China – weird, right? They're making a stand-alone spin-off of The Peacemaker. And a team-up movie, with Marshal Eagle, Deadbolt, Axeman *and* Rock-Face.'

'Okay, okay,' I said. 'Enough.'

She smirked, went on: 'So anyhow, then I called Glyn's wife . . .'

'Bijou.'

'Right, Bijou Perkins.' We both smiled at that: Bijou's maiden name was Benoit; now she was burdened with Perkins. Poetry to prose. 'She pretty much hung up on me. Said she hadn't seen him, didn't know where he was, didn't *care*.'

'Well, that's a new development.'

'I know, right? So look, Glyn probably has a bunch of friends. But I only know you. Which is why I was hoping you could track him down. Call Bijou. Find out what's going on. I'm worried about him, is all. He's always been so . . . so *reliable*.'

That was a pointed remark: historically, I have not been so reliable.

'Bijou would rather get a cold call from her oncologist than from me. You realise I'll get even less information out of her than you did.'

'Maybe. Maybe not. But I didn't know who else to ask.'

'Todd? He's still Glyn's agent, isn't he?'

'Right. But Todd took my leaving DCM as a personal slight. Far as he's concerned, we're rivals now. I'm just another shark in the water. Besides, he's too busy to schedule even a walk'n'talk. You know he reps Chris these days?'

I supposed I ought to know which 'Chris' she was talking about.

'I don't read the trades anymore, Abby.'

'Whatever. He is very busy. And I don't feel comfortable telling him how to deal with his own client . . . Wait, what the fuck is *that*?'

'This? It's an e-cigarette.'

'An *e-cigarette*? C'mon.'

'What?'

'If you're gonna quit, Lucky, just quit.'

We drank and talked some more, and Abby asked how I'd been – I think she was a little scared to hear the answer, so I put her mind at rest on that score. She told me she was still waiting on her lawyer boyfriend to propose. I told her he sounded like an arsehole. We reminisced awhile, and she laughed about the first script of mine and Glyn's that she'd ever read: *Blood*, a bold but ultimately unfilmable period saga that began during the English Civil War and ended with the Great Fire of London. She admonished me for my failure to open a Facebook account, and made me promise to join her for brunch sometime.

Eventually we ran low on wine and conversation, and, as the sun dipped, so did my mood. It was fully dark by the time I walked Abby out to her car, so I kept on walking, down to Guisados on Sunset to get myself some tacos for supper. I ate them alone at the pavement counter, watching the game traffic start to trickle away from Dodger Stadium, contemplating the steady rhythm of the cooks as they transformed corn mush into fresh tortillas.

Back home, I set to work on the rest of the six-pack. It was Sunday night and some of my favourite shows were waiting for me on the DVR, but I found myself staring instead at the slow-rotating hands of the nineteenth-century Parisian carriage clock that once belonged to my great-great-grandfather, the first Lucius Kluge. It's out of place in Angelino Heights, just like its owner, but it's the only heirloom I have that isn't in England or in storage, so it enjoys pride of place on the shelf above the television. A lot of the antiques from the Somerset estate have been sold, and now doubtless reside in the London townhouses of the recently wealthy: oligarchs, sheikhs, investment bankers. But those with the greatest sentimental value are still in the family, somewhere.

The Kluges have long wobbled on the parapet of aristocratic impoverishment, so my father is forever cooking up crackpot schemes to scare off bankruptcy. He leased a parcel of land to a wind-farm, even converted the big house at Tinderley into a venue for management team-building weekends. My parents live in the old stables now. When I was a boy, grown-ups would tell me I'd inherited the Viscount's brains and my mother's looks – which might have been a compliment, if only my mother weren't also the smart one. It was her idea to advertise the estate as a film location, which turned out to be the most lucrative scheme of all.

Every summer I'd return home from school to find actors in period dress roaming the lawns: country-house mysteries, medieval epics, Austen adaptations. By the time Glyn and I crossed paths in the university drama society, and saw in each other a similar tragicomic sensibility, I was already versed in the world of professional film production. We wrote some skits together, and then some shorts, and then Mater, on our behalf, kindly contacted one of the Hollywood producers who'd taken a shine to her while shooting a wartime drama in the grounds. The rest is history – though it was once the future.

I was on the last of the Tecates when I tugged open the bottom drawer of the Imperial desk that takes up way too much of my sitting room. That drawer contains several unfinished manuscripts that nobody knows about but me, including *Chief*, my noirish, non-linear William H. Parker biopic, and a meditative Western about a Mexican bandit fighting back against California's Gold Rush profiteers, which I'd conceived as an allegory for US adventurism in the Middle East. I skimmed *Chief*'s unwieldy second act. No, I thought, I have not been writing. Well, not *much*.

At some point, I must have expunged Glyn's phone number from my contacts list, but Abby had noted it down for me, along with Bijou's details and their home address. His answerphone greeting was brief and generic, but it was a shock all the same to hear his voice after so long, like smelling an ex-girlfriend's perfume on a stranger. Then came the beep, and I spoke into the impatient silence.

'Hi Glyn, it's Lucius. Er . . . This is odd. Been a long time. Listen, you don't have to call me back or anything, but I've just had Abby Musker at my place, and she's wondering where you are. Says she hasn't heard from you in weeks, and she's becoming a little concerned for your welfare. So maybe you could just give her a call, put her mind at rest? That's all. So . . . Er, she told me they're making *Marshal Eagle 3*, which is funny. I mean, it's not *funny* . . . You know what I mean. Anyway. Good luck with that. I, er . . . Hope you're well, I guess . . . Okay. Bye . . . This is Lucius. Bye. Call Abby.'

I put my phone down on the coffee table and stared at it, half-expecting him to call me back. But after five minutes it had failed to ring and I flicked on the late-night local news for some distraction. A family of bears were roaming the far eastern suburbs, a minor brush fire blazed in the Santa Monica Mountains, an eighteen-wheeler had jack-knifed across the 210 near Tujunga.

I passed out on the sofa again, lulled by the rhythmic cadence of the A B C 7 sports anchor . . .

'. . .*thelakersthreegamewinningstreakbouncedawayfromkobeandco lastnightinoklahomabuttheclippersremainedonarollathomeafteraslow firstquartertheypoweredaheadofthewarriorswiththisdeandrejordan alleyoopcontributingtoasatisfyingseventeenpointvictorymeanwhile awhackyweekendforthedodgersathometocincinnatiwithyaselpuighitting histhirdhomerofthesummeratthetopoftheninthforafivetothreewinand inhockeynewstheducksmadeasplash* . . .'

. . . And then my phone buzzed me awake. I watched as it inched steadily towards the far edge of the coffee table like a prisoner crawling for the fence, snatching it up just before it reached freedom. But it wasn't my old partner on the line; it was my new one.

'Raúl? What time is it?'

'Zip your fly, Sir Lucky. Bart got beat up.'

5

Who likes hospitals? Me neither. Raúl and I hustled from the car park at Good Samaritan to the Emergency Room, where, after a near-altercation with an unhelpful orderly, we finally found Bart behind the curtain in a private cubicle, propped on a gurney with a mass of white medical tape holding his purpled face together. He seemed smaller than I'd always imagined him, like a famous actor spotted in the flesh. He had two black eyes, five stitches and a broken nose.

To one side of the gurney stood his wife, Karen, smoothing his matted hair; to the other a pair of uniformed cops, who introduced themselves as Officers Schooley and Park. Schooley was a lanky, nervy white guy with a notepad at the ready; Park was Korean, and apparently so dazzled by the ward's strip-lighting that he still had on his wraparound sunglasses. His short-sleeved dress shirt looked a size too small, so snugly did it cling to his sculpted biceps.

They both wore black shoes with the heft and shine of London taxis, and utility belts high on their waists loaded with handguns, cuffs and Christ knows what else. The presence of the LAPD made me instantly anxious, seeing as how I'd just drunk several cans of lager and then DUI'd to the hospital at high speed. I tried my best not to breathe in their direction.

'Well,' Bart said woozily when he saw us, 'if it isn't Butch and Sundance.'

The broken nose was giving him trouble pronouncing his 'n's.

Officer Schooley's pencil hovered an inch from his notepad.

'I'm sorry, sirs,' he said, addressing Raúl and me. 'Was that "Mr Sundance", or . . . ?'

'He's just kidding, Officer,' I replied. 'My name's Lucius Kluge – K-L-U-G-E – and this is Raúl Gupta – G-U-P-T-A. We're Bart's employees at the store.'

Officer Park peered at Raúl through his shades: 'Gupta, huh? Is that, like, American Indian?'

Schooley tensed and grimaced at the floor.

'Indian American,' Raúl replied, unfazed. 'Close, but no cigar.'

'So what happened?' I asked.

Schooley relaxed. 'According to the doctors,' he said, 'it appears that somebody struck Mr Abernathy across the face with a heavy object – could be a tyre iron, something like that. He blacked out, and the injuries to the back of his head were likely sustained when he fell.'

'And this was at the store?'

'In the parking lot,' said Bart.

Seeing him in this diminished state, awash in a baggy blue hospital gown, my gut mixed a highball of guilt and pity, with a healthy dash of hot rage. Raúl puffed out his chest and started to pace the tiny room. 'Did you see the guy?' he said. 'Was it a crackhead? Fuckin' crackheads.'

'I don't know,' Bart replied. 'I don't remember.'

Karen rounded on Raúl. She's tiny but deceptively formidable, a derringer in a clutch bag, a former dental nurse with little patience for dawdlers or the discourteous. 'He doesn't *remember*,' she said, poking a finger at my partner, and then at me. 'What if he's *brain-damaged*? Why weren't either of you *there*? HE'S AN OLD MAN!'

'Mrs Abernathy,' said Schooley, trying to placate her. 'Please. I don't think this is the time for recriminations. Just . . . think of your husband.'

'I *am* thinking of my husband,' she replied.

'He was found unconscious by a Mr Peter Smales,' Schooley went on, reading from his notepad.

'Sasquatch Pete,' said Raúl.

'Shit,' I mumbled. 'I forgot to move the truck.'

Raúl snapped his fingers. 'It was probably *Pete* who attacked him!'

'No!' Bart cried, holding up his hands. 'Officer, do *not* write that down. Pete is a passionate man, but not a violent one. Raúl is simply being overzealous.'

He sighed, fatigued by his own outburst. Raúl opened his mouth to say something else and then thought better of it. Schooley made a note nonetheless. 'Mr Abernathy believed something may have been stolen,' he said, turning to me. 'Possibly from your truck? It would be very helpful if you could perform a stocktake, let us know whether this was a theft. Mrs Abernathy has my card. And I've told Mr Abernathy that he ought to consider installing some security cameras.'

'Sure,' I replied. 'Of course. I'll look into it.'

'Thank you, Mr . . .' He consulted his notes again. '. . . Klewj?'

My great-great-great-grandmother married a Viennese concert pianist, if you must know. 'It's Kloo-guh,' I said. 'With a hard "g".'

'Kluge,' Officer Park repeated. 'What is that? Swedish?'

When the cops had gone, Bart told us the story again – or what he remembered of it – stopping now and then to catch his breath or sip water through a straw. He'd taken some hefty painkillers, so I had my qualms about the reliability of his account. 'After I closed the store,' he began, 'I thought I'd take a look at what you boys rustled up at that estate sale—'

'Bart, it's a Sunday. I told you we'd empty the truck in the morning.'

'I know, Lucky, I know – but I was curious. Sue me. So I went out back to the parking lot and opened up the truck. First thing

I see is that wonderful desk. Lucky was right, Raúl: you really should have demanded more for it.'

Raúl bowed his head. 'Sorry, boss.'

'Well, no use in crying over spilled milk. At any rate, I opened one of the packing boxes, and what should I find inside but those Native American baskets you were talking about, Lucky. It's after sunset, so I take them into the store to inspect them in the light. What a find! Early twentieth century, I'd say—'

I interrupted him again: 'Bart, just tell us how you got whacked.'

'I'm *getting* to that, hold on. So then I go back out to the truck, thinking that perhaps I'll investigate one more box before I go home. And, as I recall, there's a strange new smell in the air — sickly sweet, like rotting fruit . . .'

'Crackhead,' said Raúl. 'Gotta be.'

'I don't know,' Bart continued. 'Could be I imagined it. Could be it was just Pete's trashcans. But then I look again at the packing boxes in the back of the truck, and I could swear that one of them is missing. Next thing I remember, I'm lying on my back with a bloody nose, Pete shaking me awake.'

Karen had been sitting stiffly in the cubicle's only chair, listening to her husband's sad soliloquy for at least the second time, but now she spoke up.

'Tell me about this estate sale,' she said, staring at me.

'The sale today? Huh. It was in the Hills. Nice place. Belonged to a production designer who drank himself to death. Or that's what Cleo Habibi says, anyway.'

'I knew it,' Karen said, and she shook her head grimly. 'Bad juju.'

I fought the urge to roll my eyes. Despite a career dedicated to the scientific discipline of dental medicine, Karen is an amateur spiritualist, who claims to be capable of identifying bad juju in inanimate objects. Most of the items at Bart's Olde California came from dead people, so the store is a clusterfuck of haunted furniture. If Karen gets defective vibes from a vase or a table or an oil painting and we can't sell it soon enough, Bart makes us take it to the Goodwill to balance out the karma. Otherwise, Karen insists, awful things will start to happen. I don't think Bart even believes the mumbo-jumbo, but he loves his wife.

And listen, I don't believe it either – not for a moment. But once, when Karen condemned a classic Victorian club chair with its original leather upholstery intact, I sneered at her superstition and took the thing home with me. A week later, I fell asleep in it with a lit cigarette between my fingers. I put out the fire with a carton of milk, which was all I had to hand, and then I left the blistered remains on the street, at the mercy of the LA Bureau of Sanitation. Bad juju.

I turned back to Bart. 'Did the police ask whether anyone suspicious was hanging around the store before closing? Any dodgy customers?'

'Of course they did,' he replied.

'And? What about the girl who bought the desk? Could she have been scoping the joint, do you think?'

Raúl bristled at the suggestion. 'Whitney Blair? Dude, are you *high*?'

'Why not? Her cheque could bounce, who knows? If that porno's anything to go by, she must have some pretty low-rent associates.'

'Y'know what, Your Lordship? You really oughta update your prejudices.'

Bart struggled to clear his throat. The stark hospital lighting served only to emphasise the ugliness of his injuries, and his dark, puffy eyelids had begun to droop with the effort of conversation. 'Actually,' he said, 'there was one other customer. Yes, it's coming back to me now. A gentleman arrived just as I was closing up. He asked about Oscar. I said he wasn't for sale.'

'Oscar?' said Karen.

Raúl and I replied together: 'The ostrich.'

She tutted and put a palm to her husband's forehead. 'You should leave him alone to get some sleep now,' she said. 'He's tired and confused and he probably has a concussion. They're keeping him in tonight for observation.'

Bart raised an index finger, with one final instruction: 'You boys have to keep the store open,' he said. 'Karen will help out. Our financial situation being what it is, I cannot afford a lengthy closure. God only knows how much these medical bills are gonna cost.'

'Sure, Bart,' I replied. 'Take as much time as you need. We'll hold the fort – right, Raúl?'

'You're *sure* you don't remember the guy?' said Raúl. 'The crackhead?'

I yanked my partner from the cubicle, and he muttered obscenities all the way back to the multi-storey. He was right, though: what sort of scumbag assaults a seventy-year-old man? I offered to drop Raúl back at his place in Koreatown, but he demanded we go via Los Feliz, to study the crime scene – and I was inclined to agree.

We left the Bronco on the street, checked the front of the store was secure, and then walked around to the car park at the back. It was well past midnight and the neighbourhood was quiet. The only light came from the bare bulb above the back door, which cast a weak yellow puddle on the tarmac as if a drunk had pissed against the wall. I sniffed the air and smelled diesel oil, with a sour top-note of what was probably mouldy tofu from Pete's bins. But not a trace of the sweet, rotting fruit odour that Bart claimed to have noticed.

'You know, Raúl, you're right,' I said. 'It probably was a crackhead. Just some mugger taking a chance. We should get security cameras like that cop said.'

I wasn't sure whether he'd heard me. He was searching the ground around the truck for clues by the dim light from his smartphone screen. I stared sadly at the little set of retractable steps that Bart had fixed to the tailgate so he could climb into the vehicle more easily. Whoever locked the truck – Sasquatch Pete, probably – had left it hanging there limp. I unlocked the doors to the cube to check on the contents, and folded the steps back up.

I was faced with Marty Kann's tanker desk, majestically rect-angular, and behind it the sleek, dark outline of the Kem Weber Airline chair. On the truckbed next to the desk was a row of packing boxes, just as Bart had remembered, with spaces where two of them were missing, like the gaps in a tweaker's front teeth.

Every box was identical and had a Habibi Estates logo printed on its side. Somebody had torn the parcel tape from one of them already. It was filled with Styrofoam peanuts, but I dug further and discovered the Bill Curry bedside lamps, bubble-wrapped and packed top-to-toe. I ripped open another, to find Marty Kann's old sketches rolled and stacked inside. I knew Bart had already taken the Native American baskets into the store for appraisal. So what was left? I tugged my e-cigarette from my jeans pocket and puffed on it. I scratched my chin where my old tobogganing scar was beginning to be obscured by stubble. Raúl appeared around the side of the truck, empty-handed, absent-mindedly massaging his belly. And then it came to me.

'Son of a bitch,' I murmured.

'What? What is it?'

'I think the crackhead stole my cookie jar.'

I woke up alone on the sofa again, with the sort of hangover that sets in only after you reach your middle thirties: gone is the straightforward nausea of youth, replaced by a bubbling quicksand of shame and angst. The blinds striped sunlight into the room. A Wilco LP still twisted on the record player, the only sound the soft crackle that said it was time to flip to Side B. The crumpled beer cans stood in a ragged semicircle on the coffee table, as if staging an intervention.

I spooned two fingers of fresh Guatemalan grounds into the cafetière and left it to percolate while I hit the shower. I was already late for work, but I couldn't go another twenty-four hours without a wash and change, so I peeled off the previous day's clothes and slouched beneath the prickling hot spray. Bart's frailty had unnerved me and, as I stared down at my shapeless stomach, my wrinkled dick and the grey, soapy water pooling around my toes, I couldn't help but consider my own steadily encroaching mortality. I'm already too old to die young.

I took the coffee in the Bronco, driving one-handed and slurping at every red light along Sunset, trying not to splash any on my last clean flannel shirt. At the store I slowed into the space between the truck and someone's brand-new Tesla Roadster. As I shut off the engine, a shadow fell across the dashboard. I might have mistaken it for a rare cloud passing overhead, were it not for the accompanying knock on the driver's side window, which gave me enough of a shock to spill a blot of warm coffee on my crotch. I swore as the stain settled into the denim and made itself comfortable.

The fat knuckles on the glass belonged to Sasquatch Pete, who waited with his bear arms folded across his barrel chest as I climbed from the car. The crown of Pete's head is hairless, but the remaining six-foot-four of him is coated in dark, downy fur. His is not the normal physiognomy of a man who subsists on quinoa.

'Hey, Pete,' I said, as brightly as I could manage. 'Listen, thanks for last night, calling the ambulance and whatnot.'

'You're welcome,' he growled. 'Glad the old man's okay. Can't say I appreciate the attitude I'm getting from your co-worker.'

Pete nodded towards the back door of the store, where Raúl leaned against the jamb, hands in pockets, eyeing us both. Burgers paced at his feet. It appeared that he and Pete had been debating the events of the previous evening.

'Ah. Sorry about that,' I said.

'And another thing,' said Pete, pulling a folded piece of paper from his back pocket and pressing it into my hand. 'He has *got* to stop bothering my customers about his lousy comedy show.'

I unfolded the paper; it was a glossy handbill for *Blowing Up* at the Lo-Ball, advertising a month's worth of weekly shows, with Raúl's name among those listed in a block font beneath the headliners.

'He can get kind of carried away. I'll talk to him.'

'You do that,' said Pete, and he began to move off towards the café, where the brunch rush would shortly begin. 'Oh, and Lucky . . .'

'Yes, Pete?'

'. . . park your darned truck *properly*, would you?'

I sighed, swigged the last mouthful of my coffee, and reached into the Bronco to leave the mug in the cup holder. Raúl swaggered over, flipping the bird at Pete's back as the big man disappeared past the bins and into his kitchen.

'I still think he's a suspect,' Raúl said. 'He's acting extremely defensive.'

'I wonder why,' I replied, and I pushed past him into the store.

Karen had been cleansing the space with smudge sticks, and the air inside was thick with the scent of burning sage. To my knowledge, there's not a drop of Native American blood in Karen's veins but, nevertheless, she waves a smouldering bundle of dried herbs over the inventory once a month, to waft away any bothersome spirits. Some of our stock might have been stolen, she'll say, or else had an owner who died in unfortunate circumstances: a chair kicked away in a hanging suicide; a mirror that witnessed a murder.

She was focused on the items from the Kann house, most of which were in the narrow space beside the register where Raúl and I had stacked them the night before, waiting to be valued, tagged and photographed for the website.

'Hey, Karen,' I said. 'Thanks for coming in. You sensing some bad juju?'

She paused and scrutinised me suspiciously, trying to ascertain whether or not I was mocking her. Fortunately, she's yet to fully grasp the British sense of humour. 'I want to sell all of this as fast as we can,' she said, gesturing with the smudge stick and leaving a smoke tendril in the air above Marty Kann's belongings. 'Discount it all if you have to. Just get it out of here.'

'How's Bart?'

'Bad,' she said. 'Worse. He woke up with a *terrible* headache. Can't even open his eyes properly, they're so swollen. He's very confused by all the medication. The doctors say he can go home later today, but I'm not so sure.'

'No word from the police, I suppose.'

She bridled. '*Those* morons?'

With Karen conducting her psychic spring-clean and Raúl busy building a case against Sasquatch Pete, the only customer in the store had been left unattended. He was a slim-built twenty-something with an Ivy League air: crisp grey hoodie, jeans and deck shoes, fair hair kept in check by a fitted Giants cap, chin as smooth as one of Warren Beatty's pick-up lines.

He was studying our pre-war one-armed bandit, a striking contraption that looked like a steampunk cash register: lacquered-wood build, cast-aluminium display with colour detailing, and a frozen row of three mismatched fruit that made it terminally unlucky. It was one of my favourite items in the store, and also one of the most expensive: Bart had picked it up for 200 bucks at a yard sale, knowing full well that it was worth at least twenty-five times that. The price tag was sufficient to scare off most prospective buyers.

'Beautiful bit of Americana, isn't it?'

'What . . . ? Oh, yeah,' said the guy, looking at me and then back at the antique machine. 'Yeah. It's cool.'

'Non-operational, though. Unless you've some old silver dollars to lose in it. Did you know the first slot machines were invented in San Francisco?'

'Uh, no,' he replied, and he propped up the peak of his cap with an index finger so that I could finally see into his keen blue eyes. 'Say, are you Bart?'

'I'm afraid not,' I said. 'Bart is off sick.'

'Nothing serious, I hope.'

'Migraine. But I can help you out if you have questions. You looking for anything in particular?'

'Uh, not really. I just got a new place so I'm looking for shit to fill it, y'know?'

I was tempted to explain that if he was looking for shit, he'd come to the wrong store. But I decided it was simply an unfortunate turn of phrase. I seriously doubted that he could afford the slot machine, anyway.

'Where's the place?'

'My place? Venice Beach. Hey, *this* is awesome.'

Marty Kann's Spanish Revival-style side table had caught his attention: the one with the painted-tile panorama of pioneers crossing the desert. He leaned over to examine the design.

'It's a great piece,' I agreed. 'You like Western stuff? Cowboys and Indians?'

'Sure,' he replied. 'It's kinda like pop art.'

Karen had been eavesdropping from the back of the store, where she was now smoke-treating a potentially sinister cowhide armchair. Hearing our discussion about the table, she yelled, 'That item is on discount!'

The guy turned to me for confirmation. 'Really?'

'Really,' I said, and I looked around at the Kann collection. 'Actually, all this stuff here is discounted. That rug. The neon sign. Whatever's in those boxes.'

'Oh, yeah? How come?'

'It's new stock,' I said. 'We got it all from an estate sale yesterday. Saves us the processing costs if you decide to buy any of it now. If you want it, I could give you the table for a thousand bucks. Probably be twelve hundred otherwise.'

Processing costs. I might just as easily have told him the truth, since the idea that furniture could be cursed would seem so far-fetched to most sensible people. But he eagerly bought my white lie, and delved straight into the nearest Habibi Estates box. He came up clutching a bubble-wrapped Stemlite lamp. A handful of Styrofoam peanuts scattered across the floor. The guy looked the lamp up and down as if it were an intern he was thinking of hitting on.

'Tell you what, I'll leave you to think about it,' I said. 'Just let me know if you have any questions.'

'Sure,' he replied, kneeling to rummage in another box. 'Thanks.'

By now Raúl was behind the register, Burgers sprawled on the beanbag at his feet. He glanced up at me sheepishly as I approached.

'What?'

He grimaced. 'You're not gonna like this, Your Eminence,' he said.

'What is it?'

He'd been using Bart's desktop computer, and he pointed at the monitor in front of him. 'I looked up your missing cookie jar,' he said. 'Thought I'd put a value on it. Turns out there was one just like it sold at auction in Florida a few months back. Wait for it . . . six grand.'

'Six *thousand* dollars?' I spluttered. 'Seriously?'

I leaned over Raúl's shoulder to look at the image of the auction lot and the price alongside it. It was indeed a *Dumbo* Ringmaster, almost identical to the Kanns', though if anything its glaze was more spider-webbed with cracks – which meant ours might be worth even more.

'We should call the police again,' I said.

'Lucky, you do realise the cops will not do a thing about this? No, I am setting up a Google alert for "cookie jar" right now. Because soon enough, some asshole is going to try to sell that fat little porcelain fuck. And we're going to be there when they do.'

He turned back to the computer before I could protest, his fleshy hands like Shetland ponies trotting smartly across the keyboard. IT consulting is one of several more secure professions that Raúl has forgone in favour of comedy. As he was typing, I spotted an unfamiliar business card propped against the bottom of the computer monitor. I picked it up; it felt flimsy and cheap. On the front, there was a smudged monochrome symbol – a clenched fist bearing down on a boldface acronym: 'CRUSH.'

And on the back? ' "Jeffrey Guzman – Executive Director". This yours, Raúl?'

'Nope. Never seen it before.'

'Huh.'

I dropped the card into the drawer where we keep all our loose paperwork. The preppy young dude in the Giants cap was hovering at the register.

'So,' I said. 'Anything I can help you with?'

'Yeah, actually,' he replied. 'Do you deliver to Venice?'

'Absolutely.'

'Cool. I just can't fit everything in my car. I kinda like the fruit machine, the cowboy table, and that neon sign you said was on discount, too. So I was thinking: what if I just gave you ten thousand for all of it?'

There are plenty of reasons why a twenty-something who wears casual clothes on a weekday could be that wealthy in LA. I tried not to act surprised as he slid his wallet from his jeans pocket. There was, I now noticed, a hint of disingenuity about his outfit: the laid-back look was just a little too pristine. The hoodie probably had a Prada label hidden in the collar. Was he an actor? A drug dealer? Or just the spoiled offspring of some waspy, West Coast billionaire?

I cleared my throat. 'I'm guessing that's your Tesla out back?'

He grinned then, for the first time, and gave me his credit card, which revealed that his name was Scott Benjamin. It didn't ring any bells.

'Huh,' I murmured. 'Two first names.'

'People call me Scooter,' he said, and he held out his hand for me to shake.

'They call me Lucky,' I replied, and took it. 'You know what, Scooter? We're making a delivery to Calabasas this afternoon. If you write down your details for me, we could head to Venice afterwards, drop off your stuff then.'

'That'd be awesome,' he said, and he scribbled his address and phone number on the back of a Bart's Olde California flyer while I rang up the full $10k on his credit card. The payment went through without protest. As sorry as I'd be to see it go, I looked forward to telling Bart we'd sold the slot machine. It wouldn't make a huge dent in our debt, but at least he'd be able to settle a few outstanding bills. Scooter barely glanced at the receipt before slipping it into his wallet.

'Catch you later, Lucky,' he said, pulling his cap low over his eyes again. 'And hey – I hope your boss feels better soon.'

I glanced again at the amount on the credit-card slip, thinking: *He will now*.

7

Los Angeles traffic is too complex an organism to be dismissed merely as 'bad'. Some days, you might stumble into a fast-flowing stretch of freeway at six p.m. On others, you'll find yourself gridlocked at eleven-thirty or two, the unwitting victim of congestion patterns governed not solely by rush hours, but by school runs, lunch meetings and everyone else's afternoon spin class. Yet while the city's sheer volume of automobiles may be unmatched, an LA standstill is seldom absolute. There's almost always movement, even if it is digestively slow.

That afternoon, though, as the truck crept along the 101, I had to wonder whether it was even worth keeping the engine turned over between each ten-foot increment. The cars stretched to the horizon, funnelling and bottle-necking through the unidentified blockages ahead, their roofs glittering in the high sun like the scales on a snake that had swallowed a cow. This was *Falling Down* traffic.

'What do you mean, you never heard of Scooter Benjamin? Did you just get here from North *Korea*? Do you even *have* an internet connection?'

Jackson Browne was in the tape deck. Burgers snored softly in his crate. Raúl was in the passenger seat. I don't often allow him to drive – too distractible.

'Who is he?' I replied, exhaling a mouthful of vapour. 'Enlighten me.'

'Lucky, the guy created Bacon Ninja!'

'Bacon *what*?'

'Bacon Ninja. The game. C'mon, you never heard of *Bacon Ninja?* It was Number One in the iTunes Store for, like, six months.'

'Raúl, I barely even know what that means.'

He sighed and mumbled and manhandled his smartphone until it started to make noises again: Far Eastern muzak, swish-swoosh, chop, slap, sizzle.

'So the game is: you're a line cook,' Raúl explained, 'and you have a cook station, and you get orders called, and you have to fit all the bacon onto the cook station and cook it without burning any, and send it out before the orders pile up too high. And the more levels you complete, the more breakfast foods you get to cook. Hash browns, tomatoes, pancakes, eggs any style . . .'

'Where does the "ninja" part come in?'

'Well, the cook is Asian, and he kinda makes ninja sounds when he calls the orders or adds more bacon. Listen.'

I listened: muzak, chop, sizzle, Hi-*Ya!*

'It's better on the iPad,' he said.

'And this is popular?'

'Dude, I can't explain it. You just have to keep playing, and keep playing, and every time you play you get a little bit better at it, but not much, and you can't frickin' stop. It's app crack. Took me a whole week to break the habit the first time I tried it. I got stuck on hash browns for like two days.'

'Huh. And this Benjamin guy invented it.'

'Exactly. When they first introduced ads and in-app purchases, I read he was making a hundred grand a day. One hundred thousand dollars. *Per. Day.* Course, he's getting sued by some college buddy who claimed it was all his idea – but that's S.O.P. for these Silicon Valley dudes. I have a cousin at Stanford. A start-up's not a start-up until there's at least one lawsuit pending.'

We'd shoved Benjamin's purchases into the truck with the tanker desk and headed towards Calabasas. Raúl was pumped about his impending courtship of Whitney Blair. I was growing increasingly irate at being hemmed in and cut up by the long-distance drivers drifting in their semi-trucks, the perma-tanned Valley girls in pastel convertibles, the industry execs in dark European coupés, the paralegals in cheap Asian hatchbacks, the Latino landscapers in battered pick-ups stacked with blowers and mowers, rakes and spades.

A news chopper buzzed overhead, following the line of the freeway west. Los Angeles: home of the televised police pursuit. Raúl narrowed his eyes to watch it shrink into the distance. 'Why the hold-up, d'you think?'

'Who knows. Fender-bender? Roadworks? There was something on the news last night about a brush fire in the mountains. It might be that.'

We had inched our way alongside the junction to the 405. The cars were thinning out as they hit the off-ramp. In my impatience, I made a snap decision, said 'Fuck this', swung the truck sharply through a brief opening in the right-hand lane before it had time to close up, and then powered on into the fluid exit stream, horns sounding in our wake. Burgers's crate slid sideways.

'Whoa! What the *hell*, man?'

'There's no point just sitting there,' I said. 'We'll hit Venice first, go to Benjamin's place. Plus there's an errand I have to run.'

'Ahem. Excuse me, Sir Lucky: an *errand*? We're on company time here. I told Whitney we were coming like a half-hour ago. She's expecting us. She texted me a frickin' smiley-face emoji! How'm I gonna look *now*?'

'Tell her we got caught up. Blame the traffic. She got a fat discount and free delivery – I think she can wait a little longer for her new desk.'

'See, this kinda thing is exactly why Bart's Olde California only has a four-star Yelp rating.'

The 405 was almost clear heading south, and I soon flicked the indicator for the Sunset exit, just past the Getty. 'Why don't you use that phone for something constructive,' I said, 'and tell me the way to 1723 Broome Street. That's Broome with an "e". It's in Brentwood somewhere.'

Raúl grumbled some more, but he put his thumbs to work and a few minutes later I stopped the truck under a ficus opposite number 1723. Broome Street was in the sort of leafy, tony neighbourhood where the only pedestrians are mailmen and rich people jogging. The house was a modern Mediterranean with terracotta roof tiles and a mustard paint job. There was a pristine, late-model German SUV parked in the drive and a guy in green overalls strimming the grass where the pavement met the front lawn. It smelled like Wimbledon Centre Court in July.

'Dullsville,' said Raúl. 'Who lives here?'

'Nobody you want to know. Mind waiting? This'll take a minute.'

I trotted up the smooth brick path to a front door shaded by honeysuckle, where a hummingbird was hopping from bloom to bloom. As I worked up the balls to ring the bell, I tried to tug the front of my shirt low enough to cover the coffee spots on my crotch. I pushed the button, listened to the chimes go *bing-bong* somewhere deep in the house and stepped away from the entrance, out of arm's reach. This was going to end badly, whoever answered the door.

I heard footsteps in the hall, the sound of a latch turning, and then there she was: Élise 'Bijou' Perkins (née Benoit), one hand rising to her hip, a model reaching the end of the catwalk. Behind my Wayfarers, I slow-panned from the floor up: long legs in tight-fit jeans, slender torso beneath a sleeveless silk blouse, tits standing to attention like a 21-year-old's. There were traces of age in her cold glare and crow's feet, but nothing some judicious Botox wouldn't fix.

'Can I help you?' she said, blank-faced, as if I were a delivery guy.

I peeled off the sunglasses. 'Hey, Bijou.'

She hesitated. Her cobalt eyes narrowed. And then: 'Ho. Lee. *Shit*. Must be my Lucky day.'

'You're looking well. Been a long time.'

Bijou's voice is husky as a coconut. 'Not long enough,' she replied.

'Yeah, well. Can't say I'm over the moon to be here.'

'And to what do I owe the displeasure?'

'I came about Glyn.'

'Of course you did.'

'Is he here?'

'No, he is not. Jesus, you look like dogshit. You'd best come in, else the neighbours'll think we have a homeless problem. Take those fucking shoes off.'

I stepped inside, yanking off my trainers and leaving them beside the row of kids' footwear at the door. A grotesque little chihuahua mix skittered into the hallway and started to yap at my heels. Bijou clapped her hands and yelled: 'Lady, NO!' The dog whimpered and backed away, still eyeing me as I followed her callipygous mistress deeper into the house.

Bijou was the first person to call me Lucky, though in the long run she only changed my luck for the worse. I met her at the Roosevelt a few months after I'd arrived in LA, when the Roosevelt still seemed like a hip place to hang out. She was a blonde alone at the bar, nursing a deathbed Cosmopolitan. I knew she was trouble right away, which is why I bought her another drink.

She said she was waiting for a friend, but they never showed. Instead, Bijou spent all night feigning admiration for my British-intellectual schtick. She was kind of an actress, kind of a model, kind of a coat-check girl. What's that old joke? *An actress so dumb, she slept with the writer*. Glyn and I shared an apartment in West Hollywood; I took her back there and we fucked each other's brains out. I was still in my twenties then, a different man.

Bijou ought to have been out of my league, but she made the

classic American mistake of assuming, because I had half a title, that I must have been rich. Mater was guilty of the same error, believing that because he lived in a house with a fancy name, my father the Viscount must also possess wealth and ambition.

But by the time I quit the industry a couple of years later, Bijou had got wise. We broke up and within weeks she'd snared Glyn – who by then must have seemed the superior prospect. He and I were already at loggerheads, and I can't say I took the news especially well. But, looking back, I have to hand it to Bijou: she made a sensible investment. Glyn Perkins has miner's DNA; he's a worker, if nothing else. And thanks to him, Bijou now had four bedrooms in Brentwood and a majority stake in a yoga-moms' fashion boutique on Montana. Or so I'd heard – I was not invited to the wedding.

The inside of the house was style-magazine chic: white walls, generic modern art. At the end of the hallway, I sneered at a framed one-sheet for *Marshal Eagle 2*, its stubbled hero approaching the viewer in a Stetson and spurs, mid-stride, packing twin revolvers. Stuff was exploding behind him.

Bijou led me past a quarry of discarded Lego into the kitchen at the back. Out beyond the terrace I could see palm trees and a pool. She perched on a high-stool and picked up a glass of what looked like iced tea from the black marble counter. High-end cookware dangled from a pot rack overhead. I took a moment to appreciate the finely calibrated a/c.

'I'd offer you a drink,' she said, sipping hers. 'But you're not staying long. Hey, put that shit *away*! There are *kids* living here.'

I'd taken a puff without even thinking.

'Oh, come on,' I said. 'It's an *electronic* cigarette. It's not even real smoke.'

'I don't care. My house, my rules.'

I stuffed it back into my jeans pocket.

'If I recall correctly, you used to have some pretty bad habits yourself,' I said.

'I've been toxin-free for years, if you must know. Which is more than I can say for you. I can smell last night's liquor, for Chrissakes. When did you last *shave*?'

'No wonder Glyn went down on one knee,' I said. 'You're still just bursting with charm.'

'Fuck you, Lucky. I have postpartum depression.'

'Aren't your kids like six years old now?'

'Five and three. What does *that* have to do with anything?'

Bijou and I make each other crazy. Always have. I glanced over at the gigantic refrigerator, where a photograph of their eldest was pinned to the door with a magnet. Glyn was in the photo as well, but his face had been obscured by a takeaway menu. I felt for the boy: Welsh father, Cajun mother, each a distinct shade of awful. He had his dad's ginger hair, and would likely inherit a bizarre accent and at least one congenital personality disorder, too.

'Did Glyn send you? I didn't know you two were talking again.'

'We're not,' I replied. 'So it's true, then; he moved out?'

Bijou looked around the room, under the counter — making a drama of it, as usual. 'Well, I don't see him here,' she said. 'Do *you*?'

'What happened?'

'Oh, please. Like I'm gonna cry on your shoulder, of all people.'

'Didn't know you had tear ducts. How long has it been?'

'A few weeks.'

'So where is he?'

She glared at me, then: 'A hotel. Probably with a woman.'

'There's another woman? That does not sound like Glyn.'

'How would *you* know? Christ, Glyn always said he thought you were still in LA. But I just assumed you'd have done the decent thing by now and left.'

I caught her glare and held it. Bijou broke first, dipped her eyes and sighed. It's been a long time, but I can still picture the little tattoo on the inside of her thigh: a ship in a storm, the waves blue curlicues.

'Tell me,' I said. 'Beej, tell me.'

'He'd been dropping off the radar a lot,' she replied at last. 'Staying out past dinner, switching off his phone. This is before he left. He told me he was working late at the lot, writing. So I checked his call history once when he was in the shower. It was all women with hooker names. Nadja. Gretchen. Bryony.'

'Those are waitress names. *Bijou* is a hooker name.'

That sucked the wind from her sails, though it gave me little satisfaction. She stared glumly into her drink, and I wondered whether there was vodka in it.

'Did you ask him about them?'

'Of course I did! He had a bullshit explanation for every one. But he's a writer: he lies for a *living*!'

'I hear the studio's waiting on a script for *Marshal Eagle 3*,' I said.

She laughed mirthlessly. 'He was supposed to direct this one, too,' she replied. 'But he pulled out. Couldn't handle the pressure. So there goes the college fund. Turns out he's a quitter, just like you. And don't even *try* to pretend like you're not enjoying this, you motherfucker.'

'Honestly? I could not care less what's going on between you two,' I said. 'But Abby Musker came to me and said she was worried about Glyn. I told her I'd track him down, so that's what I'm doing. She's the one who gave me your address.'

'*Abby?* That little prick-tease. He probably fucked *her*, as well.'

'For God's sake, Bijou. Pull yourself together.'

You'd be better off teaching a toddler Mandarin than trying to make Bijou happy; discontent is her mother tongue. But this was something deeper. Misery was scrawled across her model features. I might have said she was acting – but then, she never was that great an actress.

'He's staying at the Chagall,' she said. 'He left me a spare room-key. It's on the table in the hall. You go try talking some sense into him. Could be he'll take one look at you and see what a dumb idea it is to drop out. You are a fucking case study, after all.'

I couldn't listen to her any longer, nor look at her face like that. Too many memories, most of them bad. So I said I'd do what I could – in not so many words – and then I got the hell out, pocketing the room-key as I went and slamming the front door behind me. The guy strimming the grass from the pavement had moved on to the next-door house. Raúl stood watching as I strode towards the truck. Burgers was peeing against a tree.

8

Every kind of person washes up at Venice Beach; it's that rare LA neighbourhood where white, black and brown all rub along together. A gallimaufry of hippies and yuppies; hobos and slumming movie stars; Brits lured by the novelty of the beach, or on some misguided Isherwood pilgrimage. Lately, though, the town has a new tribe: the tech firms are moving in, their moneyed geeks gobbling up real estate – Benjamins, with Benjamins.

Our client lived in a poured-concrete cube close to the Venice canals. Bamboo sprouted tidily from behind the slatted cedar fence. A floor-to-ceiling window wrapped one corner of the top floor, and behind the reflected sky I could make out the shapes of several costly designer furnishings. It was the home of a guy who could afford his own architect, and who wanted you to know it.

There was an ancient RV slouching at the kerb out front, so I backed the truck into a spot across the street. My parallel parking is customarily impeccable, but I was so distracted that it took me three attempts to complete the manoeuvre. Raúl could tell something was up – he kept looking at me sideways.

These days I do my best to avoid emotional extremes, to swerve whenever I see drama coming down the pike. How very *English* of me, you're probably thinking. Yet there I was, unavoidably confronted by two disquieting situations in less than twenty-four hours: a mentor in a hospital bed; a partner in the wind. Anxiety unspooled into my gut, inch by inch, like a jammed VHS tape.

'Sweet pad,' said Raúl, of Benjamin's living quarters.

I raised an eyebrow. 'Alright for some.'

'C'mon dude, you grew up in a frickin' castle! And, *hashtag-just-sayin'*, it's seriously uncool to dislike somebody just because they're successful.'

'Not where I come from,' I replied. 'Besides, you can't seriously expect me to admire a guy who made a fortune from something called "Bacon Ninja", can you?'

Raúl sighed. 'What are you, a hundred years old?'

We unloaded the slot machine first, heavier than it looked, lifting it from the truck to the dolly. I hauled it across the street and onto the pavement, which was broken and uneven where the palm roots had burst through. Raúl closed the truck and came after me, carrying the diner neon: 'Burgers Fries Shakes'.

The RV parked outside Benjamin's place had seen better days. Rusted wheel arches, gunge-spattered windows, a profusion of peeling bumper stickers and a loose exhaust pipe lashed to the chassis with a length of bungee cord. There were two badly dinged surfboards strapped to the roof, and a weathered beach-cruiser bicycle on a rack at the back.

Enthroned on a folding deckchair at the vehicle's open side door was an ageing derelict wearing nothing but beads, board shorts and a pair of dirty flip-flops. He had lank, grey-blond hair and a barely tended beard. Here and there, fading tats embellished his skin, which had been browned and loosened like a baked apple by the lifelong sun. Venice teems with surfers and bums; sometimes it's hard to tell the difference. Either way, the guy plainly lived in the RV. If I were homeless, I'd probably head for the beach, too.

He was drinking a can of Pabst and gazing at a computer in his lap. It sounded like he was watching a movie. He grumbled something derogatory as we entered the front yard and steered the dolly between Benjamin's Tesla and a vast agave, but it wasn't clear whether he was talking to us or to the screen.

We'd barely rung the bell when Benjamin threw the door open.

'Hey, guys,' he said, his arms wide and welcoming. 'Thanks so much for this. *Awesome!*'

He had that aggressive Yank affability that I always distrust, a shallow performance of friendliness that they probably all learned from growing up with *Sesame Street*. He looked down at the slot machine sitting on the dolly. 'Oh boy, I love that thing. But, hmm. Any chance you could carry it? Only the floors here get scratched real easily. It's one flight up, that's all. Here, let me take that . . .'

He grabbed the neon from Raúl. 'So I'm gonna put this in my office,' he went on. 'Then I gotta finish up a conference call, but why don't you toss that thing in the den? Top of the stairs, on the left. I cleared a spot right in the middle of the wall unit. S'gonna look *awesome*.'

He carried the sign into a room off the hallway, and as the door swung shut behind him I spotted a couple of post-pubescent programmers sitting chained to their laptops. Raúl and I shrugged at one another, and then between us we lugged the slot machine up the stairs. On the landing was a life-size cardboard cut-out of what I guessed was a bacon ninja, frying breakfast in a pan. Adorning the wall of the upstairs corridor was a row of framed movie prints, each one apparently signed by the film-makers: *The Matrix*; *The Lord of the Rings*; *The Empire Strikes Back*. I rolled my eyes at Raúl, who frowned in reply.

Benjamin's so-called den spanned approximately the same square-footage as my entire house. If you stood in the right spot behind the wraparound window, you could see slivers of ocean between the buildings a few blocks away. This kid had got too rich, too young, I thought to myself. His place still smelled like a college dorm: sweat and spunk and cheap supermarket deodorant.

A shelving unit climbed to the high ceiling, and, as Benjamin had promised, there was a single clear space in the centre where the one-armed bandit would fit. We hefted it into place, and I hoped we'd found a good home for the old gadget. The surrounding shelves contained spotless coffee-table books, back issues of *Wired* and *Maxim* and various items of electronic equipment, only about half of which I could identify.

In spite of the teenage odour, the whole room was so fastidiously ordered that I figured the guy must be on the spectrum. Several of the surfaces were carefully arrayed with toys: action figures, Japanese collectibles, an original scale replica of the *Millennium Falcon*. Fortunately, most modern Hollywood merchandise is made in China, or else we'd have to make room for a dedicated section at Bart's Olde California. Apparently, Benjamin was a collector. I picked up a plastic figure with a green felt cape and tutted. Raúl elbowed me in the ribs, disapproving. He shared our client's taste for trash culture.

I heard the slap of Benjamin's flip-flops approaching down the hall before he bounced into the room, sipping a green smoothie through a straw. 'Seriously, guys, this is so *awesome*,' he repeated, for the third time, with the dubious enthusiasm of a studio exec who's about to shitcan your movie pitch.

'About that sign,' I said. 'The neons seem to work. But the wiring's pretty old, so you might want to have an electrician take a look at it, just in case.'

'Sure, sure. I'll have my guy come by,' Benjamin replied.

'Swell place,' I said. 'How long you been here?'

'Oh, like literally moved in a month ago. Y'know, I was living in Palo Alto after I dropped out of college. But then a bunch of my buddies moved to LA, so . . . This is kinda where it's at right now.'

Raúl stepped towards him, pressing his palms together: *namaste*.

'Mr Benjamin,' he began.

'Hey, call me Scooter.'

'Scooter, I just gotta say: I loved Bacon Ninja, so much.'

'You're a user? That's awesome!'

'Are you *kidding* me? I got stuck on hash browns for like a *week*!'

'Ha! Lotta people say that. That is a *tough* level.'

'So, are you working on a sequel?'

'Y'know, we *are*. We're looking into all kindsa ways to expand the Bacon Ninja ecosystem, build engagement. That success we had with the first iteration gave us a chance to develop some really cool new products for the gaming space, some AR stuff, all that. I think you're gonna love what's coming next.'

'Cool, yeah.' Raúl nodded, his brow furrowed in earnest concentration. 'Oh, and I thought the way you monetised was just so smart, so seamless.'

Benjamin gurgled the last of his juice through the straw. 'Thanks,' he said. 'The money's great and all, but I think what really matters is that we delight our users, y'know? We're looking to position ourselves as a company that's all about an *experience* – not just one app . . . Oh hey, you like Doom?'

I'd zoned out, wearied by the exchange, but now Benjamin was staring at me.

'Huh?' I said.

'Doctor Doom,' he replied, and he gestured with his empty cup at the action figure in my hand. 'He's cool, right?'

'Oh, this? Nah. No, I hate all that superhero rubbish.'

I put the figure back, on the wrong shelf.

'He's kidding,' Raúl said, glaring at me.

'Oh, I get it,' said Benjamin, manifestly not getting it.

'Actually, I'm not,' I said. 'I can't stand how all this . . .' – I waved my hand towards his toy collection, grasping for the appropriate noun – '. . . *bollocks* has infected the culture. Fantasy, sci-fi, superheroes. Fucking *Star Wars*. It's completely bloody infantilising. I mean, don't you think it devalues genuine human experience if, every time a character gets into a scrape, he can just call upon his magical ability to . . . I don't know, blow things up with his *mind*?'

Raúl looked mortified – an emotion he rarely encounters. But after a second or two of stunned silence, the young entrepreneur broke into a grin. 'Boy, I love that British sarcasm,' Benjamin said, chuckling. '*So* funny.'

My partner recovered his composure. 'This guy,' he said, jerking his thumb at me. 'I can't take him *anywhere*.'

If it seems to you like that little speech of mine was prepared, put it this way: I hadn't planned to repeat it, but that was not the first time I'd delivered it. Raúl thinks I'm a snob of sorts, and maybe I am. But some creative artefacts are just fundamentally, objectively bad – like *Mein Kampf*, or 'We Built This City' by Starship. From what I could tell, Benjamin's app fell squarely into that category, and so did his ridiculous plastic trinkets.

They both enjoyed a good laugh at my expense, so I decided to let them share their moment and went to fetch the Spanish Revival tile table from the truck. By the time I got back and set it down beside the den's Danish-style sectional, Raúl had invited himself to Benjamin's weekly Ultimate Frisbee game, and Benjamin had tentatively agreed to attend Raúl's Lo-Ball gig that Saturday night. This is how Raúl makes friends: by force of will.

The bum with the RV looked up as we finally emerged from the house. He was still sitting in the deckchair, drinking and watching his laptop. I now noticed two placards resting against the vehicle beside him: 'Yuppies Go Home!' and 'Keep Venice Weird!!' He had a face like chewed gum. I couldn't tell whether he was squinting, or whether the sun and substance abuse had just fixed his expression that way.

Raising a bony finger towards us, he croaked: 'You fellas delivering something to the dude lives there?'

'Yeah,' Raúl replied. 'What of it?'

'Goddam gentrification, that's what. Rich Silicon Valley assholes tearin' the heart out of this town. Venice Beach used to *mean* something, man.'

Raúl leapt to his new friend's defence. 'C'mon, he has just as much right to live here as you do,' he said.

'What*ever*,' said the bum, dismissing the point with a wave of his hand. 'He doesn't contribute to the *community*!'

'And what do *you* contribute to the community, exactly?' I asked.

'Hey, man, I'm part of the fabric of the *neighbourhood*.' He took a long, last swig from his can of lager. 'These Google mother-fuckers don't understand the *old* Venice. Know what I'm sayin'?'

'Not really,' I replied. 'Are *you* the old Venice, then?'

'Exactly,' the bum said, crushing the can in his hand and turning back to whatever was on his laptop. '*Exactly*.'

Raúl leaned against the RV to peer at the screen. The vehicle listed, its axles quietly complaining. 'What are you watching?' he said. 'Is that *Downton Abbey*?'

'Yeah, man. I been streamin' it. It's a great show!'

'Streaming it? You got Wi-Fi in the RV?'

'Nah, man, I steal it from *that* motherfucker.' The bum pointed at Benjamin's house. 'Ain't *my* problem if the guy has an open network, *right*?'

I laughed and started to smoke. Raúl was admiring the placards.

'Mind if I take a picture of your signs?' he said.

'Why,' the bum sneered, 'so you can put it on *Instagram*?'

'Probably,' Raúl replied, and I heard the obnoxious click of his iPhone camera.

The bum turned to me. 'The fuck is *that* thing,' he said. 'Pot?'

'It's an e-cigarette.'

'*Fuck*, man. If you're gonna quit, just *quit* already.'

By then it was too late to set out for Calabasas again, and Raúl had received another smiley face from Whitney Blair, who assured him that she would gladly wait one more day for her desk. So, at my partner's insistence, we took Burgers for a walk on the beach instead.

The bulldog chased a spittle-damp tennis ball onto the sand

and ogled the bikini babes who clustered to pet him. Raúl lapped up the proxy attention, telling jokes, polishing his act. He even laid a few torn-out pages from an old *Reader's Digest* on the ground to demonstrate Burgers's bizarre house-training. Some of the spectators groaned with disgust as he shat; some applauded. Maybe they thought it was a street performance.

Music and marijuana scent wafted across the beach from the Boardwalk souvenir shops. I stood back from the crowd and soaked up the view. Evening surfers were bobbing in the shallows, waiting for a satisfactory set. Gulls pecked at picnic leftovers. And far off, where the Santa Monica Mountains curve west over Malibu, a thin scrim of black smoke had started to creep along the ridge. A helicopter whirred above the wildfire, visible only as a pink-orange pinprick, glinting in the setting sun. No one else seemed to have noticed.

9

We headed back east, stopping to grab dinner at Bludso's on La Brea: hot links and thick slivers of low, slow-cooked Texas brisket; smoky rib tips and a heap of pulled pork. Shared sides of mac and cheese, collard greens and cornbread, all washed down with a cool pitcher of craft beer. Seriously, screw jazz – sometimes I think barbecue might be the Great American Art Form.

We sat at the bar, half-watching a Dodgers game on TV as hipsters jawed around us. Raúl's moustache was heavy with hot sauce.

'Sorry we didn't get to Calabasas,' I said.

'Dude, don't sweat it,' he replied, once more sinking his fork into our heap of meat. 'Tomorrow is another day. And get this: *TMZ* says Whitney just broke up with Marcus.'

'Is that right. And who is Marcus when he's at home?'

'Guy she was dating on *BTHTV*, before it got cancelled. He's some kinda club-promoter-slash-businessman-slash-DJ-slash-whatever. Total douche.'

'*BTHTV*?'

'*Beyond the Hills: The Valley.*'

'Huh. So was Marcus the guy in the porno?'

'The sex tape? Nah, that was Chad. She dated him in Season One.'

'And what happened to Chad?'

'Got fired from the show after Whitney kicked him to the kerb. Not an audience favourite. That's when he leaked the tape. Another douche.'

'Sounds like it.'

'So, my liege,' Raúl said, licking his fingers. 'What's with the detour to Brentwood? Who was that chick?'

I chewed on a rib tip and stared again at the Dodgers game, taking none of it in. I still have absolutely no idea how baseball works. 'Huh,' I said. 'What chick?'

He belched. 'C'mon, Lucky. I have eyes. The blonde who answered the door. She a new squeeze, or an old one?'

I swallowed, wiped my sticky hands on a napkin, sipped my beer and decided to relent. 'An old one,' I said. 'She shacked up with my best friend.'

'Ouch. That's gotta hurt.'

'Yeah, well. That was a past life. Ancient history.'

'But you're still friends? With the dude, I mean.'

'Glyn? Nah. If we're anything, it's enemies. But I don't even think we're that anymore. He's just . . . some guy I used to know.'

When Glyn and I first fell out, I spent a long time worrying that I might bump into him unexpectedly – in the produce aisle at Trader Joe's, for instance. But after a while, I realised: in Los Angeles, people never just *bump into* each other – especially not after one of you pens a blockbuster franchise, moves to the Westside and starts shopping for groceries at Bristol Farms.

'Sorry,' said Raúl. 'But then why the house call? You stoking that old flame?'

'Ha. Absolutely not. But that reminds me . . .'

I picked up my phone and began composing a text to Abby Musker. Raúl signalled the barman, who slung a dish-towel over his shoulder and sidled up. 'Get you fellas anything else?'

'Just the check, thanks. Oh, and listen. I'm doing *Blowing Up* at the Lo-Ball Saturday night. You mind if I leave some flyers here?'

'Uh . . . No, I guess not,' the guy replied, before turning away to serve a tall, grey stranger who was looming at the far end of the bar.

'Great,' said Raúl. He reached into the messenger bag at his feet and came up clutching a stack of handbills as thick as *Atlas Shrugged*. Then he leaned in close to me and muttered from the corner of his mouth. 'Don't look now,' he said, his eyes swivelling towards the tall guy, 'but I think that's *Ted Danson*.'

Karen had closed up and was long gone by the time we got back to the store. Next door, Sasquatch Pete's café was Monday-night quiet. I made a point of backing the truck into a space that I thought he would find amenable. Roosting crows squawked conversationally atop the nearby power lines.

Raúl was trying to persuade me to go with him to a comedy club. 'Why don't we head to the Lo-Ball,' he said. 'Improv night. We can still catch it.'

I mumbled non-committally as we crossed the car park to the back door of the store. 'C'mon, come hang with some comedians,' Raúl went on. 'They'll make you feel better about yourself.'

'Thanks, but I'm not sure I feel like laughing,' I replied.

'Not by *laughing*,' he said, as we let ourselves in to grab our things. 'They'll make you feel better cause they're all such *deadbeats* . . . Wait.'

Raúl thrust out his hand to stop me in the doorway. He was carrying Burgers in the pet crate, and the dog had started to snarl: a steady, menacing rumble, like a tiny chainsaw. 'What is it, buddy?' Raúl whispered.

But for some faint rectangles of streetlight, the store was pitch dark.

'Raúl . . .'

'Shh.' He knelt and set the pet crate on the ground. 'Burgers? What is it, huh?'

'At least turn on the *lights* . . .'

'Shh!'

I shushed, but heard nothing besides Burgers, still snarling, and the blood pulsing in my ears. And then, a click: the Anglepoise beside the cash register snapped on. Looming over it was a tall, broad dude dressed all in black: black sweater; black cargo pants; black gloves; black balaclava. No, not *all* in black — he'd accessorised with a fetching yellow fanny-pack.

Chills, multiplying. Something about his quarterback shoulders seemed wrong, as if they'd been padded to make a skinny guy look wide. I could see only his eyes, wide and intense, and his mouth, breathing fast — enough to discern that he, like the outfit, was black. We all stood and stared at each other for what felt to me like a full minute, and I found myself edging bit-by-bit behind my partner.

'Are you wearing a *cape*?' said Raúl, finally. 'Hold on: is that supposed to be a *Batman* costume?'

The dog growled on, but this time the man growled back.

'Where is it?' he said, bass in register and threatening in tone.

'Where is *what*?' Raúl replied, apparently unperturbed.

'The blackbird.'

'Say *what*?'

'The *blackbird*,' the man growled again. 'Marty Kann's black-bird! *Where IS IT?*'

I stuttered quietly, 'M-Marty Kann?'

'The fuck are you talking about?' said Raúl. 'Where's our *cookie jar*, you cosplay motherfucker? And why are you talking like that?'

The man in black narrowed his eyes, stopped growling. 'Cookie jar?'

That's when I spotted the papers strewn across the counter behind him — Marty Kann's drawings, removed from their box and rifled through.

'Raúl,' I said, collecting myself. 'Raúl, just . . . calm down. Now listen, chum. Do you have a gun?'

The man in black took a moment to process the question. 'Uh, n— . . . Yeah?'

'He doesn't have a gun, Lucky,' Raúl said.

71

'He might have a gun.'

'He doesn't. Look at him. He's crapping his pants. He doesn't have a gun.'

'Hey,' said the man in black, piqued. 'How do *you* know I don't have a gun?'

'Where is it, then? In your *utility belt*?'

The instant he finished spitting the words, Raúl lunged towards the counter. The man stumbled back, swivelled and made a break for it. In a flash, my partner had rounded the cash register and reached for the antique wooden baseball bat that Bart keeps beneath it, in lieu of an alarm system. The man in black flung open the front door of the store and tumbled into the street, the opening bars of 'The Star-Spangled Banner' chiming in his wake. Raúl vaulted the counter and raced after him, brandishing the bat and yelling back over his shoulder: 'Hey, Sir Lucky – MOVE YOUR ASS GODDAMIT!'

Raúl may be squat, but he moves like Road Runner. By the time I made it to the pavement, he was already halfway down the block and gaining on his prey. I dashed after them, passing Sasquatch Pete as he emerged from his café, drawn outside by the commotion.

The European nobility are nowadays such a feeble, chinless bunch that it's difficult to imagine us having ancestors formidable enough to earn their titles. Centuries back, somewhere far closer to the fat trunks of our family trees, there were warriors and gifted statesmen. But the last time a Viscount Wonersh excelled himself on the battlefield was at Waterloo – and neither his courage, his stamina nor his selflessness has survived the intervening generations. My legs are long and I can maintain appearances in a sprint, but as soon as the race became middle-distance, I started to flag.

Up ahead, I saw the man in black reach Hillhurst and canter into traffic. Brakes screeched, horns sounded. My lungs were suffering the consequences of twenty-five years' accumulated tar.

Raúl paused at the kerb, but then the lights turned red and he booked it across the street before I could reach him. I stopped and clung to a lamp post to catch my breath, watching helplessly as he plunged down one of the unlit side streets on the far side of the avenue.

Wheezing, I jogged onward, but I'd already lost sight of them both in the dark. The side street was residential, two pin-drop silent rows of homes animated only by the blue flicker of flatscreen TVs from between venetian blinds. I made it about fifty yards before I had to drop to my knees on someone's lawn, chest about ready to cave in. As my breathing slowed, I could hear footsteps fast receding, a shout – and then I spotted them.

Beneath the streetlamp at the other end of the block, the man in black had turned to face his pursuer, long cape fluttering as they circled one another, he the matador and Raúl the bull. I tried to cry out to my partner to be careful, but I couldn't summon sufficient oxygen for the task.

Raúl raised the bat, ready to strike, but he hesitated just long enough for the man in black to get behind him, blur-quick. I heard my friend howl with pain and watched him collapse on the pavement – *whump!* The clatter of the bat on the concrete echoed like distant gunfire: *toka-toka-toka-tok*. 'No,' I croaked. '*No!*'

I fought my way upright and staggered forward, slaloming with exhaustion. The man in black had vanished into the night, but Raúl was still hollering – which at least meant that he wasn't dead. He was on the ground when I reached him, writhing in pain and clutching his rear. 'He stabbed me in the ass!' he cried. '*Batman* stabbed me in the FRICKIN' *ASS!*'

Nearby porch-lights flickered into life, bewildered Los Felizians peering past their door-chains at the unfolding scene. Raúl gritted his teeth as I reluctantly pressed my hand to his butt-cheek, but it came away clean: no blood. My nostrils caught an acrid scent. I sniffed the air. Something was burning.

Officer Park hefted the wooden bat in his hand, testing its weight.

'So this is a genuine Dodgers bat?' he said.

'That's correct,' Raúl replied, wincing, still in pain despite having wolfed a handful of Advil tabs. He sat in the chair behind the register, two plump cushions beneath him and Burgers mewling in his lap. 'It was Moose Skowron's – that's his signature right there. Swung it against the Yankees at the '63 World Series. Comes with a certificate of authenticity. To *you*, Officer: a thousand bucks.'

Park nodded, suitably impressed, and set the slugger down on the counter. Officer Schooley cleared his throat, read from his notepad: 'So, Mr Kluge, you said that the front door to the store was left unlocked?'

Karen stifled another sob with a soggy Kleenex and leaned into Sasquatch Pete, who'd wrapped his arm around her in consolation. 'I'm so sorry,' she whimpered. 'I thought I locked it. I didn't know how to work the latch!'

'Karen, seriously, this is not your fault,' I said. 'I should have shown you how to close up properly. It's complicated.'

It is not the least bit complicated. But I saw no reason to make her feel worse than she already did. The five of us – Karen, Pete, Park, Schooley and myself – stood among the antique clutter, encircling Raúl: the hero, the victim. It was two hours since I'd peeled my partner off the pavement and helped him to hobble back to Bart's Olde California. I'd called Karen, Pete had called the police.

'See,' said Officer Schooley, 'the thing is, that means we can't really get the guy on breaking and entering. This is a store, after all . . .'

'You have *got* to be kidding me,' said Raúl. 'It was *dark*! It was past nine! *Way* after business hours.'

'Y'know, some stores are still open then,' said Officer Park. 'Like 7-Eleven.'

Raúl fumed. Park folded his arms, steroidal pecs bulging beneath his uniform.

Schooley said: 'Was anything stolen, to your knowledge?'

'We don't think so,' I replied. 'He just went through some boxes.'

'And Mr Gupta,' the lanky cop went on, 'could you clarify – did the man attack you first, or did you attack him?'

'Well, I chased him out the store.'

'With the baseball bat.'

'Officer, the guy tazed me in the ass! I have a welt down there the size of the Staples Center. You wanna see it?'

'But *technically*,' said Schooley, 'he was acting in self-defence.'

Raúl threw his hands up. Burgers yipped in sympathy.

'Hang on, Officer,' I said. 'Just hang on. Even if the perp didn't break in, didn't steal anything, and even if he tazed Raúl in self-defence, surely he's got to be the same person that attacked Bart last night? The same person who stole our six-grand cookie jar?'

Schooley pondered that, but then dismissed it. 'Circumstantial,' he said.

'Circumstantial?' I replied, beginning to share Raúl's indignation. 'Come on, that's two nights in a row!'

'I see what you're saying, Mr Kluge, but it might just be bad luck.'

'Bad *juju*,' Karen muttered.

'Hey, Raúl,' said Pete, scratching his heavy beard as he ruminated. 'Didn't you say the guy was dressed as Batman?'

'Yes!' Raúl cried. 'He was doing Christian Bale, doing Batman. Y'know, that deep-voice thing he does? No . . . ? *Anyone?* Oh c'mon, has nobody here seen *The Dark Knight? SERIOUSLY?*'

I tutted – *superheroes.* Park raised his hand: 'I saw it. Good movie.'

'Fuck me,' said Raúl, exasperated.

Schooley again: 'But he was wearing gloves . . .'

'Yeah,' I replied. 'So no fingerprints.'

'. . . and a mask?'

'A balaclava,' I said.

Schooley licked his narrow lips, frowned, murmured: 'And could you tell whether he was, uh . . . ?' He tailed off.

'What?' said Raúl. 'Whether he was *what?*'

Park took over: 'He means was the guy white, brown, yellow or African-American.'

Raúl and I shared a look that I believe encapsulated the rich history of black people and the LAPD. 'Dunno,' Raúl shrugged. 'It was pretty dark.'

'He kept saying something about a bird,' I added. 'And I'm pretty sure he mentioned a dead guy called Marty Kann.'

'Kann,' Park repeated. 'What is that, Pakistani?'

'Not Khan,' I replied, '*Kann.*'

'Bad juju,' Karen muttered again.

Raúl stood up abruptly, cradling Burgers. 'You know what, Officers? It doesn't matter,' he announced. 'I think you have all the salient information. It's late, and I would like to get home so that I can put some lotion on my sore butt.'

Schooley and Park exchanged a glance. 'Of course,' Schooley nodded, flipping his notepad closed. He seemed relieved to be allowed to escape. 'We'll be in touch. And in the meantime, I really recommend you install those security cameras. How is your husband, Mrs Abernathy?'

'Resting up,' Karen said. 'He's still not himself.'

'Well, at least he's back home now. That's the main thing. You have my number in case you think of anything else.'

The cops made to leave, Park pausing on his way out to peer curiously at Oscar. He prodded the fibreglass beak, almost tentative, as if it might bite him. Schooley opened the front door, setting off the 'Star-Spangled Banner' chimes. Park chuckled and called to his partner as he followed him out to their squad car: 'This store is *wild*, bro!'

With uncharacteristic compassion, Sasquatch Pete agreed to see Karen home. She was upset, but: silver lining – her guilt about the unlocked door would keep her sweet for a few days. Raúl and Burgers stood at the window, watching them go.

'Y'know what,' Raúl said. 'I think we can strike Pete from the list of suspects.'

'I wholeheartedly concur,' I replied. 'But listen. The guy definitely said something about Marty Kann, didn't he? You heard that, too. I wasn't imagining things. Shouldn't we have told them about the Kann estate?'

'Dude, those cops are about as much use as a vegan at a gun range.' He turned from the window with a gleam in his eye that instantly had me worried. 'You want my opinion?' he said. 'We can catch this guy ourselves.'

'Raúl, come on. This isn't a game . . .'

'And I'm not playing. Did *you* get tazed tonight? C'mon, hear me out.'

'Ugh, alright,' I sighed, still apprehensive. 'What are you suggesting?'

He put a hand on my shoulder, drawing me in. 'So, I've been thinking . . .'

'Oof. Did it hurt?'

'Good one, Grandpa. Listen, I've got a Google APB out on Ringmaster cookie jars. I think *you* ought to go talk to Cleo

77

Habibi, work the Marty Kann angle. It's her sale connects the dead guy to the store, could be she can join some dots. She'll talk to you – she likes you.'

'What's that supposed to mean?'

'Don't be so British. You know what it means.'

I considered Raúl's strategy. It was hare-brained, but it possessed a certain logic. I decided to humour him. 'Fine. I'll call her tomorrow,' I said. 'But I want it on the record that I think this is a stupid idea.'

He grinned and slapped me on the back. Burgers wiggled his rear in solidarity. At the counter, we began to gather up the mess of Marty Kann's drawings that Batman had unpacked. I leafed through the stack absent-mindedly.

'So, the guy was clearly looking for something,' I said. 'Agreed?'

'Agreed,' said Raúl.

'Something he thinks we have. "The blackbird"?'

'Whatever that is.'

I pulled on my e-cigarette. Marty Kann was a superlative draftsman – and versatile, too: architectural sketches, scenic visualisations, character renderings. I preferred his production designs to most of the movies they'd been used for. But as I worked deeper into the stack, I started to notice something else. Among the finished drawings, in corners and on flipsides, were countless doodles arranged as sequential rectangles. Some of them took up entire sheets. Dynamic action scenes, dialogue speech bubbles – even, to my distaste, several characters clad in what appeared to be spandex. I plucked one of the doodles from the pile.

'What are these, movie storyboards?'

'Hate to break it to you, Sir Lucky,' Raúl replied, 'but I think they're comics.'

If I asked you to lie back and think of Hollywood, perhaps you'd picture the Sunset Strip, that broad, fabled thoroughfare that skirts the rim of the Hills. Above it, A-listers lurk like big game among the trees and shrubs, while downslope stretch the city's endless shimmering boulevards.

The Strip is where Mickey Cohen laundered his fortune. It's where Led Zeppelin rode Harleys through the lobby of the Chateau Marmont. Its pavements were once peopled with junkies and hoodlums, its storefronts filled by tattoo parlours and titty bars. The Rainbow Grill, the Roxy, Whiskey a Go Go: they each teem with the ghosts of dead celebrities. But today all that tradition, romance and tragic glamour is being cemented over with chain eateries, office blocks, *Spider-Man 5* billboards and cheesy new hotels like the Chagall. So you'd be right – because that's Hollywood in a nutshell.

I scanned the laundry-white lobby. At reception, a troupe of Asian guys with designer luggage were checking in: Chinese film investors, or perhaps a Korean pop group. A tiny, made-up girl in an even tinier dress hovered in a square of sunlight near the glass entranceway, flicking her hair and glancing at her phone: budding starlet/teenage call-girl. A gym-fit dude sporting nothing but swimming togs and a two-ton Rolex strode down a corridor towards the pool, rolled towel under his arm: celebrity trainer/superstar DJ.

And here was Abby, perched on a pink couch that looked like

a vagina, checking her watch. She saw me and waved. My Chuck Taylors squeaked on the slick marble floor as I strolled over.

'Must be my Lucky day,' she said. I get that a lot.

'Sorry I'm late. It's turning into a hell of a week.'

'Y'know, when I said we should have brunch, I never imagined you'd get back to me so soon. Had to tell my assistant I was meeting a hot young writer.'

'Instead of an old, washed-up one?'

'You're not *that* old.'

'Thanks for coming, Abby.'

She stood and smoothed her work clothes: a fitted suit, kitten heels. She has the wardrobe of a Hollywood agent and the heart of a kindergarten teacher.

'Funny thing is,' she said, 'I just heard back from Todd's PA yesterday. He said he spoke to Todd, who told him *he* assumed Glyn was back in England, working on the *ME3* script at his mom's place. Keeping a low profile.'

'Wales.'

'What?'

Call me pedantic, but I sometimes find Boston to be the eastern boundary of even the smartest American's geographical knowledge. 'His mum lives in Port Talbot,' I said. 'That's in Wales, not England. Crucial distinction.'

'Alright, fine,' she replied, bemused: '*Wales.*'

'Well, Bijou thinks he's here, with another woman. If that's the case, and I go in alone, it might end in a fistfight. But with you in the mix, I thought we'd both act a little more civilised . . .'

Abby raised an eyebrow.

'What?'

'I'm sorry. It's just the thought of you or Glyn in a *fistfight*. Kinda far-fetched.'

How right she was. I resolved to keep the previous evening's events to myself. The room-key I'd lifted from Bijou's place was not a key, as such, but a magnetic keycard in a paper sleeve, which bore the number 610. We hopped into an open lift and hit the button for the sixth floor. I studied myself in the stainless steel while Abby tapped her foot to the tinny muzak. I still hadn't got around to shaving, and my facial hair was beginning to look intentional. As the lift rose, Abby chuckled to herself quietly, which I took to be a prompt.

'Something funny?'

'Aw, nothing,' she said. 'Todd texted me, too.'

'Oh, yeah? When?'

'After I talked to his PA. Told me to back off Glyn. Just waving his dick around, I guess. Probably thinks I want to poach his client.'

'Well, don't you?'

She smirked at her reflection as the lift pinged for our stop. The sixth-floor hallway was deserted save for a housekeeper's trolley, some discarded room-service trays and a couple of ice buckets containing upturned bottles of champagne. The Chagall has a rep as a party hotel: the worst kind. Room 610 was at the end of the corridor. There was no 'Do Not Disturb' tag dangling from the door-handle, but I knocked all the same. No answer. Abby tipped her head: *try again*. I knocked once more, waited, put an ear to the wood panelling. Silence.

Abby bit her lip. I think she feared what we might find beyond the door: the aftermath of extramarital coitus, or another Hollywood OD. The keycard worked first time, and we slid quietly into the room. It was a south-west corner suite, open-plan, all cool whites and blues and velvet-upholstered, faux-mod furniture. A soft-porn photograph hung over the bed. I stuck my head into the wet room. Nobody home. The suite didn't seem to have been used since it was last cleaned: the bed was made; the towels fresh. I checked the wastepaper basket – empty.

And yet, and yet. It was plainly occupied. A suitcase lay open on the luggage rack, filled with dirty underwear. A phone charger was plugged into the wall. A selection of lifestyle magazines were stacked on the desk, with some chewed pencils, a handful of screener DVDs and a set of cuff-links. Abby opened the wardrobe; there were clothes hanging inside, and two pairs of smart-casual shoes. I sat in the desk chair and swivelled to face her.

'Does this look like Glyn's stuff to you?'

'I think I recognise this,' she said, tossing a starchy, lilac-striped Oxford shirt onto the bed, still on its coat-hanger. Upper-class menswear was one of Glyn's signature working-class affectations. Through the open window came the breakfast hubbub from the poolside restaurant, several floors below. The soft curtains billowed on the breeze, and as they parted slightly I could see the silhouettes of Century City in the far distance. One of those skyscrapers contained Todd Carver's corner office – Glyn could see his script deadline from his desk.

'Well, looks like we just missed him,' I said.

Abby picked up a book from the bedside table.

'What's he reading?'

She read out the title on the spine: '*The Hero with a Thousand Faces*, by Joseph Campbell.'

'Wanker.'

I opened the desk drawer and fished out the hotel notepad. I picked up one of the pencils and began to scrape the graphite lightly back and forth across the top sheet of the pad, wondering whether the old indentations-in-the-paper trick would actually work. To my joy and amazement, letters began to appear. 'Holy shit,' I laughed. 'Abby, there's a name on this . . .'

'Is it "Evelyn"?'

I glanced up. 'How did you . . . ?'

Abby was holding Glyn's book open in one hand, and a sheet of the hotel notepaper in the other, with the same letters scrawled on it in Glyn's handwriting: 'EVELYN'. He always made notes in all caps; I remembered that. As if nobody ever taught him joined-up handwriting.

'Huh,' I said. 'Yeah, I guess it is. And is that . . . an address?'

'Melrose and Robertson,' she read aloud. 'Ten a.m.'

I glanced at the analogue alarm clock on the bedside table. It was nine-thirty.

'Is there a day? A date?'

She turned the note over and looked at the back. I could see it was blank.

'No,' she said. 'But there's this . . .'

From the same open page in Glyn's edition of Campbell, she picked up another scrap of paper, which she handed to me. It was a valet ticket from the Chagall's parking garage. 'Isn't that a little weird,' Abby said, 'to leave without his car?'

'Maybe he just went to breakfast. The blueberry pancakes here are to die for.'

She put the book back on the bedside table and scanned the room, her arms crossed, tapping an index finger against her lips in thought. There was a knock at the door, and we guiltily locked eyes until we heard the timid voice from the hallway: 'Housekeeping!'

Abby crossed to the door and opened it halfway. 'Hey there,' she said, to the hotel employee outside. 'Haven't you already cleaned this room today?'

I could hear the young woman's nervous, accented denial.

'Okay,' said Abby. 'Could you come back in a half-hour . . . ? Thanks.'

She closed the door and turned to me, frowning.

'So he's been gone at least a day,' she said.

'Maybe he's with the woman,' I replied. 'Evelyn.'

'Without his car?'

'Maybe he took a taxi,' I said, and I pointed to the charger in the wall socket. 'His phone is gone. There's no sign of his wallet, his laptop. His glasses. Check the bathroom; I didn't see a toothbrush. It's not as if he packed an overnight bag and then jumped out the window. He just flopped somewhere else last night.'

'He doesn't wear glasses anymore,' she said. 'He wears contacts.'

'Come on, Abby. We've established that he's staying here, at least some of the time. Let's leave him a message at reception, tell him he has to call you pronto.'

'Aren't you the slightest bit concerned,' she said, her plucked eyebrows pincering, 'about your friend who has gone *missing*?'

'Listen,' I replied, counting the points off on my fingers. 'One: he's not missing. You just don't know where he is. Plus, two: he's *not* my friend. Equals, three: no, I am not concerned.'

I stood and strode over to the minibar in the sitting-room area, where I pocketed a packet of nuts and several of the miniatures from the refrigerator. I could feel Abby's glare warming my back like afternoon sun.

On the shelf beside the snacks, I noticed one item that could not have been from the hotel's inventory: a half-empty bottle of Ribena. Glyn used to buy the blackcurrant concentrate in bulk from the British deli in Santa Monica, along with his regular supply of chocolate Hobnobs. He was always more homesick than me. After a good day's writing, we'd mix the Ribena with vodka and soda and toast our future success.

While Abby left her message with the hotel receptionist, I took a stroll through the Chagall's facilities, but there was no sign of Glyn in the restaurant or the spa. I caught up with her again at the valet stand and stopped her before she could ask for her car. 'Hang on,' I said, and I searched my pockets until I found Glyn's ticket and handed it to the valet. Abby's eyes widened.

'Might as well be thorough,' I said, under my breath.

Glyn's car was a white, convertible BMW 6 Series, this year's model. I put the roof down and flicked on the radio. It was set to a hip-hop station with the volume up, and I kept it there as I roared out onto the Strip, soaking up the lifestyle. Glyn had achieved everything we'd imagined for ourselves when we first put pen to paper: movie career, model wife, soft-topped sports car. This might have been my life, I thought to myself as I wove through traffic. If only things had gone a little differently, I could have been the guy who races away from the stop-light, instead of the guy left stalled in the dust.

'Lucky,' Abby yelled over the music and the rushing air, 'I'm going to be late for my next meeting! Where are we *going*?'

'Melrose and Robertson,' I said. 'It's almost ten a.m., right?'

She was still annoyed with me, but I could sense her beginning to soften. She checked her wristwatch. 'Right,' she replied. 'Good idea.'

Melrose Avenue and Robertson Boulevard met just a few short blocks away, and we arrived almost exactly on the hour. I nosed the Bimmer into the car park on the north-east corner, facing the intersection. We sat and watched the pedestrians, but none of them was Glyn. Abby pointed at the sleek, white building across the street, set back behind a manicured hedge. 'That's Cecconi's,' she said. 'Best kale salad in WeHo.'

I offered to go take a look. One good thing about Hollywood: no waiter can afford to turn away a diner in jeans and trainers, just in case he turns out to be the director at their next audition. I smiled confidently at the staff as I strode into the restaurant and searched for a head of ginger hair among the breakfast crowd. No such luck. I buttonholed the maître d' at front of house.

'Excuse me, do you have a breakfast reservation for Glyn Perkins, ten a.m.?'

He glanced at the book. 'I'm afraid not, sir,' he said.

'What about "Evelyn"?'

'No, nothing under that name, either. But I have a table if you'd like to wait?'

When I got back to the car, Abby looked downcast.

'What is it?' I said. 'Did you see him?'

She held out her hand – and in it: an iPhone in a plastic, Union Jack case.

'Glyn's phone. It was in the glove compartment.'

I took it from her and made to switch it on.

'I tried that,' she said. 'Battery's dead.'

I stared at the phone, as if Siri might suggest a rational explanation.

'Alright,' I said finally. 'Now you can be a little concerned.'

'Thanks, I think,' she replied. 'Weird, isn't it?'

'It is kind of weird.'

'Shit.'

'But let's not get carried away. I'm sure this is all still completely innocent. I'll charge the phone and check it later. Maybe this Evelyn person will be on it.'

'Okay,' she said. 'Yeah, I mean I'm sure he's fine. And y'know, he probably did go back to England like Todd thought—'

'Wales—'

'And I guess he left in a hurry and figured, screw it, the studio is paying for the hotel room – so . . . Don't you think?'

'Sure,' I replied. 'Works for me.'

She was trying to convince herself, but I saw no reason to disabuse her. Her theory seemed plausible. Besides, I didn't want to get myself too worked up about the guy I'd thought of as my nemesis for the past few years.

'Abby, I really have to get to work,' I lied.

'Yeah, of course. Me too,' she said, and I started the engine.

We avoided eye contact as I drove back to the hotel, slower this time, both of us hoping to disguise our mutual doubts. The parking valet seemed disappointed to see us again so soon, and positively baffled when Abby asked him to bring her own car from the garage. I told her I'd go back up to room 610 to fetch the phone charger, and to slip Glyn's valet ticket back between the pages of his book. Then I watched her leave, wondering just what our next meeting might bring.

As soon as Abby had disappeared around the curve, I made my way back into the lobby. I was hungry, and the studio was picking up Glyn's tab: the Chagall may be full of dickheads, but you can't argue with those pancakes.

12

When I finally arrived at the store, Karen was dusting, Burgers was napping, and Raúl was hopping from foot to foot as if he needed to pee.

'Dude,' he said. 'Where have you been? You gotta see this. C'mon!'

He took me by the arm and dragged me bodily to Bart's computer, where a browser window lay open, displaying a poorly lit photograph of a Ringmaster cookie jar standing upright on a patch of mown grass. Raúl gestured to the screen in triumph: 'I found it!'

I peered at the item on the monitor. It was certainly the same make and vintage as our Ringmaster, but it was impossible to identify without examining it in person for the flaws I'd spotted when I picked it out at the Kann house.

'Huh.' I sucked my e-cigarette, blew vapour. 'How do we know it's ours?'

Raúl grimaced as he lowered his tender behind into Bart's chair. He clicked the mouse, minimising the photograph and backing up to a Craigslist classified ad. It was illustrated with just the one inconclusive image, and accompanied by the words: 'Garden Nome, gd condition – $100 ONO (Los Angeles)'.

'Okay,' said Raúl, eager to explain his methodology. 'So I was getting nothing back on my Google alert for "Cookie Jar". But the store's been pretty quiet, so I just started surfing Craigslist. Five minutes in, up pops this guy. Posted this morning, in Los Angeles. The seller clearly has no clue what he's got – I mean, *garden gnome?* And he's only asking a hundred bucks, which sounds like a number somebody pulled out of their ass.'

'You think this is our Batman? The guy who attacked you and Bart?'

'Or one of his associates. Like Robin.'

'Huh?'

'You know, Batman and Rob— Ah, forget it.'

'Is there a name on there, an address?'

'It's an anonymous listing, but I already pinged the guy a message, said I was a gnome collector. Called myself "Ralph". I offered a hundred twenty dollars for the jar, figured that would make sure he'd sell it to us, so now – knock on wood – we set up a meet. You impressed, my liege?'

I was. 'Hey, Karen,' I said. 'You see this? Raúl's got a lead!'

Karen broke off from dusting a pair of Paul Frankl nesting tables to raise an eyebrow in our direction. 'I saw,' she said. I gave Raúl a questioning look: *What's with her?* He shrugged, murmured: 'Mercury's in retrograde.'

The LA freeway system works in mysterious ways. Whereas the previous day it was gridlocked at around the same hour, the 101 now flowed like a waterslide, spitting us out at our exit after thirty minutes. We trundled through old-town Calabasas and wound our way up into the canyons above. Somehow this sleepy enclave at the arse-end of the Valley has become the Beverly Hills of crap celebrities: Jack Nicholson wouldn't be seen dead scouting real estate around here but, the way Raúl tells it, the paps are forever prowling the outdoor malls and juiceries in search of its resident reality stars and tacky teen-pop sensations.

Whitney Blair lived in a plush gated community called Jacaranda Groves, a recently constructed cluster of landscaped McMansion tracts accessible only via a wide lane with high, pruned hedgerows on either side. As we approached the cast-iron gates, a whiskered private security guard in a pressed grey uniform emerged from the hut at the side of the road. He looked at least sixty, probably a retired desk cop, and he stood blinking in the sunlight like a woodchuck awakened early from hibernation. As we pulled alongside I could hear the talk radio turned up loud in the hut behind him. A CCTV camera peered at me through the driver's side window.

'You hear about this *fire*?' he yelled cheerfully, jerking a thumb back over his shoulder at the sound of the hourly news bulletin. 'Twenty thousand acres and spreading! Hope the wind doesn't blow this way! What can I do for you boys?'

'We're delivering an antique to one of the residents,' I replied.

He cupped a hand to his ear. 'Hah?'

'WE'RE MAKING A DELIVERY,' Raúl yelled back, rightly surmising that the guy was at least half deaf.

'Issat right? Who to?'

'Ms Blair,' I said.

'Hah?'

'WHITNEY BLAIR,' said Raúl.

'Well alright then,' said the guard. He disappeared into the hut, returning several seconds later with his spectacles on, studying a clipboard. He took his sweet time. 'Hmm,' he said, looking up at last. 'She didn't put you on the list.'

'What is this,' I muttered, 'a fucking nightclub?'

'Hah?'

'SHE KNOWS WE'RE COMING. COULD YOU CALL HER UP?'

The guard stared askance at me for a moment, then he went back into the hut. The volume on his radio decreased a notch. I drummed my fingers on the wheel. The pet crate rocked on the seat as Burgers shifted his weight. Raúl was fidgety with anticipation. Out came the guard again, wearing an expression that was one part apologetic, one part antagonistic, two parts delighted with himself: a cocktail I like to call the Jobsworth.

'She's not answering,' he said, and he folded his arms.

'Look,' I replied, in my politest Queen's English. 'Would you mind awfully just letting us through? Please? She really is expecting us. She's writing a book, you see, and the desk is terribly important to the creative process.'

'*Hah?*'

Incapable of containing himself any longer, Raúl barked: 'DUDE, JUST LET US THE HELL IN!'

At that, the guy came over all schoolmarmish. 'Now listen here, fellas,' he said, peering at us over his specs. 'We've some extremely important people living in this community. Just what exactly do you think they pay me for? I can't let any old pair of low-lifes through these gates with a removals truck. You could make off with half the valuables on the estate, for all I know!'

This was getting us nowhere. I turned to Raúl. 'You call her,' I said.

Raúl took a deep breath and clamped his phone to his ear while the ornery old git stood staring us out, as if we were gravel he'd just shaken from his shoe. Meanwhile, an SUV with tinted windows pulled up behind the truck. I had to assume it contained yet another C-list superstar.

'No answer,' said Raúl, with a mournful sigh.

'You'll have to get out of the way, boys,' the guard said, gesturing to indicate the other car.

I gritted my teeth, resisted the urge to make a rude remark, and swung the truck into an ungainly five-point turn. We drove away and I watched in the wing mirror as the guard waved the SUV through with a smile.

'Fucksake,' I said. 'That ditzy cow. All she had to do was put us on a list. Does she want the bloody desk or doesn't she?'

'I'll text her,' Raúl replied, hangdog.

To cheer us both up, I made a diversion to Burbank on the way back to the store. Chili John's is an unassuming lunch joint at the corner of Keystone Street, which has survived since the '40s, with barely an update, by serving variations on a single dish to generations of studio folk. I held the door open for the big black guy in a baseball cap who was coming out as we arrived. Raúl stared after him as he walked away. 'Hey,' he said. 'Was that *Laurence Fishburne*?'

We sat at the horseshoe counter while a young longhair in an AC/DC T-shirt produced two bowls of Wisconsin beef chili over spaghetti, which we sprinkled with grated cheese and oyster crackers. We cooled our tongues with soft rolls and root beer. Raúl's phone pinged, and he read what looked to be a lengthy, illustrated text message.

'She said she's *really*, *really* sorry she forgot to put our names down on the list,' he said. 'Then there's a sad-face emoji. She said she'll make sure we're on the list all week so we can come back anytime. Then a smiley face. She said she'll give us a *biiiiig* tip, exclamation mark. Then two thumbs-up. Oh, and she says the reason she didn't pick up when we called is because she was in the shower . . .'

He tailed off mid-sentence, and I knew that he was thinking about Whitney Blair in the shower, naked and sudsy. 'Sorry, chum,' I said. 'Guess you'll just have to jerk off to that sex tape one more time.'

He grinned and dispatched another mouthful of chili. 'She was at the beach in Malibu yesterday,' he said.

'How do you know that?'

'*MailOnline* had bikini shots of her at El Matador. Then she got lunch at the Country Mart. "Whitney Blair puts on a brave front after latest break-up from *BTHTV* beau." Something like that.'

'You sound like a stalker. And you plan to be her rebound?'

'Why not? I'll bet regular guys never ask her out. Probably intimidated.'

'Not a problem for you,' I said. 'She's very attractive, I'll give you that. But say she agreed to go on a date with you. What would you even talk about?'

'What do you mean? What does *anybody* talk about?'

'I mean what are her interests? Besides fame and shopping.'

'Jeez. You really do think everyone else is a frickin' moron, don't you? Just because she doesn't own a copy of the Cassavetes Criterion Collection or whatever. She's writing a *book*, dude! Does it never occur to you a celebrity can be smart?'

'Some celebrities, sure. Not this one.'

He looked at me the way a trucker looks at a vegetable, but then his phone sounded again, this time to herald the arrival of an email.

'Hey, Lucky: it's the Craigslist guy!' He punched the air. 'Bingo! *Gotcha*, asshole! He says to come collect the cookie jar in Mid-City.'

'You got his name?'

He scrolled to the bottom of the message. 'Just an address,' he said.

'When does he want to meet?'

'Uh, Friday. But screw that. Let's surprise the motherfucker tonight!'

I swabbed the bottom of my chili bowl with the last of the bread roll. 'I was planning to meet Cleo Habibi this evening,' I said.

Raúl's eyes went wide and he turned to me, smirking. 'Oh, *really*?'

'*You* told me to – remember? You said she might have the scoop on the Kann sale, the "blackbird" Batman was looking for . . .'

'Riiiight, of course.' He nodded.

'But if we're going to catch this guy anyway, then I guess I can cancel.'

'No way, don't do that!'

'Why not?'

'*Because*,' he replied, winking. 'Where are you meeting her?'

'At her place, I think.'

He whistled. 'Wow. That's kinda forward.'

'It's not a date, Raúl.'

'Does *she* know it's not a date?'

'Of course she does. Cleo and I are business associates.'

Raúl snorted with laughter, spraying root beer onto the counter in front of him. 'Oh boy,' he said. 'That is *priceless*. "Business associates"! I love it.'

He wiped his mouth with a paper napkin and put a firm hand on my shoulder. 'She *likes* you, Sir Lucky. And she's a fox. In fact, you should bring her to my show Saturday! You are coming to my show, right?'

He had segued straight from one awkward subject to another. Yes, Cleo is an attractive woman. And maybe, just *maybe* she enjoys my company on a more than merely professional level. But no: I was not planning to go to Raúl's show. I could not bear to watch him bomb, nor could I quite stomach the idea that he might actually be good. 'Umm,' I said, and then I bottled it: 'Yeah, I think so.'

'You *think* so? As if you have other plans.'

'No,' I replied. 'No, I'll probably come.'

'Excellent,' Raúl said, and he slurped the last of his root beer. I had resisted RSVPing for weeks leading up to that moment, but I knew that he would now take my response as a firm commitment. Angelenos are a notoriously flaky breed: a social engagement in this city is impossible to confirm until it's actually, verifiably happening. But if Raúl says he's going to be somewhere, he'll be there. He'll probably be late, mind you, but he'll be there.

13

The truck was too conspicuous for our purposes, so after shutting up shop that evening I drove us both in my Bronco to the address our suspect Craiglist seller had unwittingly supplied. Mid-City, no more characterful than its name suggests, is part of the shapeless swathe of charisma-free burb that sandwiches the 10 freeway from Downtown to the beach. Somewhere in there we found Colfax Drive, running north to south in a grid of flat, unvarying residential streets.

We parked under a flickering streetlamp a hundred yards from number 826. The high tension wires hummed overhead. Dead palm fronds littered the pavement: the telltale sign of a neighbourhood that nobody much cares about, least of all its own inhabitants.

Earlier, Raúl and I had agreed between us to leave the Abernathys out of the loop. They had enough to worry about with Bart still semi-invalided and the rent to pay, so I'd sent Karen home early and promised to visit Bart the next morning, deliberately neglecting to mention the developments in our investigation. I didn't even tell her that we'd failed again to dispense with Marty Kann's tanker desk – I knew she'd only blame the bad juju.

We snuck surreptitiously along the odd-numbered side of Colfax Drive. Raúl was carrying Bart's antique baseball bat and ducking behind the parked cars so as to approach the perp's home undetected, which only made him look more suspicious. In fact, there was nobody around to see us – and besides, as we drew abreast of the building, our cover was blown by a pitbull woofing indignantly from behind a nearby chain-link fence.

Go anywhere on foot in this city and you'll likely be barked at; the dogs here are enraged by pedestrians. *Get the fuck back in your car, asshole*, they seem to shout. *Who walks in LA?* Burgers, straining at his leash, yapped back at the pitbull, and before long several local mutts were howling a dusk chorus.

No matter; number 826 was dark and silent. It was your classic Los Angeles dingbat – a rectangular, two-storey walk-up built with no more durability than a movie set: wood, chicken wire and stucco, painted a shade that might once have been pastel before the weather turned it dishwater-brown. It had no front lawn, just a few scraps of crab grass poking from the cracks in the blank concrete parking square, and behind that a sheltered carport with room for three cars, occupied only by a single rusted El Camino station wagon.

We crossed the street to take a closer look. The building comprised three apartments: one on the ground floor at the back and two up a set of steps to the side. The faded plaques at the foot of the staircase suggested the ground-floor apartment was number 826½, while the one upstairs at the back was 826A. Number 826 was at the front, above the carport. We crept up to the door, but the lights were off and, as far as we could see, no one was home. There were bars on the windows, which rounded out the shabby vibe. It looked like just the sort of place that might accept a reprobate as a tenant.

The only signs of life were coming from 826A, just along the upstairs landing, behind the perp's. A light from inside cast a pale rectangle across the plaster balustrade and a few sorry pot plants. I could hear a TV with the sound turned up, and I smelled something frying. In spite of my whispered objections, and with Burgers at his heel, Raúl tiptoed along to the window and peered in. A moment or two later he returned, shaking his head. I followed him back to the street.

'Anyone in there?'

'Just a woman, making chicken,' he replied. 'Couple kids watching cartoons. You wanna hang out, see if our guy turns up?'

I checked the time on my phone. 'I should probably go meet Cleo.'

He clapped me on the back, beaming. 'Godspeed, bro,' he said.

Raúl decided to Uber home with the dog, so I went straight to Cleo's place. She lived in a modest condo on the seventh floor of a Westwood high-rise. As I knocked at her door I realised that I'd brought no bottle, no flowers – nothing to clarify the status of our meeting, date or otherwise. But when she opened up, she didn't appear to be disappointed.

'Must be my Lucky night,' she said, and then: 'Sorry. I bet you get that a lot.'

I smiled. 'Never.'

Cleo stepped back to let me in. Her outfit was nothing fancy – a casual sweater and jeans. But she'd put on mascara and fresh lipstick, and she smelled like citrus and sandalwood. 'I have some wine,' she said. 'But I guess you're driving?'

'Thanks,' I replied. 'I'd love some.'

She pointed me towards the sitting room while she went to fetch the plonk. The space was subtly sidelit by retro lamps, and on the stereo a soft-rocker strummed an acoustic guitar, crooning something about fathers and daughters. There were crudités and dips arranged in matching ceramic bowls on the coffee table, which was a single varnished slab of sequoia on the shagpile rug. I sank into the sofa behind it, dipping a celery stick in hummus as I studied the decor.

Cleo's style was what you might call ethnic-contemporary. On the bookshelves a scented candle burned alongside some exotic-looking *objets*, such as a little Ganesha elephant god, which might have come from Goa, or from the Venice Beach Boardwalk. She had pictures of parents and siblings, nieces and nephews. On one wall hung a pair of Chinese scrolls, and on another a trio of tasteful black-and-whites: the Parthenon; Angkor Wat; Machu Picchu.

She came back from the kitchen with two fat glasses of claret and arranged herself at the far end of the sofa, watching me assess the room.

'You're wondering how much of this stuff comes from my clients, right?'

'Huh,' I chased the hummus and celery with a mouthful of wine, 'I suppose.'

'Actually, none of it,' she said. 'I don't mind selling dead people's things, but *owning* them? Now that gives me the creeps.'

'Bad juju,' I muttered.

'What?'

'Nothing, doesn't matter.'

'What is that, one of those e-cigarettes?'

'Oh, this? Yeah, sorry. You mind?'

'No, go ahead. It's smokeless, right?'

I nodded, exhaling. 'People keep telling me I ought to just give up altogether.'

'Easier said than done, I'll bet.'

Cleo and I had known each other a good while, but our interactions rarely rose above banter. At her sales she's all sass, but now that I had her at home I suspected the tough-dame demeanour disguised delicate heartstrings, which a true gentleman would not pluck roughly. I asked her about her family photos, and soon she was giving me the deep background.

The Habibis fled from the ayatollahs to California in '79, when Cleo and her brothers were just kids, too young to remember life in the old country. Her parents still lived a stone's throw away in the Tehrangeles district; they'd stopped asking her about grandchildren. She danced across the subject of her divorce – married too early, to a guy who expected she'd quit her career. Things went south between them, so she went east, 'found herself' on the far side of the world, came home a year later and threw everything into her business. She'd seen enough to know happy endings were just intermissions.

I poured another glass and reciprocated, sketching my own thumbnail bio: idyllic Somerset childhood, climbing trees and prodding frogspawn. Five-year stretch at boarding school. Pimm's cocktails and probationary adulthood at Oxford. The short-lived screenwriting career. The best friend who stole my girl and abandoned me for the Big Time. Stasis in Southern California, where disappointment is easily disguised as Development Hell.

I was enjoying the wine, how it smoothed the edges off a rough couple of days, how it permitted my gaze to stray to the curves under Cleo's sweater; to the painted toenails tucked beneath her on the sofa; to her kale-green, kohl-framed eyes, staring and then darting away. Love-wise, since Bijou, I've been like Tom Hanks in that desert-island movie: bedraggled and alone on a raft in the open ocean, clinging to the frail hope that I'll one day drift into a shipping lane. Cleo was smoke on the horizon.

She set her glass down, and I wondered whether she was about to scooch towards me, but instead she said to hold on, and then disappeared into another room. I dipped a carrot in tzatziki before she returned carrying her tablet computer and a file box, from which she tugged a slim, manila folder. She flipped it open on the coffee table. 'You wanted to ask me about the Kann estate?'

I'd almost forgotten why I was there. 'Huh?' I replied. 'Oh, yeah. Yes: Marty Kann.'

She picked up the top document from the file – several sheets of paper stapled together. 'This is the hard copy of the inventory,' she said, and handed it to me.

I skimmed the list, spotted the Airline chair and the juncus baskets, the desk destined for Whitney Blair, and the diner neon that now hung in Scooter Benjamin's home office. Cleo sat close to me, trying to read my expression.

'What's this about, Lucky?'

I came clean. 'We've had a couple of break-ins at the store,' I said, meeting her eyes. 'Somebody clocked Bart in the car park on Sunday night.'

She gasped: 'Oh my God.'

'He's okay,' I went on. 'Just a few cuts and bruises. Doesn't remember much. But anyway, the guy who attacked him stole that cookie jar. The *Dumbo* one, remember . . . ?'

She nodded.

'And then, last night, Raúl and I got back to the store late and found the guy in there, going through the Kanns' stuff.'

'Oh my *God*,' she said again.

'Yeah. He ran off. We chased him, but he got away.'

'Wow.' She put a comforting hand on my arm. 'I'm glad you guys are okay.'

'Thanks,' I said, adopting a thousand-yard stare, as if I'd been more than an audience member for last night's action. I took a deep breath, full of her perfume.

'You called the cops, right?'

'Yeah, but we don't think they'll put a lot of manpower on it. So we're doing a little investigating of our own. Nothing risky. Just following up a few leads.'

'I see. Such as . . . ?'

'Such as: the guy last night said something about a *bird*. "Marty Kann's blackbird". I don't see anything like that on the inventory, but maybe you remember something? Could be an ornament? A painting?'

'Blackbird?' She looked at her lap, thinking hard, but finally shook her head. 'No, sorry. So you *talked* to the guy? What did he look like?'

'He had a balaclava on. A whole costume, actually. Black guy. Tall-ish. Had an inch or two on me. Does that sound like any of your customers? The people at the sale on Sunday?'

She withdrew her hand from my arm, suddenly defensive. 'My *customers*?'

'Cleo, the guy knew that we had some of Marty Kann's stuff. The only way he could have linked Bart's store to the Kann estate is through your sale.'

She furrowed her brow. 'I guess you're right,' she replied. 'But honestly? I don't remember seeing any tall black guys at the Kann sale. Here . . .' Her long nails clickety-clacked across the touch-screen as she pulled up a spreadsheet on her tablet: 'This is my customer mailing list. Should be up-to-date.'

I cast my eye over the list, but it was just email addresses, arranged in alphabetical order. A few contained what appeared to be full names, but none of them set off alarm bells. Perhaps this was a wild-goose chase, after all. I shook my head, handed back the tablet and gulped down the last of my wine.

'Y'know,' Cleo went on, 'most of my customers are regulars, but there's normally one or two new people at every sale.'

'Oh, yeah?'

'Yeah. And I think a couple signed up to the mailing list last week, just after I advertised the Kann estate.'

'Huh.'

She scrolled through the list on her tablet. 'This guy,' she said, and she pointed to one of the email addresses. I leaned in to read it: JG@villainsLA.ir.

'I thought it was interesting,' she went on, 'because dot-I-R is an Iranian domain. And he introduced himself at the sale. I think he said his name was Jeff?'

'*Jeff?*'

'I think so. He was Latino, I guess. Big guy, with a straggly beard. I thought he looked kinda like an actor . . . Oh, who *was* it . . . ?'

Now I remembered: the heavyset dude in the Kanns' garage. He'd been standing there with Cleo that morning, watching the truck as we drove away. Raúl had pointed him out and insisted that he looked like . . . 'Paul Giamatti?'

She squinted, perhaps trying to picture Giamatti. 'Uh, no,' she replied. 'I wasn't thinking of him . . .' and then she snapped her fingers: '. . . Jack Black! Yes! He looked kinda like *Jack Black*.'

'I thought you said he was Latino.'

'Yeah, but like a Latino Jack Black.'

I sighed and munched on another celery stick. This 'Jeff' was certainly not our Batman. 'What about the son?' I said. 'Marty Jr. You said he lived in Reno, right? Maybe *he* knows what the "blackbird" is.'

'Could be. I probably have his number around somewhere. But I didn't deal with him.'

'No?'

'No. Technically my clients were the lawyers. But the executor is a guy called . . .' She reached back into the Kann file, found the document she was looking for, and then the name: '. . . Frank Waggoner.'

A chunk of celery stuck in my throat. *Frank Waggoner*. Now there was a name I hadn't heard in a while. I spluttered, gulped and forced the bothersome canapé down at last with a dry swallow. My eyes were watering.

'Lucky, you okay?'

'Did you say "Frank Waggoner"?'

'Yeah. You know him?'

'Huh. How common a name is that, d'you think? *Waggoner*.'

'Not very. Why?'

The name had torn a slow puncture in my state of mind; my mood began to fold in on itself like a deflated paddling pool.

'Lucky, what is it?'

'Umm,' I said. 'Listen, thanks so much for the wine and the, er . . . This was really helpful. I think I should go now, or I'll be too sloshed to drive.'

'Oh.' Cleo was taken aback, but she quickly regained her composure. 'Of course,' she said. 'Are you sure you're okay? Is there something wrong?'

Frank Waggoner. Mention him again and it might stir memories that were better left repressed. I was seized by the overwhelming urge to breathe fresh air, to be alone with my self-pity. I stood too quickly, lurched for the exit and mashed my shin on the corner of the coffee table.

'Nah,' I said, wincing and wondering whether I'd drawn blood. The pain cut through my angst like salt through tequila. 'Nah, I'm fine. Just, er . . . Think I might be coming down with something. Slightly feverish, you know?'

I staggered to the front door of the apartment and struggled dumbly to decipher the sequence of locks. Finally, Cleo had to reach around me to open it up. I stepped out into the hallway, sweat prickling the palms of my hands.

'We should . . . I dunno,' she said. 'Call me?'

'I will,' I said, meaning it. 'Sorry.'

Cleo stared at me, mystified. I didn't know whether to shake her hand or kiss her, so I did neither, and in the end she just smiled forlornly as I limped away.

14

I drove home with the windows wound down, but the freeway rush did little to chase away my funk. *Frank Waggoner*. Hearing his name was like tasting a dish that once gave me food poisoning, and my thoughts turned again to finding Glyn.

When I arrived back at the cottage in Angelino Heights, I went straight to plug my old partner's smartphone into the wall. As it was booting up, I pissed loudly, put *Nebraska* on the record player and poured several measures of single malt over a handful of ice. I drank and paced the kitchen until the phone began to ping and buzz with a steady stream of stored messages. Wary, I approached the desk, while The Boss blew a haunting riff on his harmonica.

On the phone's screen was a photograph of Glyn's kids – two boys, both blessed with their mother's bone structure and cursed with their father's Factor 400 complexion. What would mine and Bijou's kids have looked like, I wondered. I swiped to unlock the phone, but it was password-protected. I dredged my former friend's date of birth from the depths of my recall and tapped in several possible combinations without any joy, unsure of how many attempts the phone would allow before it shut me out permanently.

After three or four tries, I decided on a different tack. I had no idea of the children's birthdays, but I remembered Bijou's just fine. My heart rattled my ribcage as I punched the numbers: 0, 2, 1, 4. At last, the screen slid open, smooth as a new box of dominoes.

I checked the voicemails first. The latest appeared to have been left the previous afternoon, and it came from Glyn's home number. I listened to the first few seconds: '*For Chrissakes. Answer your phone once in a while!'* It was Bijou; she sounded drunk and a little weepy. *'You're not gonna believe who just showed up here looking for you. I barely recognised him . . .'*

I deleted the message before I could hear her damning verdict. Next, I found my own call from Sunday night: *'Hi Glyn, it's Lucius. Er . . . This is odd. Been a long time. Listen, you don't have to call me back or anything, but I've just had Abby Musker at my place, and she's wondering where you are . . .'*

I too had been audibly tipsy. It's disconcerting to listen to one's own voice played back: mine now sounds like my father's, but marinated for a decade in booze and Americanisms. Among the other messages backed up over the past fortnight were two from Abby: the first, breezy; the second, a week later, tinged with concern. *'Hey Glyn, it's Abby. Just checking you're still alive, ha-ha . . .'*

The earliest voicemail on the log, more than two weeks old, was from somebody named Bryony. I recognised the name as one that Bijou had considered suspicious, so I listened back to the message. *'Oh hey Glyn, it's Bry,'* the woman said. She sounded young, wholesome, West Coast. *'Weren't we supposed to be meeting today? Anyway, gimme a call when you get this.'*

It was getting too late to call a stranger's home under normal circumstances, but this was a special case: Glyn was a day or two away from having his picture printed on the back of a milk carton. I held my breath and pressed the call-back button. It rang a few times and I almost hung up, but then there was a click – and that voice again, soft and surprised: 'Hello?'

'Hello, is that Bryony?'

'Hi. Glyn?'

'Er, no. Actually, my name is Lucius. I'm . . .' I swallowed, suddenly uncertain as to how I ought to introduce myself. 'I'm a friend of Glyn's.'

'Oh.'

'Listen, I'm sorry to call so late, but Glyn has gone AWOL and I'm trying to locate him.'

'Oh my God, is he alright?'

'Yeah, it's nothing to worry about, really. I just . . . I'm calling the people listed on his phone, and you left him a voicemail . . .'

It sounded as if she was watching television, and I could hear the volume being lowered as she focused her attention on the call.

'Oh my God! Where *is* he?'

'That's what I'm trying to establish, Bryony. I'm sure he's fine. But, listen . . . *how* exactly do you know Glyn?'

'Oh. Well, I mean. I'm his Pilates instructor.'

'I'm sorry, did you say "Pilates"?'

'That's right.'

I was a little thrown. 'Huh. And how often do you guys meet?'

'I guess once or twice a week,' she said. 'We have one-on-one classes. He comes to my house. My studio is in Mar Vista, so it's more convenient.'

'Okay. And when was your last session?'

'Uh, hold on. Let me check my schedule . . .'

I heard her moving around, and the chime of a computer starting up. I tried to picture her in her home: watching *The Bachelorette* in sweatpants. Did she have a cat or a boyfriend? Also: Glyn did *Pilates*?

'Hey, you still there?'

'Still here,' I said.

'So, it looks like our last session was four weeks ago. Yeah, he normally comes to my place Mondays and Fridays, so it was Friday – like, four and a half weeks ago. Oh my God, has he been missing that *long*?'

'I . . . We don't know.'

'But have you called the *police*?'

'Not yet. It's complicated.'

'Oh my God. I've never known anybody to go *missing* before.'

'Bryony, how did he seem? Glyn. When you last saw him.'

'Oh, I don't know. God. Fine, I guess? He had some back pain. He's a writer, right?'

'Right.'

'So he spends a lot of time sitting down. Sitting is the new smoking, right? He was planning to get himself a treadmill desk, or that's what he said. We were working on his core strength. But anyway, I think a lot of his problems aren't . . . physical.'

'What do you mean?'

'Well, y'know. He seemed like he was in peak physical condition.'

That couldn't be right. 'This is Glyn *Perkins* we're talking about?' I said. 'British, red hair, not very tall?'

'Yeah, exactly,' she replied. 'So he was super fit and healthy. But y'know, back trouble can be caused by other things, like stress or anxiety.'

'Huh. Listen, Bryony – I'm sorry to ask, but did you and Glyn ever . . .'

'What?'

I tried to phrase it delicately. 'Well, was your relationship ever, I don't know, more than . . . Pilates instructor and, er, pupil?'

There was a brief silence as she digested the question.

'Oh my God, NO! Who told you *that*? He's *married*! Isn't he married?'

'He is. Nobody said anything, but I'm just checking . . .'

'Oh my God, no.'

'I'm sorry, I had to ask.'

'Why?'

'Because . . . Listen, Bryony. I apologise. Don't worry about it. I've a few more calls to make but I'm sure I'll track him down soon. You've been very helpful.'

'Oh, okay. Well, when you find him, tell him to stay mindful of his posture.'

'Er. Yeah, sure.'

'Oh my God.'

'Okay, goodnight. Bye, Bryony. Bye.'

I hung up, confused. The Glyn she had described, albeit briefly, did not sound like the Glyn I had known. Peak physical condition? He was a guy who always planned to get the chop salad but ended up ordering the cheeseburger. Stress, anxiety? I mean, sure: Glyn had worries – don't we all? But I had always been the neurotic half of our partnership. He was the stoic.

I checked his call log. His last contact was weeks ago – an outgoing call to his agent, Todd. Before that, calls to Bijou and to his mother. I kept scrolling, thinking I might come across the Evelyn whose name Glyn had scribbled on the note at his hotel bedside. Instead I found more of the names Bijou had flagged.

Despite the late hour, I decided to go for broke and pressed the call-back button for "Nadja". The call went straight to an answering service: '*Hello. This is the office of Dr Nadja Perelman,*' droned a nasal secretary, presumably reading from a prepared script. '*Our office hours are nine a.m. to . . .*'

The message included an out-of-hours emergency number, but instead I opened my laptop and googled 'Dr Nadja Perelman'. The top result was a therapist in Los Angeles. I skimmed her bio:

For more than thirty years, Dr Perelman has welcomed individuals, couples, children, families and pet-owners to her inclusive private practice based in Beverly Hills. She provides counseling to current and former military personnel, including veterans of the conflicts in Iraq and Afghanistan. Dr Perelman has a particular interest in dreams, which she firmly believes are a valuable and rarely tapped source of solutions to the unresolved problems in our everyday, waking lives. Using Spengler's Manifested Subconscious method, she also leads a bi-weekly dream group aimed at helping artists to uncork their creativity.

At the top of the page was a headshot of a thickset, severe-looking, middle-aged brunette. If Glyn was cheating on Bijou, it was not with Dr Perelman.

* * *

There was one more recurring woman's name in Glyn's log: a 'Gretchen'. I checked the dates and times of the conversations; they were regular – about once a week, outside work hours. Booty calls? I punched the call-back button again, but this time a man's voice answered: 'Yo.'

'Huh. Hi. Is this Gretchen?'

'Uh, *no*.'

'Who is this?'

'Who is *that*?'

'Er, I was hoping to speak to Gretchen.'

'Gretchen ain't here.'

'Okay. With whom am I speaking?'

'Say *what*?'

'I was hoping to speak to someone about Glyn Perkins . . .'

'Glen *who*?'

'Perkins. Glyn Perkins. My name is—'

'Aw, riiiight. *Glyn*.'

'You know him? You know Glyn?'

'Sure, kinda.'

'*How* do you know him?'

There was a pause, and then: 'Pfft. Fuck you, cop.'

The call was cut off. He must have hung up, I thought, but I tried to call back anyway. It rang and rang and finally went to a generic voicemail. I considered the ramifications. The guy could have been a friend or relative of this 'Gretchen', screwing with me for sport. Or a pimp. More likely, though still implausible, he was a dealer. The late, regular calls suggested as much, although Glyn had never been a Class-A kind of guy. In fact, he'd positively disapproved of Bijou's cocaine intake. Always was a killjoy, Glyn.

Either way, it seemed the call log was a cul-de-sac. Maybe Glyn was shacked up somewhere with the mysterious Evelyn. Or maybe Bijou had been wrong after all, and there was no other woman. I browsed the apps on his phone: Uber, Facebook, Bacon Ninja, a program designed to help with meditation.

108

I glanced at my carriage clock and number-crunched the time zones: it was far too early for me to call Wales. Besides, if Glyn turned out not to be there, I didn't want to be the one to break the news of her son's disappearance to an elderly lady, thousands of miles away.

Glyn's steelworker dad had died young from chronic emphysema, and he spent his teens with a single mum in a pebbledash terrace in Port Talbot. Mrs Perkins and I didn't exactly hit it off on the few occasions we met. I don't know whether she was intimidated by my privilege, or whether she just resented my spiriting away her only child like a fly-by-night fiancé. I thought that phone call best left to somebody more suitable: Abby, or Bijou.

I sat at my desk, pressing my thumbs to my eyelids. By now, Springsteen was chugging through 'Open All Night'. I set the smartphone down on the desk and refilled my whisky glass as another name returned to me: *Frank Waggoner*. Depression shambled ever nearer, arms outstretched, with the grim inevitability of a Romero zombie.

The bottom desk drawer was still jutting open from when I'd delved into my store of unfinished scripts a couple of nights earlier. It seemed like an invitation, so I plunged my hand to the bottom and teased out the document from the very foot of the stack. It was slimmer than the rest of the screenplays: seven pages in total, if memory served. The edges had crinkled over time, but the words at the top of the first page were still perfectly clear. I sat slumped in my chair, staring at them and waiting for sleep:

MARSHAL EAGLE

A Treatment for a Feature Film Screenplay

by

LUCIUS KLUGE & GLYN PERKINS

15

Glyn was driving; I was smoking. His old blue Honda took the swooping bends of Mulholland with the grace of a Jamaican bobsled. The car-seats were speckled with cigarette burns. Some of them had been there when he bought the banger, a few weeks after we arrived in LA. Some, I confess, were down to me.

'I thought you were trying to give up,' he said.

'Huh? Oh, yeah. Maybe next month,' I replied, flicking ash from the open passenger's side window.

My hands shook and my teeth chattered, even though it was the middle of May and 80-something Fahrenheit in the shade. Bijou had chosen that morning to start a fight about how best to fill the dishwasher at her place. My girlfriend thrived on conflict, but it was the last thing I needed before such a crucial meeting.

I envied Glyn's composure. He drove us calmly towards our destiny with the confidence of a guy convinced that he's already made it. And, in a way, he was right – even our poky West Hollywood apartment was a world away from the home he grew up in. Born for black and white but living in glorious Technicolor: for Glyn, further success would be a bonus prize.

My partner had the build of a prop-forward in an amateur rugby team: stocky and going to seed. His trendless oblong specs sat on a thick nose made thicker in a pub-fight with some Oxford-shire farmers shortly after our finals. He'd cut his hair and bought new clothes for the meeting: brogues, pleated chinos, a blazer. His jowls spilled over his crisp shirt collar like a scoop of vanilla melting on a cone.

I too had put on a shirt, done up to the top-but-one button, but I had left it untucked atop my jeans and Chuck Taylors. Glyn had tutted when he saw the outfit, but I thought I understood Hollywood better than he did: the industry likes its creatives to look casual, or so I assured him. Glyn and I were close friends, maybe the best, but we saw the world in slightly but significantly different ways. He likes comfort; I prefer style. Sometimes it bothered me to be seen with him in a roomful of beautiful strangers.

If you'd known me as a fresher at Oxford, you might have described me as a Bright Young Thing, or something less polite. I was a marginal socialite, an associate of several semi-secret drinking clubs. The politics were unsavoury, but the carousing was delicious. Among the unapologetic rahs of my acquaintance were a handful whose names you'd now surely recognise: two cabinet ministers, a magazine editor, a former Bond girl.

When I first met Glyn, I paraded him like a mascot, proof that I was capable of commingling with the lower classes. Maybe he saw me similarly: as a sign that he'd transcended the social barriers which so intimidated the historical hoi polloi. Slowly but surely, my gross condescension had given way to genuine friendship, but a little of that old hierarchy was still ingrained in our alliance.

The car slowed as we came to a pair of squat wooden totems, flanking a driveway on the city side of the road. Mulholland weaves along the ridge that splits Hollywood from the Valley, and the turn-off seemed to lead straight over the edge of the ravine. Glyn peered at the house number carved into one of the peculiar gateposts.

'Is this it?'

'I don't know,' I replied. 'You checked the address, didn't you?'

'This is it,' he said, answering his own question.

He swung the Honda through the open gate and down the steep driveway, which soon levelled off and curved into a courtyard in front of the house, a modernist bungalow with a warm, redwood facade. Several sports cars were parked in a row outside, and among them I recognised our agent's Merc. As we pulled up, Todd Carver and his young assistant, Abby, climbed from the vehicle. I watched Todd don his shades, button his dark suit and unconsciously smooth the top of his head where his hair used to be; he suffered prematurely from severe male pattern baldness, and had recently opted for the full Bruce Willis.

I opened the door and dropped my spent cigarette on the gravel. Glyn stared daggers at me from the driver's seat, so I picked up the butt, tossed it over the low wall of the courtyard into the canyon and returned his glare: *Satisfied?*

If Todd had been born in New York, he'd be an investment banker; DC and he'd be a lobbyist. But he was born at Cedars-Sinai, so he was a Hollywood agent. He chuckled at the sight of the Honda and looked us both over. Abby sidled up beside me and squeezed my arm, probably sensing my anxiety.

'Gentlemen,' said Todd. 'This is it! You psyched? You should be. Glyn, I love the jacket. Is that *new*? Where'd you get it?'

Before Glyn had time to tell Todd that his blazer came from J. Crew, the front door of the house opened behind him, and a young Asian man in an immaculate two-piece and an anime T-shirt emerged to usher the four of us inside. As we moved through the entrance hall, it became evident that what had appeared to be a single-storey bungalow was in fact the top floor of several, with the rest of the house descending on concrete steps and cantilevers, clinging to the hillside like Cary Grant to Mount Rushmore at the end of *North by Northwest*.

The hall opened onto a mezzanine, with a set of spiral stairs leading down into the double-height living room. Like the building's exterior, the walls of the room were clad in rich, varnished redwood. It had the vibe of a cabin in the Rockies. A woven Navajo rug spanned the floor between the oxblood leather sofa and the hearth, over which hung a tall portrait of a stubbled man in a Stetson and spurs, striding towards the viewer, one hand on the revolver holstered at his hip. He wore a US Marshal's badge on his lapel and his eyes glowed with reflected fire. Glyn nudged me in the ribs and pointed: was the painting for our benefit?

At the back of the room, a concertina door led to the broad sundeck beyond. There were two men seated on Barcelona chairs at a glass patio table, and they rose to greet us as we approached. Behind them, a third figure stood at the far edge of the deck, silhouetted against the blue sky and the city view. Todd made the introductions: 'Guys, you both know Bob and Dash . . .'

Bob Erickson, a big dude in an expensive suit, was the studio's creative exec in charge of pulling together the project. Chiselled Dash Smith, in triple denim and a baseball cap, had already been hired to direct. We all shook hands, made nice.

'And this, of course, is Mr Frank Waggoner.'

The third man stalked across the deck towards us. He was slim and grey, somewhere in the afternoon of his middle sixties, wearing a pale, innocuous sweater and sensible trousers. As he came closer, I noticed an unsightly purple birthmark splayed across one side of his neck, like Carrie's dead hand clawing at his throat.

'Mr Waggoner,' Todd went on, 'may I introduce our writers: this is Glyn Perkins, and this is his sidekick, Lucius Kluge. Oh, and I believe you've already met my assistant, the lovely Abigail.'

'Delighted,' said Waggoner, shaking each of our hands in turn, beaming like a benevolent uncle. His teeth were several decades younger than the rest of his face. I hoped he wouldn't notice how clammy my palms were. He turned to his manservant: 'Hiro, would you fetch our guests something to drink?'

It was only after I'd asked for a G&T that I noticed everyone else was ordering soft drinks. Abby smirked at me, Todd and Glyn frowned, but by then it was too late to change my mind without looking ridiculous. Besides, I needed something to take the edge off. I noted that Todd had taken to introducing me at meetings as Glyn's 'sidekick', as if I were no more than Sancho Panza to his Quixote, Eli Wallach to his Clint. Looking back, I suspect the fix was already in.

It was at least three years since Glyn and I had arrived in Los Angeles, bursting with adolescent ambition. We came here – or I did, anyway – to write personal, meaningful films, rooted in people and relationships, ideas and moral complexities. I grew up on Mater's VHS collection: *The Graduate* and *Apocalypse Now*; *The French Connection* and *Coming Home*; *Badlands* and *Five Easy Pieces*; *McCabe & Mrs Miller* and *The Last Picture Show*. I guess I was born a few decades too late, kicking and screaming into consciousness just as *Star Wars* came along to blast away the last true golden age of American cinema.

We had sat on a lot of couches in a lot of corner offices, clutching a lot of tiny bottles of mineral water. Everybody just *loved* our voices, *believed* in our vision, felt sure we'd be *perfect* for this or that project. We sold one screenplay, *The Underground*, a highbrow heist thriller set in London under the Blitz, which got us our Writers Guild membership and the coveted health insurance that came with it. But the script languished in the filing cabinet of an acquisitive, uncaring producer.

Otherwise, we were yet to receive a single solid job offer. Glyn had been working as a barman and a dog-walker, which to me seemed undignified now that we had reached our thirties. I was living on my wits – and on my modest allowance from the Kluge family trust fund.

Confounded by our failure, conflicted about its causes, we hit on a new tactic: working alone. We'd each go away and write a script of our own, put both our names to both works, like Lennon and McCartney, and then see whose solo effort proved the most resilient in the Hobbesian Hollywood marketplace.

I spent several months researching PTSD, opioid addiction and the hillbilly culture of the Appalachians and eventually came up with *Peach Creek*, a social-realist drama about an Afghan war vet who turns vigilante after coming home to find his coal town crippled by a heroin epidemic. Glyn, on the other hand, took all of a fortnight to vomit up a blockbuster about the lost city of Atlantis, featuring a roguish helicopter pilot, a beautiful marine archaeologist, a cruel Libyan colonel and a whole heap of cod science and symbology.

Somewhat against my better judgement, we presented them both to Todd, who glanced cursorily at my 150-page manuscript before gravitating to *Atlantis*, which he declared precisely the sort of pandering tosh that would qualify us for the job of writing a prospective superhero franchise: *Marshal Eagle*. He was right.

This is how a Hollywood writing career can begin: some desperate studio executive comes across your name at the bottom of a long list of people who already said 'No', and he or she delves a hand into the DVD bargain bin, hoping it'll come up clutching *Casablanca*.

Sure enough, after three other screenwriters had passed or asked for fatter paycheques, we were now on the brink of our big break. Our treatment was admired by the studio, which believed it could be brought in at $150 million; and by Dash Smith, the helmer-for-hire. We'd hit all the right notes at the pitch meeting with Erickson and his colleagues. But there was one last hurdle to clear: Frank Waggoner. Todd had explained to us that Waggoner, the publisher of Thunder Comics, personally retained the IP to many of the most celebrated titles in the Thunder stable, including *Marshal Eagle*, *Axeman* and *Deadbolt*.

The *Axeman* movie had barely washed its face at the box office, and was already expected to suffer a reboot. But the first *Deadbolt* had been a huge success for the studio – the third biggest opening weekend of the year – and they were keen to continue their arrangement with the old man and his superheroes. Waggoner was shy of the limelight, but he still demanded script approval, a producer credit and a veto over the principal cast and crew of any film based on a Thunder property. I got the sense he had power the way the Queen has power: possessed but rarely wielded. He didn't write the laws; he just signed them. Todd had assured us the meeting was a mere formality. But he also warned us that Waggoner had notes on our treatment, and that we would be well advised to humour him.

By the time Hiro the manservant returned with our drinks, Erickson was excitedly telling Todd and Glyn about an upcoming breakfast with the movie star whom he insisted was circling the title role. The others had taken their seats around the table, while I stood at the edge of the deck, peering over the rail at the pool set into the concrete promontory below.

When someone handed me my G&T, it took me a moment to realise it was not Hiro's hand but Waggoner's, contoured and liver-spotted. He smiled and sipped from his own glass, his dark eyes dancing, and I got the sense that the old man was sizing me up. I mumbled my thanks and tried not to stare at his birthmark. I already craved another smoke, but I gulped down a mouthful of the drink instead. It tasted like it was all tonic.

'That's so great,' Abby was gushing. 'Brad would be *perfect.*'

'Although,' Erickson replied, '*Russell* is also looking for the right project.'

I never really got to know Erickson. He's the sort of guy it paid to be intimidated by if you cared about your future in Hollywood, one of that elite breed of Spago-lunching studio execs whose names everyone who's anyone ought to be familiar with. When he retires, every two-bit talent agency, management firm and production house in town will take out a full-page ad in *Variety* to congratulate him on being such a swell guy. Maybe he's a true cinephile, not just an accountant. Maybe he wrote his college thesis on the Nouvelle Vague, I don't know. But what I do know is that he answered to a studio chief who'd probably never read a subtitle in his life.

Todd, who looked as if he was close to soiling himself with

excitement, chimed in: 'Bob and I have discussed it, and we think we can get Benicio for the Shaman,' he said. Everyone cooed approvingly.

And then Waggoner fixed his eyes on me. 'So, Lucius,' he said. 'Do you mind if I call you Lucius? Did you notice the portrait of Marshal Eagle over the hearth?'

'I saw it,' I replied, swallowing.

'It was sent to me by a talented fan,' he went on. 'Normally I keep it in the garage, but I thought I'd hang it today, seeing as it's a special occasion.'

'Huh.'

'What did you think?'

What did I *think*? Well, here's the logline – *Marshal Eagle* was a heap of shit. Our treatment was a version of the character's origin story: John Eagle, a US Marshal from Houston, lives in the twenty-first century, but still carries a Colt revolver like a relic of the nineteenth. Tasked with tracking a terrorist mastermind known as the Shaman, he pursues his quarry to an Indian reservation in West Texas. The Shaman demonstrates superhuman strength and agility, shooting John Eagle several times and killing most of his colleagues in a warehouse explosion.

Mortally wounded, Marshal Eagle moves through the spirit world, but eventually returns to life to find he's being tended by an old Comanche woman. His recovery is swift, and he soon learns that during his vision quest, he has acquired the powers of several spirit animals: the cunning of a wolf, the speed of a stallion, the strength of a buffalo and the senses of – you guessed it – an eagle.

Meanwhile, the Shaman has been plotting an attack on Washington, and a scarred but reborn Marshal Eagle blah blah blah. You get the picture. The source material was derivative, lowest-common-denominator claptrap. Worse than that, it was jingoistic, militaristic and more than mildly xenophobic. What did I *think*?

117

I shrugged. 'It's alright.'

'You know, I very much enjoyed your treatment,' Waggoner said.

'And we're so glad you did,' Glyn interjected. Usually, I was the pitch-man, but this time we'd agreed that Glyn would do the talking. 'Mr Waggoner,' he went on, 'you and the guys at Thunder have such a marvellous character here. Classic but contemporary; tough but deep. I think he really speaks to the heart and soul of America. But I – *we* – also think that, in spite of our outsiders' perspective, we can make Marshal Eagle our own.'

Encouraging smiles all round. I thought Todd might burst into applause.

'Well, gentlemen, I agree,' Waggoner said. 'And I also think the more contemporary changes you've proposed for the Shaman are very sensible.'

Erickson nodded, adopting a sombre tone. 'Absolutely,' he said. 'The terrorism angle just feels, I don't know . . . *relevant*.'

'Oh, yeah,' Todd grinned. 'Super relevant.'

'It really gives the script an urgency,' said Dash, throwing shapes with his hands. 'Y'know, I truly believe that Marshal Eagle is gonna be *the* superhero for 2007.'

The best movie directors ought to be a blend of psychopath and therapist: they need to fake empathy to work with their actors, but they need to switch it off at will if they ever hope to master the crew. Watch the average tentpole these days, though, and you'd think the psychopaths were winning.

Todd held his pomegranate juice aloft. 'To *Marshal Eagle*,' he said, and the others joined him in the toast – everyone except Waggoner.

'There is one thing,' the old man said, raising his voice to be heard over the chinking of glasses. 'About the treatment – which, as I say, I enjoyed very much. But I sense at times that you resist some of the very things Marshal Eagle's fans love most about the character: his superpowers; his wrestling with otherworldly forces.

I would love to see some more of that mysticism in the finished script.'

Glyn opened his mouth to reply, but I was seized by the urge to butt in. 'Actually, it's funny you should say that,' I said, smacking my lips. I could taste the gin now. 'Because Glyn and I had some disagreements on that very point.'

'Oh, really? And which side of this disagreement were you on, Lucius?'

My breath grew short. The ice in my drink began to clink as my hand trembled. The truth is, I was upset we were even there. I had never wanted to take on the project in the first place, and I felt as if my partner had abandoned our creative principles to participate in hastening the cultural apocalypse. The people sitting at the table had gone quiet as they awaited my response. I didn't look at Glyn, but I could feel his eyes like a kitchen knife tickling my ribs.

'Honestly, Mr Waggoner? I can't stand all that superhero crap. It's a power fantasy for high-school losers. Hobbits, wizards, bloody *Star Wars*. It's all completely infantilising. Surely it devalues genuine human experience if, every time a character gets into a scrape, he can just call upon his magical ability to . . . blow stuff up with his mind.'

Waggoner smiled, which struck me as somehow inappropriate. 'But these things can be metaphors,' he said. 'You're a writer, Lucius — surely you can appreciate a metaphor?'

'I'm sorry, Mr Waggoner. But I don't believe there's meaning in any of it. It's just shapes and colours and loud noises designed to appeal to people with the mental capacity of . . . I dunno, a puppy chasing a roll of toilet paper. There's no complexity, no ambiguity. It's all about good versus evil, which if you ask me is a dishonest reading of the world. And, look: maybe it sells Happy Meals. But from where I'm sitting, it's all just sound and fury, signifying nothing.'

He laughed. '*Shakespeare!* How wonderful.'

I wiped a hand across my brow. Glyn was jonesing to interrupt, but he couldn't seem to summon the words. Erickson had half-risen from his seat as if to defend Waggoner's honour. If there's one thing you should never share with a studio executive, it's an aversion to *Star Wars*. But the old man waved him off.

'What if I proposed that the superhero was an expression of man's own best qualities,' Waggoner said. 'An ideal to strive towards, like the Greek gods?'

'An *ideal*?' I replied. 'Half the Greek gods were serial rapists.'

Abby breathed in sharply and I glanced at the group. Todd, his face frozen in horror, was gripping his glass of pomegranate juice so tightly that I thought it might shatter. Trouble was, the more horrified Todd looked, the more it encouraged me. Because I'd never fucking liked Todd in the first place. He was rude to waiters. My anxiety had peaked and was tipping over into euphoria.

Waggoner smiled again, steelier now. It seemed to me that the purple shade of his birthmark had deepened, as if his blood was running higher while he defended his life's work. 'Take Superman,' he went on. 'In Clark Kent, we are offered an image of ourselves: vacillating, weak, insecure – all but invisible to the opposite sex. And yet, a hero waits just beneath those spectacles, ready to emerge under the right circumstances. Super-heroes can teach us many things, Lucius: selflessness, sacrifice, responsibility.'

Into the silence that followed, Dash Smith decided to insert his two cents. 'Also,' he said, looking to the others for support, 'they're really *cool*. Right?'

I downed the rest of my drink and turned to face him. 'See, Dash, I don't think they *are* cool,' I replied. 'At *all*. I think Jack Nicholson in *Cuckoo's Nest* is cool. Brando in *The Wild One* is cool. Lauren Bacall in anything: cool. But *superheroes*? Superman wears his underpants on the outside!'

Dash lowered his head and mumbled something at the floor.

120

'What was that?' I barked.

He looked up at me again. 'I *said*, Marshal Eagle is cool.'

'Marshal Eagle is bullshit American exceptionalism personified. He's John Wayne: Jedi Master. He's Dick Cheney in a fucking cowboy hat. I mean really, Dash, would you just grow the fuck up? Thanks again for the drink, Mr Waggoner. You have a beautiful home. I'll show myself out.'

Todd stood up as I passed him on my way back into the house, and I thought he might hit me. His domed head throbbed pinkly, like a thumb caught in a door. But it was Glyn who caught up with me at the top of the spiral staircase. He grabbed me by the shoulder and spun me around. I raised my hands to defend myself, but he didn't look angry; he looked devastated.

'Lucius, what the hell . . . ?'

'I can't do it, Glyn. I *told* you I couldn't do it.'

'We've discussed this a hundred times, Lucius! They want us to write a film. A real bloody feature film! I thought this was what you *wanted*.'

'A *superhero* film?'

'Is this about *Peach Creek*?'

'Fuck you.'

'We moved to bloody Hollywood. What did you *expect*? No one is trying to trick you! We do one for them, and then we do one for us.'

'That's bollocks, and you know it. We do one for them, and then we do another for them, and then another. There's no "us" in this town.'

I saw a dark thought pass across Glyn's face. 'Did you plan this? Your big bloody exit?'

'Not exactly,' I replied, which was true. Not *exactly*.

In the early days of our friendship, Glyn had been in awe of me. I was, after all, wealthier, wittier, taller, better-looking. And yes, I guess I enjoyed basking in that awe. When I'd agreed to write with him, I felt as if I were taking him under my wing. I never questioned which of us was the senior partner. It was me, obviously. It was always me. Until it wasn't.

'Please don't leave, Lucius,' he said. 'We can fix this. We can still make it together, I promise. Would you just bloody *try*?'

Glyn likes films where the dog lives and the good guys high-five at the end. He may have had tears in his eyes.

'I'm sorry, Glyn. It's over.'

It was only after I left Waggoner's house that I remembered Glyn had done the driving, and that I didn't have my car. You can't exactly hail a cab up in the Hills, so when I got back to Mulholland I started walking west along the side of the road. I wondered whether anyone would follow – whether Todd would send Abby out in the Merc to find me – but after a while I gave up wondering.

You probably saw *Marshal Eagle*. To judge by the box-office numbers, I'm about the only person who didn't. I bet you're asking yourself why I even stayed in LA after all that. Maybe I just like the sunsets.

I walked until I could see the Capitol Records building in the distance, and I clambered over the crash barrier onto what looked like a trail leading through the chaparral. I lit a cigarette, the last in the pack, and then I headed off into the Runyon Canyon scrub, the dust scuffing my favourite trainers, the thorns scraping at my best pair of jeans as I scrambled downhill, away from everything.

PART TWO

THE VILLAIN'S LAIR

16

I blinked awake at my desk, to find that certain clues had coagulated while I was asleep and navigating the spirit world. Something Bart had said; something Cleo had shown me; something about our run-in with Batman. I clung excitedly to the crucial pieces of dream flotsam as I floated up into consciousness. The *Marshal Eagle* treatment had slid from my lap to the carpet; I scooped it up and stuffed it back into the bottom drawer. The sun was barely up, so I had time to shower, floss, brew coffee and mull over my next move. I took a raincheck on the shave: maybe I'd let the stubble grow, maybe I wouldn't. I hadn't decided yet.

Glyn's smartphone had charged overnight, so I took it with me in case anyone new tried to call him. I checked my mailbox: nothing but coupons and catalogues. I backed the Bronco out of the driveway, e-cig clamped between my teeth. A dumpster-diver with a rusty shopping trolley full of her soiled belongings was scavenging for empties in my recycling bin. I figured she'd find a few.

It took me fifteen minutes to drive to Atwater Village, and I stopped first at Tacos Villa Corona, a local hole-in-the-wall, to pick up two of LA's finest breakfast burritos. As I parked on the street outside the Abernathys' cottage, Karen emerged from the front door, headed to the store. We edged around one another on the narrow, aloe-lined path.

'He's in the den,' she said. 'Don't wear him out.'

'Thanks, Karen,' I replied – and then, sweet as the Stevia in her coffee: 'Oh, and thanks again for all your help this week. We couldn't have kept the store open without you.'

She paused as she reached her Corolla, keychain trembling at the driver's door.

'Lucky . . . ?'

'Yes, Karen?'

She hesitated, battling her natural inclination never to apologise. 'I feel terrible about the other night,' she said at last. 'I was so sure I'd locked up properly.'

'Don't be. Listen: Raúl and I might be out and about running errands for the next day or two. Are you happy manning the fort?'

'Of course,' she said, and guiltily waved goodbye. Bingo.

The Abernathys' cottage is beloved but boxy, built for convenience not posterity. If this were Kansas I'd consider it a tornado risk. The den was at the back of the house: a dark, cluttered cubby-hole free of Karen's influence and decorated with several yards of groaning bookshelves, a selection of junk too obscure for the store, and a 64-inch flatscreen television. Bart was reclining on his La-Z-Boy with a blanket across his lap, watching news footage of the fire in the mountains: a plane vainly dumping red flame retardant over a roaring hillside. The news ticker at the foot of the screen had given the blaze a name: the Overlook Fire. Bart switched the TV off when he heard me come in, twisting his stiff neck as he tried to face me.

'Woodward! Good to see you. What, no Bernstein?'

'Hey, boss. How are you feeling?'

His face was still swollen, the bruises turning the colour of urine. One eye was still half-closed, the other bloodshot. His glasses rested lop-sidedly on the Band-Aid that traversed his fat nose, and a bandage was taped over the stitches on the back of his head, where the doctors had shaved his hair, leaving a vivid pink rectangle of bare scalp.

'Ach, terrible headaches,' he said. 'And I'm not too steady on my feet. But I'll be back at the store next week.'

'No need to rush.'

'Well, perhaps the week after.'

It wasn't so much the scars that concerned me – more that Bart seemed to have shrivelled beneath the blanket, like a date wrapped in bacon. His pyjamas were too baggy, his skin semi-translucent from several days out of the sun. I'd seen it in other older men: that moment when the lights first flicker, and the darkness begins to creep into the corners of the room.

My grandfather, the 15th Viscount Wonersh, ploughed his Land Rover into a rhododendron on the estate at Tinderley, broke his leg and gave himself a nasty gash on the forehead. The injuries were not immediately life-threatening, but he was diminished by them. His vigour and pride deserted him, and after that it was only a matter of time.

I did not tell Bart that story. Instead, I held up the brown paper bag containing our burritos. 'Brought you breakfast,' I said.

He grinned and gingerly removed his specs. 'That's m'boy,' he said. 'Karen has been wonderful these past few days. A real trouper. But she insists on making me oats. I tell her I need a hearty breakfast; she tells me I need a healthy one. But I don't care how you dress 'em up – almonds, bananas, syrup – nobody should have to eat *oats* every darned day.'

I opened the little plastic tubs of dipping sauce that came with the meal and set them on the coffee table next to his painkillers, then I went to the kitchen to pour us each a glass of orange juice. When I returned, Bart had already taken a bite and was sighing with pleasure.

'Sure hits the spot,' he said. 'So, how's business?'

'You know about our big sale?'

'I heard somebody finally bought the one-armed bandit. Ten grand, Karen said.'

'Yeah. Some Stanford frat-boy who got rich from a video game. Took some things from the Kann estate off our hands, too.'

'I also heard about Monday night. Sounds like we have a crime wave on our hands. Is Raúl okay?'

'He's fine. His ego's a little sore,' I replied, pulling up a chair and unwrapping my own burrito. 'Actually, that's kind of what I wanted to talk to you about.'

'Oh, yeah?'

He took another bite and waited for me to speak.

As I thought about where to begin, my eye was drawn to a familiar old photograph framed on the wall behind him. Believe it or not, snapshots can mature into valuable antiques. This one was taken on Mount Baldy, highest peak in the San Gabriels, around 1912, when there was a modest encampment at the summit. The photograph depicts a trolley arriving at the camp station. Not long after it was taken, a fire broke out in the cooking tent, gutting the so-called Baldy Summit Inn. The camp was never rebuilt, and there are just a handful of extant images of the site before the conflagration – including Bart's. History moves fast here; memories are fragile and all too easily mislaid.

'Did you remember anything else about the other night?'

'No,' he said forlornly. 'It's still hazy. But I keep waking up with that smell in my nostrils: you remember the smell I told you about? In the parking lot, before they hit me? Sweet – like a vase of cut flowers that's been left out in the sun.'

'I remember. I've been thinking about a couple of other things,' I said. 'That night, at the hospital – you told us that a man came to the store at closing time, before you were attacked . . . ?'

'That's right. He wanted to buy Oscar. I told him Oscar wasn't for sale.'

'Bart, I want you to think carefully. What *exactly* did the guy say?'

He frowned. 'I'm not sure that I understand.'

'Well, did he say, "I want to buy Lucille Ball's fibreglass ostrich?" Or did he point at Oscar and say, "How much for that thing?" What were his *exact* words? I know it's probably hazy, but try to remember. It might be important.'

Bart chewed another mouthful. His mind was working hard behind his watery eyes. 'I think he said, "I'm interested in the bird." Yes. No, wait. He said "the *black* bird". Yeah, that was it: "I'm interested in the black bird." '

I almost punched the air: we were getting somewhere.

'That's great, Bart. That's what I thought. Tell me, can you remember what the guy looked like?'

'Well, sure. He was . . . uh. He was overweight, certainly. He was wearing a T-shirt with some sort of design on it, I don't recall the details. He was Latino, I believe. And he had a beard, I guess you would say. In fact, he rather reminded me of an actor . . .'

'Paul Giamatti?'

'No . . .'

'Jack Black?'

'No . . . not Jack Black. I would say, Philip Seymour Hoffman. Yes.'

'Philip Seymour Hoffman? Didn't you say the guy was Latino?'

'Mm-hm. But Hoffman had such *range*, didn't he?'

'Okay, Bart, forget Philip Seymour Hoffman. Did the guy say anything else? After he asked about Oscar, and after you told him Oscar wasn't for sale.'

'Not really. He acted a little peeved, then he gave me his card and left.'

'He gave you his *card*?'

'Well, yeah. What's this about, Lucky?'

I almost laughed. 'You know what, Bart? I have to go. This has been great. I'll come back tomorrow or the next day, tell you all about it then.'

'You're leaving already? You barely even touched your breakfast!'

'I'll eat it in the car.'

I drove to the store, the burrito in my free hand. For now, the name Frank Waggoner had faded from my thoughts, and my heart raced not with anxiety, but with anticipation. I parked the Bronco and hurried inside. Karen was rearranging the items in the front-window display. Raúl was nowhere to be seen. I made straight for the desk by the register, pulling open the drawer where we keep the loose paperwork. There it was, at the top of the pile: the business card I'd deposited, unthinking, two days beforehand.

'Lucky?' Karen had noticed I was there, and that I was triumphantly brandishing the card. 'Everything okay?'

'Everything's fine, Karen. Bart's napping. Have you seen Raúl?'

'Pah! No,' she replied, and went back to her work.

I sat behind the counter and turned my prize over in my hands. It was printed on cheap, slender card. On one side was a logo that I didn't recognise, smudged like newsprint by somebody's sweaty thumb – a clenched fist, pressing down on a five-letter acronym: 'CRUSH.' On the other was his name, Jeffrey Guzman. It said he was 'Executive Director', but of *what*, precisely? The email address was the same one I'd seen the night before on Cleo's mailing list: JG@villainsLA.ir.

There was a phone number, too. I tried to guess what Raúl would have done if he were there. That didn't take me long: I dialled the number.

'Yes.'

'Hello there, I'm trying to get hold of Jeffrey Guzman.'

'This is he.'

'Huh,' I said, realising that I'd neglected to formulate a strategy. So I told the truth: 'Mr Guzman, my name is Lucius Kluge. I'm calling from Bart's Olde California in Los Feliz. I believe you enquired about the black bird?'

I heard a slurp; it sounded like the guy at the other end was drinking something through a straw. Finally he responded, in a gloomy monotone: 'I've been expecting your call, Mr Kluge.'

'Oh, really?'

'I rather think we ought to meet. I wonder: would you be

prepared to come to my place of business today – at noon, say?
It's not far.'

'Er, I suppose so.'

'Very good. Do you have a pen?'

I wrote down the address Guzman gave me. He hung up before
I could ask any more questions, so I called Raúl.

'My liege.'

'Did you sleep through your alarm again?'

'No.'

'Then where are you?'

'I'm on the bus.'

I don't know how he does it; I've lived in Los Angeles for years
and never once taken public transport.

'To the store?'

'No, to Santa Monica.'

'What? Why?'

'I told you, dude. I'm playing Ultimate Frisbee with Scooter.'

'Scooter?'

'Scooter Benjamin, remember? He invited me to his weekly
game.'

'Christ, okay. Listen: I'm coming to pick you up.'

'Oh. Cool, thanks. Game finishes at eleven.'

I finally found the game in full flow at a small park a few blocks
from the beach, on a rise with a view across the roofs to the shimmering Pacific. A sea breeze carried the scent of cut grass, with
a smoky undertone. By now the wildfire in the mountains was
clearly visible from miles away: a dark cloud loomed over the
coast to the north. With the blaze's acreage still growing, the radio
bulletins had turned to which celebrities' homes were in danger
of obliteration. A ranch where they once shot Westerns had
burned. A horse sanctuary had been evacuated.

Raúl was in his Clippers vest, hurling himself around the pitch
with impressive efficacy, given his diminutive stature. That's how

he pursues new friends: like he's diving to catch a Frisbee, enjoying the leap without knowing the outcome. When somebody you've just met in LA says *We should hang out sometime* or *Come join my Ultimate Frisbee game*, what they really mean is: *Nice meeting you, but I have enough friends already.* Raúl nevertheless takes them at their word – either he believes them, or he's simply bloody-minded. Or both.

Benjamin, who appeared to be the captain of Raúl's team, was one of the more skilful competitors on the pitch, his lean, youthful frame swathed in box-fresh, breathable sportswear. He grinned and winked to me as he jogged back downfield from scoring a goal. The opposition team descended into finger-pointing and recrimination, while one of their number trudged glumly to pick up the plastic disc from the grass a few dozen feet away.

The remaining players were all twenty-something tech-industry oxpeckers of varying athleticism and ethnicity. I'm no sports pundit, but they didn't look like top-drawer Frisbee-tossers. To a man, though, they were rabidly competitive: hard-fouling, rage-propelled, yelling orders, complaints, trash-talk – loud enough to unsettle the children in the playground at the far corner of the park. I found it hard to identify the fun in a casual game played with such naked aggression.

The Frisbee, of course, is another Southern California invention. We have a short-stack of original 1950s Wham-O 'Pluto Platters' in a glass cabinet at the store. They can fetch $400 if they're still sealed in their packaging; $200 if not. Better value than a game of Bacon Ninja, if you ask me.

The players' designer kitbags were heaped at the touchline. Burgers guarded them obediently, licking his chops and pacing back and forth as if keen to bound after the Frisbee himself. Close by, orange quarters and scraps of torn clingfilm lay strewn across the grass like the losers of some bloody medieval battle; I guessed the dog had polished off the half-time snacks. The commotion had drawn several other spectators: a jogger and a couple of bums. I smoked my e-cigarette and checked my watch every few seconds.

The game finally ended just before eleven-thirty. Raúl's team exchanged triumphant high-fives. Most of the players grabbed their kitbags and made for their Priuses, but my partner gulped long and deep from a litre of Gatorade and strolled my way, rubbing the sweat from his brow.

'I think that was Ryan Seacrest,' he said, and he pointed past my shoulder at a fellow spectator, who was jogging away towards Main Street.

'Ryan Seacrest,' I replied. 'That's a famous person, right?'

'You're kidding. Tell me you're kidding.'

Burgers whined at his ankles, hopping from paw to paw.

'Hang on, buddy,' said Raúl, and he fished a water-damaged old issue of *National Geographic* from his bag. The magazine fell open as he chucked it onto the grass. Burgers, true to his Pavlovian instincts, trotted over and squatted on it.

Benjamin appeared topless beside me, towelling his toned torso with way too much pride. He was both jock and nerd at once, an unsettling hybrid, like one of those preposterous portmanteau dog breeds. He produced a can of Axe Africa from his kitbag and sprayed his chest and underarms exhaustively, seeding a cloud of the cloying scent thick enough to make my eyes water.

'That dog is so dope,' he said, watching as Burgers finished emptying his bowels onto a photo essay about the Amazon rain-forest. 'It's Lucky, right?'

'Right,' I said, and shook his outstretched hand. 'How's that slot machine been working out for you, Scooter?'

'Oh, *awesome*,' he replied. 'I love it. That neon sign, too. Lotta great feedback from the guys in my team.'

'Good. I'm delighted.'

'And hey, I'm always in the market for cool shit. You ever get anything new at the store you think I might be interested in, gimme a call. Money is no object.'

'So I gather,' I replied.

He was grinning at me with wide, caffeinated eyes, cultish self-belief coming off him in waves. Convince yourself that you're destined to do great things, and you might design yourself a million-dollar iPhone app. Or you might just shoot up a high-school cafeteria. It's a fine line, in my opinion.

'So it looks like Gupta's our new star quarterback,' he said, nodding at my partner, who was now carrying the shit-laden periodical to the nearest bin. 'You should come join us for next week's game.'

'Not sure my knees could take it,' I said, and took a drag on my e-cigarette. 'Or my lungs. Seems like kind of a competitive crowd.'

He laughed. 'The guys? Don't mind them. They all read the Steve Jobs book. Now they think they have to be assholes to be successful.'

'Guess they got that backwards,' I said.

Benjamin laughed again, a little less self-assured than before. He and Raúl bade each other a fist-bump farewell, though not before my partner had extracted another promise from Benjamin to attend his stand-up show on Saturday.

Raúl grinned as he climbed into the Bronco. 'So, how'd it go with Cleo?'

'Don't ask,' I said, starting the engine. 'Tell me: what do you see in that Scooter guy, anyway?'

His face fell. 'Enthusiasm,' he replied. 'You should try it sometime.'

17

By the time I'd presented all my findings, Raúl was riding a Gatorade high.

'Holy crapola,' he said, slapping the dashboard. 'So let me get this straight: this Giamatti-looking dude, Guzman, is at the Kann estate sale Sunday, introduces himself to Cleo. And then that night he turns up to the store, asks Bart about this "black bird", gives him a business card. And then Bart gets beat up and the Ringmaster cookie jar gets stolen. So you think this Guzman guy did it?'

'Doesn't really make sense,' I replied. 'Why leave your card when you're about to nick something? Also, he's obviously not our Batman.'

'Hmm. True that. So the next night, Batman breaks in . . .'

'Technically, he didn't "break in", but yeah . . .'

'Whatever.' He palmed the perspiration from his face like a squeegee man wiping a windscreen. 'Batman breaks in, asks about "Marty Kann's black bird", tazes me in the rear. Then this morning, you put all this together in a frickin' *dream*, find the business card, and set up a meet? You know what this means?'

'No, what?'

'It means you're one of those asshole savants. Like Sherlock. Or House.'

Guzman's address was on a fly-blown stretch of Sunset in Little Armenia, several blocks west of Scientology HQ, Hollywood's big blue butt-barnacle of misguided belief. Our destination turned out to be a storefront in a strip mall, between a laundromat and a Thai place rated a 'B' by the health department. As Raúl hopped from the Bronco, I heard him exclaim: '*Seriously?* You have got to be shitting me.'

I closed the driver's side door, leaving Burgers to doze on the back seat, and looked towards where Raúl was pointing. In the shadow of a striped awning, two life-size cardboard cut-outs appeared to be guarding Guzman's store. One wore body-armour and wielded a broadsword; the other was sheathed in spandex, bunched fists emitting silver orbs of electrical energy. Both had square jaws and implausible musculature, and they flanked an elaborate window display made up of – and here my heart sank – comic books. It was not the display that had so agitated my partner, though, but the sign above it, which was painted in crisp, black gothic lettering with red and gold trim: The Villain's Lair.

'I mean, c'mon,' he chuckled. 'Kinda on the nose, don't you think?'

But for the tinkling bell that announced our entrance, the store was as silent and cool as Steve McQueen, dimly lit by old filament bulbs and with patterned carpet squares underfoot. Along one wall ran narrow wooden shelves, holding what looked to be the latest issues of several dozen superhero titles, their violently colourful cover art an affront to my sensibilities. On the opposite wall were deeper shelves that carried squarebound graphic so-called 'novels'. A table in the middle of the room displayed special editions, vintage issues and rarities, and under the glass counter at the back was an assortment of over-priced, mass-manufactured merch. I thought I spotted some Marshal Eagle collectibles.

Raúl plucked off his Ray-Bans and whispered loudly: 'This place is *outstanding*.'

Needless to say, I disagreed. There were three other people in the store. A guy in a tweed waistcoat and winklepickers stood restocking the alphabetised shelves. A pretty girl with purple hair and a death-metal T perched on a stool behind the counter, poking her phone. A skinny teenager sat cross-legged on the floor, leafing intently through a fresh comic. He did not look up as we came in.

'Can I help you guys?' said the girl.

'We're looking for Jeffrey.'

She nodded over her shoulder. 'In the office.'

Raúl followed me through a beaded curtain behind the counter, into the little back office beyond. Daylight filtered greyly through a venetian blind, sketching the outlines of a plywood desk, and behind it the substantial figure of Jeffrey Guzman. I remembered him from the sale, standing with Cleo in the maw of Marty Kann's garage. His eyes were dark and liddy, his beard tufted around the jowls but scant on the cheeks, his thick, middle-aged frame crumpled and careworn like an old couch left at the kerb. Despite my friends' varied claims, I could see no obvious resemblance to any award-winning character actors.

The air was oily and sweet with lunch smell, a half-eaten burger and fries nestling on the desk in their waxed-paper wrappings. Guzman sat among stacks of comics and spine-cracked paperbacks. Atop his filing cabinet was the fireman's helmet from the *Axeman* movie. I recalled him clutching it like a trophy at the Kann sale, and I wondered how substantially Cleo had ripped him off. He rose to greet us with a grunt of exertion, wiping his greasy fingers on a takeaway napkin.

'Mr Guzman? I'm Lucius Kluge. Sorry we're a little late.'

'No matter, Mr Kluge. As you can see, my schedule is flexible. And this is . . . ?'

'Raúl Gupta,' my partner replied, shaking his hand.

'We work together at Bart's Olde California,' I added.

'Of course,' Guzman said. 'Sit down, please.'

His arse-cleft nosing over his waistband, he hauled a heap of rucksacks and skateboards off a beat-up vinyl sofa and dumped them roughly in a corner. As I sat in the vacant spot, I noticed an old ketchup stain deep in the weave of the office rug. A black walking cane topped with an intricate silver gargoyle rested against the edge of the desk; I wondered whether it was an affectation or a medical necessity. Guzman sank back into his office chair with a sigh.

'Is that an In-N-Out?' said Raúl.

'It is.'

'Animal Style?'

'Indeed.'

'You mind?'

'Please, go right ahead.'

'Thanks,' said Raúl, helping himself to a handful of Guzman's fries before he, too, took a seat. 'I just played ninety minutes of Ultimate Frisbee; I'm hungrier than a supermodel.'

'This is your place?' I said.

'I am the owner and manager, yes.'

' "The Villain's Lair",' Raúl said, his mouth full. 'Cool name.'

'You were at the Kann estate sale last weekend,' I said, hoping to guide the conversation towards the point.

'I was,' Guzman replied. 'I saw your truck and I noted down the details of your store. I understand you enjoy some special privileges with Ms Habibi.'

Raúl snickered childishly at the turn of phrase, and almost choked on his fries.

'Cleo gives us first look and a fair price,' I said. 'Why do you ask?'

The fat man poked the last of the cheeseburger into his gullet and eyed me levelly, as if trying to discern whether my question was disingenuous. He washed the mouthful down with a long slurp of his milkshake. He had an old-fashioned manner, a borrowed politesse that belied his trashy milieu.

'I believe you may have acquired an item from Mr Kann's home that interests me,' he said. 'I had hoped we might come to some sort of arrangement.'

Raúl leaned over and purloined a napkin from the desk.

'You mean the black bird,' my partner said, mopping Thousand Island from his moustache.

'That is correct. Mr Abernathy did not seem eager to discuss it when I spoke to him on Sunday. But perhaps I caught him at an unfortunate time.'

'He thought you were talking about Oscar,' said Raúl.

'Oscar?'

'Lucille Ball's ostrich . . . Never mind.'

I interrupted: 'Listen, Mr Guzman. You're going to have to help us out here. This "black bird" we're talking about? We don't have it. Not only do we not have it, we don't even know what it *is*. Is it a piece of jewellery? A painting? What?'

Guzman stared at me, disbelieving. He steepled his fingers.

'You really don't know?'

'We have no idea,' I replied. 'But some real funky stuff has been going on and we'd like to get to the bottom of it. So, enlighten us: what is the black bird?'

He smiled. 'Look around you, Mr Kluge,' he said. 'What do you think it is?'

I was about to tell him sternly that I was in no mood to play Twenty Questions, when Raúl suddenly clapped his hands and grabbed me by the shoulder. 'Hold on!' he said. 'It's a *comic book*! Am I right?'

Guzman was still smiling. 'Very good, Mr Gupta,' he said. '*The Black Bird* – also known as *White Lightning vs The Black Bird, Part Four* or, to give it its proper name, *White Lightning #88* – is indeed a comic book. A very rare and significant comic book.'

'A comic book?' I groaned. 'Christ Almighty.'

I took a long pull on my e-cigarette.

'Thing is, Mr Guzman,' said Raúl, 'I'm no expert, but I read plenty of comic books, and I'm pretty sure I never heard of *The Black Bird*.'

'Worry not, Mr Gupta. Nor have many of your generation. But you are aware, I take it, that Marty Kann was a comic-book artist? Briefly one of the better-regarded pencillers of the late Silver Age.'

'Huh,' I said, taking an interest in spite of myself. 'You don't say.'

'Oh, yes. Wroblewski and Kann were the partnership that kept Crusader Comics in business. Perhaps you've never heard of Crusader, either? It was what you might call a boutique publisher by industry standards, but it had some popular titles during the 1960s. For much of that decade, *White Lightning* was the most successful of them all. Ring any bells, Mr Gupta?'

Raúl racked his brains. 'Nope, sorry. I don't think so.'

'He was Crusader's answer to Thor. You've heard of Thor, of course. Well, White Lightning's alter ego was Sandy Starr, an unassuming New York architect. But when he repeated some magic words of Ancient Greek, Starr transformed into White Lightning: last surviving descendant of Ares, the god of war. He was blond, blue-eyed, wore a toga and a feathered helmet, carried a shield and spear. I know it sounds a little silly these days, but at the time he had quite a following.'

'As far as I'm concerned, Mr Guzman, it sounds no more silly than any other superhero,' I replied, still vaping.

'Freddy Wroblewski was responsible for the storylines,' Guzman continued. 'He was Crusader's editor-in-chief. The concept was a shallow Kirby pastiche, but the craft was not without merit. Kann had a gift for convincing emotional portraiture. His action was eye-catching, his panel-work often ingenious. His draftsmanship gave Wroblewski's characters a depth they did not deserve.

'But no amount of artistic skill could have rescued *White Lightning* from the debacle of 1972. That was when Wroblewski and Kann introduced a new villain to the *White Lightning* universe: the Black Bird. She was the evil queen of an ancient African tribe from a remote, magical island. They portrayed her as a rageful savage, bent on attacking America. Her creation was likely intended as an homage to blaxploitation pictures – but if so, it was grossly misjudged.'

'Huh.'

'Perhaps forty years earlier, such a thing would have seemed acceptable. But the early 1970s was an intensely political time. Social issues pervaded many superhero stories: poverty, racism, drug abuse, women's liberation. In that climate, the Black Bird went entirely against the grain. An angry black woman, battling an Aryan superman – can you imagine such a thing?

'*White Lightning vs The Black Bird* was conceived as a four-issue storyline, but as soon as the first part was published it provoked outrage in the progressive comics community. By issue two, the brouhaha had gained the notice of the wider world. There were heated protests at Crusader headquarters in San Francisco. And then, after issue three, the offices were firebombed. A breakaway Black Panther faction was suspected, though the culprits were never caught.

'The final issue proved too controversial to publish, so the print run was pulped. White Lightning had been Crusader's standard-bearer, but now he was a disgrace. The fire gutted their offices, and the company was forced to declare bankruptcy soon after – which is why, Mr Gupta, you have never heard of Crusader Comics.

'*White Lightning #88* never went on sale to the public, and only a handful of copies are thought to have survived. One was sold at auction for a shade over ninety thousand dollars in 1996, to an unnamed European buyer, by an anonymous vendor widely believed to be Freddy Wroblewski. It is my understanding that Marty Kann never worked in comics again, but the consensus among the comics fraternity is that he died in possession of one of the few other remaining copies of *The Black Bird*. So you see: a rare and significant volume.'

His potted history concluded, Guzman allowed the facts to linger in the air with the burger smell and my e-cigarette vapour. It struck me that this was not the first time a toxic comic book had caused me grief. *Bad juju.*

Raúl whistled. 'Ninety *thousand* bucks?' he said.

Guzman nodded grimly.

'It's an intriguing story,' I said. 'But we still can't help you, Mr Guzman. We don't have the comic book. And if I had seen it at Cleo's sale, trust me: I would not have bought it.'

Guzman sighed, rueful but resigned.

'What about the son?' I said. 'Marty Jr. Wouldn't he have inherited it?'

'I contacted him, naturally,' Guzman replied. 'He insisted – in no uncertain terms – that he did not have *The Black Bird*. I was inclined to believe him.'

'So maybe it doesn't exist, after all. Maybe Marty Kann never had a copy.'

'It's possible. Or perhaps he did have it, but divested himself of it at an earlier date. Nevertheless, we have reason to believe there may have been a copy left in his estate. There were certain other items among the effects at Ms Habibi's sale that suggested to me he had not entirely left his past in comics behind.'

I thought back to the estate sale, and to the superhero doodles Raúl and I had discovered on the backs of Marty Kann's production-design sketches.

'Mr Guzman,' I said. 'No reason you'd be aware of this, but we have suffered some break-ins at Bart's Olde California since the Kann sale.'

Guzman peeled the lid off his milkshake and began to stir what was left with the straw. 'Hm,' he said, peering into the cup. 'I thought that might come up.'

Raúl and I shared a look. My partner's face darkened.

'What do you mean?' he said. 'How did you know?'

Guzman stood, gripping his cane for balance, and shuffled to the beaded curtain, parting it slightly with his free hand. 'Winslow!' he called through to the store. 'Would you come in here for a moment, please? Thank you.'

Guzman returned to his chair. A few seconds later, the curtain parted again, and in walked the teenager who'd been reading a comic on the floor when we arrived. Now that he was standing I could see he was a tall, rangy black kid, wearing J. J. Hunsecker specs and a gilet. He had a bum-fluff moustache and ungainly limbs, still apparently waging the last desperate campaign of the war on puberty. He clasped his hands in front of his crotch and stared hard at the ketchup blot on the rug.

'This is Winslow,' Guzman said. 'He works here on weekends and during high-school vacations. Do you have anything to say to these gentlemen, Winslow?'

The kid shifted his weight from foot to foot, and then grumbled, barely audible, 'Uh . . . yeah.'

Raúl sprang to his feet. 'Holy shit!' he said.

'Whoa, Raúl. What is it?'

'Lucky, don't you see? This scrawny fucker is Batman! He's the one tazed me!'

He pointed at the kid, who finally looked him in the eye, his jaw set.

'What?' I said, sceptical. 'This kid?'

'Mr Gupta,' Guzman said. 'With all due respect: as I understand it from Winslow, he entered an open store and made an enquiry, at which point you threatened to do him bodily harm – with a baseball bat, no less. He merely deployed his stun gun in self-defence.'

'Are you kidding me? He was wearing a balaclava and frickin' football pads!'

'Wait a second,' I said, finally standing myself. ' " *Winslow?* " '

'As in "Homer",' Guzman explained. 'His father teaches art history at UCLA.'

'Huh.'

He went on: 'I understand that you're upset about what occurred, Mr Gupta. But I would ask you not to complicate a fifteen-year-old's life by involving the police. Winslow is a fine young man whose zeal at times gets the better of him, and I do not trust the criminal-justice system to treat him with the leniency he deserves. I trust we can find some other way to make amends. I hope you appreciate my position. Now, Winslow: what do you wish to say to Messrs Gupta and Kluge?'

The kid's defiant glare was softening. Eventually, he returned his eyes to the floor and murmured, 'Sorry.'

'I'm not sure they heard you, Winslow.'

He glanced up and said it again, embarrassed: 'Sorry.'

I put a hand on Raúl's arm to placate him, but he still wasn't satisfied. 'Listen, Bruce Wayne. It's all well and good you apologising to us: my ass is almost healed,' he said. 'But our boss, Mr Abernathy? He's in a bad way. Broken nose, stitches in the back of his goddam head. You put an old man in the hospital. *And* you stole Lucky's cookie jar. We can't just let that slide.'

The kid looked fearful now. 'Cookie jar?' he said, and at last I recognised his voice from the other night. This was the man in black who'd had me petrified.

Guzman frowned. 'I'm sorry, Mr Gupta,' he said. 'I'm afraid I don't know what you're talking about. Winslow, can you throw light on this matter?'

'No!' said Winslow. 'I never saw the other dude! Just these two.'

'Mr Abernathy was assaulted?'

'That's right,' I said. 'He was roughed up at the store on Sunday night. His attacker stole a cookie jar – which also came from the Kann estate, as it happens.'

'*Sunday* night? At what time?'

'About an hour after he spoke to you.'

'Well, then. Winslow couldn't possibly have been involved.'

'Why not?' said Raúl.

'Because I came straight from meeting Mr Abernathy to our weekly book group, here at The Villain's Lair. I have several witnesses who can tell you that Winslow was with us all evening. His mother picked him up around ten.'

'Oh, yeah?' I said. 'What book were you reading?'

'*Born Again* and *The Man Without Fear*,' Winslow replied.

144

'Daredevil,' said Raúl. 'Cool.'

'Huh?'

'They're comic books, Sir Lucky.'

'For God's sake,' I said. 'Those aren't *books*.'

Guzman opened his desk drawer and passed me a handmade, photocopied A4 leaflet. *CRUSH book group*, it read. *Sundays, 7.30 p.m. @ The Villain's Lair. Email JG@villainsLA.ir for more information.*

'My condolences to Mr Abernathy,' Guzman said. 'But if we might return to the issue at hand: I have already docked Winslow's pay. With his parents' permission, I would also be prepared to loan him to you as an employee on a part-time basis for, shall we say, a month? He would be paid by me as normal, but he would work for Bart's Olde California. A kind of informal community service.'

Raúl was now simmering on a low heat. 'I have two conditions,' he said.

'Name them,' Guzman replied.

'One: I want that taser. Kid of fifteen shouldn't be walking around with an offensive weapon. Also it's kinda cool and I wanna try it.'

'Agreed. Winslow?'

I almost felt sorry for the kid, hands in his pockets, specs a little steamy. He was reluctant, but a sharp look from Guzman persuaded him to cross to the corner where the bags were heaped. He knelt and rummaged in his rucksack.

'Two: I'm doing a stand-up set at the Lo-Ball on La Brea Saturday night. I would like to leave some flyers on your counter, and a poster in your window.'

'Done.'

The kid stood and handed my partner the stun gun: a black, boxy device with a pair of small metal prongs at its business end. Raúl pressed the trigger; a spark danced between the two points, accompanied by a loud clicking sound.

'Well, alright then,' he said, grinning.

I handed the photocopied book-group ad back to Guzman. 'So what is CRUSH, anyway?' I said. 'It was on your business card as well.'

'I'm glad you asked,' the fat man replied, and he unbuttoned his shirt, yanking it open like Clark Kent to reveal the familiar symbol on his vest: a fist bearing down on the five-letter acronym. 'We're a campaign group. CRUSH stands for "Comic-book Readers for Understanding, Sensitivity and Humaneness".'

'Hold on,' said Raúl. 'Isn't "comic book" two words?'

'Is "humaneness" even a word at all?' I said. 'How many people in this group?'

'Four, so far,' Guzman replied. 'Myself. Young Winslow here. Tyler and Skye, whom I expect you met in the store. Tyler has a soft spot for *The Savage Dragon*, but we shan't hold that against him. Skye appreciates gloomy British writers like Gaiman and Moore. Perhaps the two of you would hit it off. We hope to sign up some new members at Comic-Con.'

'And you're campaigning for what, exactly?'

'We're an organisation devoted to collecting and contextualising problematic titles from comics history. In the long term, it is our intention to display *The Black Bird* and other examples in some form of not-for-profit exhibit. We believe such artefacts should not be allowed to become commodities, afforded monetary value simply by virtue of their notoriety.

'Had you been in possession of *The Black Bird*, I hoped I might have persuaded Mr Abernathy to part with it for a nominal sum. Given that you, Mr Kluge, hold a somewhat vaunted status in the field of comic-book ethics, I thought you would be amenable to my offer. But, believing that you were being deliberately obstructive, Winslow took it upon himself to—'

'Hang on a sec. A vaunted status in the field of *what*?'

'Comic-book ethics.'

'Who, me?'

'Why yes. For your decision to decline involvement in the *Marshal Eagle* movies. Quite admirable, I must say.'

'How do you know about that?'

'Oh, a simple internet search. It appears to be quite a well-known story among superhero aficionados, Mr Kluge.'

Raúl turned and stared at me with a strange new fascination; I don't think I'd ever told him the full story of my aborted film career.

'I don't understand,' I replied. 'Why would that make me . . . popular?'

'The film version did its printed predecessor a great disservice, in my opinion. Wouldn't you agree?'

'I never saw it.'

'It kinda sucked,' said Winslow. 'Sequel was okay.'

'It did suck,' Raúl agreed. 'Sorry, Lucky.'

I was unnerved by this news of my online fame, not least because it stemmed from a chapter of my life that I'd done my level best to forget. I sagged back onto the sofa and rubbed my eyes with the heels of my hands.

'Don't apologise to me,' I said. 'Apologise to Glyn Perkins. He wrote it.'

'A philistine,' Guzman said.

It was odd to be on the same side as Guzman in a debate about taste. Yet I also felt obliged to defend my old writing partner. And so I found myself explaining to Guzman, to Raúl and to Winslow how Glyn was from a hardscrabble background that made it more difficult for him to pass up an opportunity like *Marshal Eagle* than it was for me, with my lofty artistic principles and my modest family trust fund. How we hadn't spoken in years – and how he now appeared to have vanished on the eve of his *Marshal Eagle 3* script deadline.

They were all so fascinated, it almost made me feel better.

18

Karen cheered up when she heard that Bart's Olde California would be taking on an unpaid intern while her husband recovered. I told her Winslow was a friend's son and left it at that, figuring the less she knew about our new hire, the better. Raúl and I said we'd close up the store and sent her home early.

In spite of my partner's heated protestations, I insisted it was too deep into rush hour to make another attempt at delivering the tanker desk to Whitney Blair in Calabasas – but I opened the truck to look it over once more, just in case it contained a secret compartment or a drawer liner concealing Marty Kann's copy of *White Lightning #88*. It was empty, down to the shallow pencil drawer, which was still in need of a new lock.

Inside, Raúl sat with Kann's sketches arrayed on the counter. He was tinkering with his new toy, watching the white electric charge leap from point to point with the wide, excited eyes of a schoolboy stumbling across his dad's *Playboy* collection.

'Find anything?'

'Nope, just drawings.' He sighed. 'Ninety grand, Sir Lucky. Ninety grand.'

After leaving Guzman's, Raúl had immediately referred to his smartphone and scoured the internet for Marty Kann and the Black Bird. His search confirmed what Guzman told us: Marty Kann and Freddy Wroblewski, the creators of White Lightning, were players in the comics business between the late '60s and early '70s, but both vanished from the timeline following the Black Bird affair of 1972. Kann quietly resurfaced some years later, with his first film credits as a production illustrator; Wroblewski appeared to have faded into total obscurity.

As for *The Black Bird*, that too was all too true: the controversy, the fire, the swift demise of Crusader Comics. And then, a quarter of a century later, a single copy of *White Lightning #88* was sold anonymously at auction, to some interested European party with money to burn, for $92,500.

'My guess? It doesn't exist,' I said. 'Guzman said Marty Kann never worked in comics again – you think he'd want to hold on to something toxic like *The Black Bird*? If he ever had it, I think he flushed it down the toilet or sold it. Maybe it paid for some of that Craftsman bungalow.'

'And what about whoever beat up Bart? You believe that kid Winslow's alibi?'

'The book-group story stands up.'

'Which means the cookie-jar rustler is still out there somewhere.'

'Yup.'

'You have any plans after work?'

A few hours later we were back in my Bronco, parked across and a little way down from the low-rise apartment building in Mid-City where our Craigslist suspect claimed to reside. I had bought two cups of bad coffee and a bag of four freshly baked crullers from SK Donuts over on Third to maintain our spirits during the stake-out. The pastries lasted all of twenty minutes. The neighbourhood dogs started barking again as the streetlamps came on and the sky turned to strawberry gelato.

We had already checked on the other apartments. The carport still contained a single vehicle: the same rusted El Camino, which we guessed belonged to the woman upstairs in 826A. There was as yet no sign of the perp in number 826.

'This coffee's awful,' I said, and I cracked the driver's door to pour the last of the tepid beverage out on the kerb.

'I'm working on a bit about that.'

'About what?'

Raúl was watching Burgers lick pastry crumbs out of the foot-well. 'How we're all obsessed with espresso coffee, even though it tastes like bitter-ass piss,' he said. 'I drink coffee, you drink coffee, we all drink frickin' coffee. But the first time you tried it, you hated it, right? Give a kid coffee, they'll spit it out. A lot of life is kidding yourself into enjoying stuff you really hate. You know what Kopi luwak is?'

' "Copy loo-whack"? No.'

'It's coffee, made from beans that were eaten and then crapped out by a furry creature from the jungles of South Asia. Land of my forefathers. You can get it at a place in Santa Monica. Sixty-five bucks a cup. You believe that? Westsiders will pay *sixty-five bucks* for a cup full of warm shit . . .'

'Huh.'

'And here's the twist: turns out the kopi-luwak trade is now so lucrative that the producers stack the furry creatures — palm civets, they're called — they stack 'em in cages and force-feed 'em the coffee beans. So all these rich liberals discover they're actually drinking the *foie gras* of coffee.'

'Really.'

'And then, y'know, I talk about my parents. It's gonna be like two to three minutes of the act. It's a sophisticated bit.'

'Sounds like it.'

'But funny, though. You'll see on Saturday.'

'Of course,' I replied. 'Saturday.'

I had yet to formulate a satisfactory excuse not to attend his stand-up gig. Raúl licked his index finger and thrust it into the paper bag that had lately contained the crullers. It came out coated in cinnamon sugar, which he licked off absent-mindedly, and then repeated the process.

'So you and this Glyn dude were writing partners,' he said.

'Correct.'

'How does that work? One guy types, the other guy spitballs?'

'Sometimes.'

'So which one were you?'

'Either. Both. It depends. We had different ways of working, though. I was kind of a perfectionist, liked to produce two clean pages per day. Glyn's a churner: write twenty pages, throw out eighteen of them. Oh, and the other big difference between us? I have taste.'

'Jeez. Remind me never to write with *you*. Wait, is that—?'

He froze. A decrepit green Nissan sidled into the carport and took the spot next to the El Camino. The engine shuddered to a halt. We both held our breath, waiting to see which apartment the driver would head towards.

He was a tan young dude, tall, blond and buff, wearing a gym vest and carrying a shopping bag. His face was too pretty for anyone ever to have landed a punch, and I would've bet against Raúl or myself in a fight with the guy. He walked with a dancer's deportment from the car to the staircase, and then he started to climb.

Before I could say a word to stop him, Raúl was out of the Bronco and halfway across the street, Burgers blinking up bewildered at the now-empty passenger seat where his master had been a moment before. I hauled my arse from the car as fast as I could, but once again found myself trailing behind my partner in hot pursuit, lumbering like Murtaugh after Riggs: *I'm too old for this shit*.

When the guy heard Raúl's rapid footfalls and turned to see him charging up the outdoor stairs, he must have suspected what was in store, because he started to fumble frantically for his door-key. He turned it in the lock just as Raúl reached him and jabbed the stun gun right into his kidneys. I heard the guy yell in distress over the sound of kids' television from 826A, and watched aghast from the foot of the steps as he tumbled straight back through his front door.

'Raúl!' I shouted. 'What the *fuck*?'

The guy was cursing and mumbling for help, but my partner was not to be deterred. 'Where is it?' I heard him growl – and again, louder: 'WHERE IS IT?'

'Where is *what*? I don't have any money!'

'Cookie-jar-thieving mother*fucker*!'

'You've got the wrong gu*ARGGHH*!'

There was a crackle of electricity and a high-pitched squeal as he tazed the guy again. I got to the door to find Raúl in the narrow magnolia hallway, standing over his quarry, who was scrabbling to reach his dropped smartphone. His shopping bag had spilled its contents across the laminate: protein shake; instant ramen; turkey slices; loo roll.

'Raúl,' I said. 'Raúl, STOP!'

Raúl paused, brandishing the stun gun.

'Don't,' the guy said, holding his hands up in front of his face, which was contorted with pain and terror. 'Not again. *Please!* Just tell me what you want!'

'Hold on a second,' Raúl said, his tone suddenly light. 'Weren't you in *NCIS*?'

The guy's fear turned to confusion, and his features began to realign themselves. His soul patch quivered, clinging to his bottom lip like a koala to a branch. Tears sprang to his eyes as he slowly lowered his hands.

'You saw that episode?' he said.

'Sure,' Raúl replied. 'Didn't you get shot, or something . . . ?'

'Yeah, by the—'

'— By the guy with the—'

'— That's right!'

'Of course, I remember. Hey, Lucky, he was in *NCIS*!' Raúl said, half-turning towards me, and then back to the fellow on the floor. 'Y'know, you had your hands up just then, and I was like, "I *recognise* that dude!" Isn't that wild?'

'Yeah,' said the guy, grinning tentatively. 'Pretty wild.'

I leaned against the jamb, breathing hard and hoping my heart rate would slow.

'Seriously – great job, dude,' my partner went on. 'That episode was tight.'

'Thanks! But, uh . . . Who are you guys . . . ?'

'Oh,' said Raúl, looking from the horizontal actor to the stun gun in his hand and back again, coming over all sheepish at long last. 'Right, yeah. We're here about the cookie jar.'

'Cookie jar? What cookie jar?'

His name was Hal Green, another actor you've never heard of and needn't expect to. He had a solid alibi for Bart's assault: every evening, Thursday through Sunday, he was in the back room of a bar-restaurant in Culver City, performing a one-man show of his own devising about William Faulkner's Hollywood years. He showed us a photocopied playbill to prove it. Los Angeles supposedly hosts more theatre productions per annum than any other city in the world. And, in my limited experience, they are almost all godawful. LA theatre? Come off it.

To supplement the scarce pro acting jobs, Hal did some side-work as a personal trainer at a gym on Pico, but it can't have earned him much. I guessed the rent on the tiny apartment was no more than twelve hundred a month. He had a fridge that hummed as loud as heavy construction, though not quite loud enough to drown out the cartoons on next-door's TV. The walls were bare, as if he'd never quite admitted to himself that he lived there, and an archipelago of mismatched yard-sale furniture was spaced across the living-room's expanse of faux-wooden flooring. We sat on his cheap futon, drinking his cheap beer.

Think writing is a poor career choice? Try acting. The actor's life is a pimply kid's prom night: 99 per cent rejection. Hal was an educated man who spoke fondly of Faulkner's *As I Lay Dying*, yet his career high was playing a dead body on a mediocre network cop show. If he squinted, he could probably see the Hollywood sign from the end of his street, taunting him with its proximity. He was young, but not *that* young. I wanted to tell him he'd be a whole lot happier if he packed a suitcase of whatever mattered most to him, and drove his crappy Nissan back to Kansas or Iowa or Minnesota or wherever it was he came from in the first place. But then, who was I to talk?

Satisfied that he wasn't our man, we asked him about the neighbours. The downstairs apartment, 826½, had long been empty due to water damage. 826A was occupied by a single mum and her kids. The landlady lived out of town. Neither of them sounded like a viable suspect. We checked the Craigslist ad again on Raúl's smartphone: it was definitely the right address. But Hal pointed at the picture of the Ringmaster jar, standing upright on a patch of grass.

'Looks like it was taken on someone's lawn,' he said. 'I don't recognise that spot. And heck, there sure ain't no mown grass on *this* property.'

When it was time for him to show us out, I almost felt more guilty for leaving him alone in his shabby apartment than for being an accessory to his assault an hour beforehand. He and Raúl swapped improv stories and invitations to their respective shows as I stood vaping out on the balcony at the top of the stairs.

'E-cigarettes, brother,' Hal said, as he lingered in the doorway to wave us off. 'I tried 'em. But in the end I said to myself, "Hal, you oughta just quit."'

'You know what, Hal?' I replied. 'That is excellent advice.'

19

I was sitting alone in the shadows on Glyn's front step when my phone rang.

'Hello?'

'Lucky, it's Cleo. How's it going?'

'Hey, Cleo, I'm good. You?'

'Never better.'

'Just wanted to hear my voice?'

'It's about the Kann sale. You know you asked me about the son, Marty Jr?'

'Oh, yeah. Lives in Reno.'

'Actually, no. Turns out he's back in LA now.'

'Really?'

'That's why I'm calling. He returned my message today.'

'Huh.'

'So do you still want to talk to him?'

'You know what? That might not be necessary, after all.'

'Oh? How come?'

'Long story.'

'Alright. Well, I have his number if you want it.'

'Why don't you text it to me, just in case.'

'Okay. He sounded cool, but tread lightly. This is kinda unprofessional of me.'

'I will Cleo, thanks. And listen, I'm sorry about last night. I don't know what happened. That guy, Waggoner. You gave me a shock bringing him up, that's all.'

'I noticed. My coffee table is still convalescing. How do you know him?'

'Another long story. But it was weird of me to leave like that, I know.'

She was quiet on the far end of the line.

'Cleo?'

'You busy tonight? Wanna grab some dinner, tell me one of your long stories?'

'Ah. Kind of, yeah. Busy, I mean. Sorry.'

'That's cool. I was thinking I should stay in and wash my hair, anyway. Find myself a Meg Ryan movie on Netflix.'

I smiled. 'Very funny,' I said.

'Are you going to Raúl's show Saturday?'

'Christ, you know about that?'

'Of course. He sent me a Facebook invite. Will I see you there, then?'

'I guess you just might.'

As I hung up, I heard Bijou's heels clacking along the pavement beneath the ficus trees. I stood when her sleek, moonlit outline came into view at the end of the path, her little mutt's leash in one hand, a plastic bag full of its turds in the other. The chihuahua mix saw me first, and it yapped and skittered around her ankles. 'Holy shit,' she said with a start, when I stepped into the porchlight.

'Hi, Bijou.'

'*Asshole!* Hiding in the dark like a fucking rapist.'

'I would've called, but you wouldn't have answered, so . . .'

'It's late. What the fuck do you want?'

I slid the hotel keycard from my pocket and handed it to her.

'Is that all? You could've left it in the mailbox, y'know.'

'But where would be the fun in that?'

She turned it over in her hand. My pocket buzzed: Cleo's text arriving.

156

'Kids are in bed,' Bijou said finally. 'You need a drink? Because I do.'

'I thought you were toxin-free.'

'Yeah, well. Vodka doesn't count. Hold this.'

She handed me the still-warm sachet of dogshit while she unlocked the front door. The chihuahua mix kept eyeing me and growling, like a lairy old drunk picking a fight in a dive bar. It was all I could do not to punt it into the flowerbed.

Bijou poured me a bourbon over rocks and herself a vodka tonic, and we stood fondling them under her stark kitchen lights. The industrial-sized dishwasher was running; it made the floor quiver enough to register on the Richter scale. The kitchen counter had a child's handprint on it: a dried red smear of pasta sauce. I grimaced as I swallowed a dram and sucked air in through my teeth. She tutted.

'Still drinking it neat to impress me?'

'You haven't asked me how Glyn was,' I said.

She rolled her eyes. 'You saw him? How is he?'

'He wasn't there.'

'Wasn't where? At the Chagall?'

'That's right.'

She sipped her drink and studied me. 'You mean he wasn't there when you visited, or he's not staying there anymore?'

'He still had a room. Some of his stuff is in it. But I don't think he'd been there for at least a day or two. You should call his mum in Port Talbot.'

'And why the fuck would I do that?'

'Because Todd Carver thinks he's there, working on *Marshal Eagle 3*.'

'You talked to Todd?'

'You must be joking. Todd would rather sign Lindsay Lohan than take my calls. No, Abby Musker told me.'

'Of course she did. And did she tell you Glyn already blew

through two script deadlines because he's *depressed*, or because he's busy screwing some Victoria's Secret model? Or did Todd not pass on that particular bit of information?'

'Not my problem, Bijou.'

'Oh, but this is?'

'Like I said before, it's a favour for Abby. I'm just trying to help.'

'That is priceless. You, *help*?'

I tried to breathe evenly. Bijou doesn't just know how to press my buttons, she has the nuclear codes. 'You know what? I don't buy this Glyn-screwing-a-model theory,' I said. 'I checked out some of those names you mentioned, the "hooker" names? Turns out Bryony is Glyn's Pilates teacher. And Nadja is some kind of dream therapist he's seeing. So: you need to call Todd, or call Glyn's mum. And if he's not at his mum's, then I don't know . . . Maybe you should call the police.'

'The *police*?' she gasped. 'What the fuck are you saying to me?'

She set her drink on the counter and steadied herself. I imagine it was not her first vodka of the evening. I felt obliged to grab hold of her by the shoulders. 'I'm not saying anything, Bijou. I just think it's a bit weird that no one knows where he is. And I think you should put your mind at rest. And Abby's, for that matter.'

Her eyes met mine; they were brimming. I was close enough to smell her perfume, the same bittersweet scent she'd always worn. 'What if I don't wanna know where he is, Lucky? What if Todd's covering for him, and he really is just shacked up with some piece of ass? You think *that's* gonna put my mind at rest?'

I thought of the name Glyn had scrawled on that scrap of paper and folded into his copy of *The Hero with a Thousand Faces*: 'Evelyn'. I chose not to mention it. 'If that really is the case, Beej, then you're going to have to find out sometime, aren't you?' I said. 'It might as well be now.'

She kissed me first. That's my story, and I'm sticking to it. She stared at me blankly, blinked away the welling tears, and then she kissed me. Kissed me sharp and violent, just like old times, tongue darting and thrusting till I could taste the vodka through the bourbon. Her firm tits were hot against my chest, her arse hard as a pair of cantaloupes as I hefted her up onto the counter.

In that moment, I may as well admit, I felt a flush of empathy with Glyn: there's a deep, dark, dangerous thrill to hooking up with your friend's girl. I hadn't got so hard so fast in a decade – not since bumping uglies with Bijou on our first go round. As we kissed some more and started to dry-hump, I recalled that tattoo on the inside of her thigh: the ship in a storm, sails full, fit to rip. I remembered how she once rode me, like John Wayne in fucking *Stagecoach*.

Maybe it was my hand moving too eagerly beneath her top. Maybe it was that she got my shirt off to find a farmer's tan and my once-trim mid-section in a state of sad disrepair. Maybe it was plain old shame. But after what seemed like thirty seconds, she pulled away, paused, and then slapped me crisply across the face.

'You fucking asshole,' she said.

'What? *What?* You kissed *ME*!'

'Shut the fuck up. You'll wake my kids.'

She pushed me off and hopped back to the floor, then she went to the sink to splash her face with water. I stood there looking like an idiot, with my shirt off, my cheek sore and my dick still tenting my jeans. 'Jesus Christ,' I said.

She brought a damp cloth back to the counter and started to scrub off her child's ingrained tomato handprint, ranting irrationally: 'What did I do to deserve *British* men? Look at me! I oughta be married to a quarterback! But no, I had to go get stuck on a couple of patronising British *writers*. You act so smart and superior, so fucking self-righteous. But underneath you're both just *eaten up* with self-doubt and insecurity. Glyn buries it deeper. I mean, my God, at least he's had to *work* for something in his life. But *you*? I see right fucking through you, Lucky. You're so god-dam self-obsessed. You make me *sick*. It's fucking *pathetic*.'

'You have a real potty mouth, Bijou.'

She hurled the dirty cloth at my face, missed.

'Y'know, you act like *I'm* the asshole,' she said, wagging her manicured finger. 'But *you* threw *me* over, remember? You *do* remember that, don't you? You were kinda shit-faced at the time, could be it slipped your fucking mind.'

I didn't have an answer for that, so I grabbed my shirt from the tiled floor. By the time I tugged it back on and downed another mouthful of her whisky, I'd come up with one: 'Well, that's no excuse for shagging my best friend, is it?'

'Oh, you mean the best friend you deserted on the most import-ant day of his life? You mean my fucking HUSBAND? And what were we supposed to do, Lucky? After you had your little *breakdown* and dropped off the goddam map?'

'Whoa there. "Breakdown"? I did not have a bloody *breakdown*.'

Bijou laughed harshly and picked up her vodka tonic. 'You just go on telling yourself whatever story tucks you in at night,' she said. 'You're the writer.'

'Not anymore, I'm not.'

She lifted the glass to her lips, took a long gulp and swallowed hard. 'When Glyn and I . . . *Shit*. It was like you'd died or some-thing, Lucky. We were *grieving*. We helped each other to pick up the fucking pieces, y'know. And then . . .'

'And then.'

She hauled herself up onto one of the high-stools, picked an ice cube out of her glass and pressed it to her temple. She looked about as exhausted as I felt.

'Where the fuck have you been, Lucky?'

'What's that supposed to mean?'

'Do you even have a job?'

'I work in antiques.'

'You're serious.'

I stared at her.

'Makes sense,' she went on. 'I guess you grew up with all that *Harry Potter* crap. Have you been in LA this whole time?'

'Not the *whole* time,' I replied. 'I go for weekends in Joshua Tree. Spent a fortnight in the Yucatán a couple of winters back.'

'That's not funny. Our eldest kid is almost six fucking years old and you've never even met him.'

'It's not as if you invited me round for dinner.'

'Would you have come?'

I thought about it. 'Probably not,' I replied.

The dishwasher had finished its cycle. The children seemed to have slept through our effing and blinding. Lady the chihuahua mix was in the next room, minding her own business. Silence is surprisingly easy to come by in Los Angeles at that hour of the night.

'I'm gonna have another drink,' Bijou said. 'How about you?'

20

I woke up on the sofa again, but this time it was Glyn and Bijou's. An imitation Mies van der Rohe – way more expensive than mine, and a lot less comfortable. I opened my eyes and blinked up at the high white sitting-room ceiling. From somewhere in the house came the salty murmur of Bijou's voice and the smell of fresh coffee, a tonic to my furred tongue and my jackhammer head. I reached down to yank off the thin quilt I'd thrown over myself before crawling into sleep in the wee hours, and then I heard a growl from nearby.

I raised my head. Lady the chihuahua mix, teeth bared, sat on the flatweave rug at the far end of the sofa. Beside her was a ginger child in gingham pyjamas, a spray of freckles across the bridge of his nose and a frown crumpling his shallow forehead. I recognised him from the photo on the refrigerator: the five-year-old.

'Hi there,' I said, sighing involuntarily as I sat upright.

'Who the fuck are you?' said the kid. He was his mother's son.

'I'm Lucius,' I replied.

He broke into a grin. 'That's my middle name!'

'Is that right? Well, you can call me Lucky.'

Before he could shake my outstretched hand, a woman's voice yelled his name from the kitchen: 'Dylan! *Breakfast!*'

The kid trotted away without saying goodbye, Lady at his heels. I rubbed my face, smoothing down the stubble that had grown another day longer. The sitting room was big and cool, furnished without taste or imagination like a Pottery Barn showroom, all decorative lanterns and distressed-effect side tables. Nothing in the house besides Bijou and Glyn could be more than ten years old.

The life *Marshal Eagle* had built was a good one, by any conventional measure. I wondered why Glyn would ever feel the need to leave it. In spite of the naff decor, I felt a pang of envy, which I intend to blame on my hangover.

When we first left home to try our luck in Hollywood, I had flown out ahead of Glyn. I remember picking him up from LAX – how soon the sunlight and the ocean breeze seemed to dispel his jet-lag. I took him straight to the In-N-Out on Sepulveda, where I witnessed the reverence with which he took his first bite of an American cheeseburger. The guy wanted to swallow Southern California whole.

I was still the frontman for at least our first year, did most of the talking at parties and pitch meetings. But I grew distracted by cocktails and cock-teases, and in our writers' room – which at the time was a Starbucks on Santa Monica – Glyn was quietly growing in stature. When I finally stopped to notice the ground shifting beneath me, the earthquake was already well underway.

On the counter in the kitchen, I found freshly squeezed juice and hot coffee, toasted bagels and almond butter. The children sat at the table eating breakfast with their Latina nanny. She saw me and smiled, and gestured for me to help myself. Then she went on spooning yoghurt into the three-year-old. 'That's Lucius,' said the five-year-old, between mouthfuls.

I poured myself a large cup of black coffee. The pool rippled in the breeze beyond the terrace outside. I guessed a morning swim would be too much to ask. It seemed I'd have to go to work in the same clothes again, and with last night's bourbon still on my breath.

'You were right.'

I turned to find Bijou in the doorway. She had on Lycra pants and a gym vest over a sports bra, which provided a fairly comprehensive impression of just what I'd missed out on the previous night. Perhaps that was precisely her intent.

'No change there, then,' I replied. 'What was I right about this time?'

'I just talked to Glyn's mom. He's in Wales, like you said. So, you can tell Abby Musker she doesn't have to worry anymore.'

'Alright, that's good. Did you talk to him?'

'No. I mean, he was—' She faltered and dipped her eyes. 'He was out for a walk or something.'

I supposed they were still on non-speakers.

'Well, one thing at a time, right?'

'Yeah. One thing at a time. But apparently the *ME3* script is pretty much done, so . . . y'know. That's all fine.'

'Okay,' I said. 'I'm glad, I guess.'

She poured herself some juice. The five-year-old brought his empty cereal bowl over to the counter. 'Mom?' he said, and she rested her hand on his head.

'Hey, Dylan.'

'So is Dad in Wales?'

'Yes, my darling. He's gone to see Grandma. You remember Grandma?'

'*Fat* Grandma?'

'That's right.'

Once I'd finished my coffee, Bijou walked me to the door and watched me work my heels back into my trainers.

'You needn't tell Glyn I came looking for him,' I said.

'I wasn't planning to.'

I stepped outside and breathed in the scent of warm honey-suckle. Fat swallowtail butterflies floated among the blooms that framed the porch.

'So, Lucky . . .'

'Yes?'

'You think you'll come round for dinner sometime?'

I cocked my head. 'You think you'll invite me?'

She smiled – a rare and dazzling sight. I put on my sunglasses, the way Rhett Butler puts on a hat. 'See you next time, Bijou.'

I texted Abby on my way to the store, to tell her Glyn was safe in Wales. By the time I got to Los Feliz, she'd responded: *Phew!! Tnx. Still weird tho, no? Ax*

Perhaps it was weird, but I hadn't seen my former writing partner in years, so I was in no position to account for his behaviour. It didn't sound like the old Glyn to skip out on his wife and kids, hop on a plane to London without telling them, and head back to the grim industrial town he'd spent half his life trying to escape. Then again, the old Glyn wouldn't have taken Pilates classes, either.

I didn't have much time to mull it over, because Raúl was waiting for me in the store car park. He approached the Bronco just as I was composing a reply to Abby, his pupils darting and dilated, as if he'd just smoked a mean bowl of sativa.

'Something wrong, Raúl? That's the second time you've been early this week.'

'Couldn't sleep.'

'How come?'

He leaned in the driver's side window and lowered his voice: 'I found it.'

'Huh? Found what?'

'Lemme show you.'

I stopped concentrating on my phone. 'What is it, Raúl? Don't muck about.'

'C'mon,' he said, opening the car door and gesturing for me to follow.

'Where are you going?'

'Just *c'mon*, Your Lordship.'

He led me over to Bart's truck and insisted we both get into the cab, but when I went to put my key in the ignition, he stopped me.

'No,' he said. 'We're not going anywhere.'

'Then what the hell is going on?'

He swept his eyes furtively across the car park, in case Karen or Sasquatch Pete should spot us. I'd never seen him so jumpy. 'You remember at the Kann sale,' he said. 'I picked up that pet crate for Burgers, from the garage – and a box of crappy old magazines for him to poop on?'

'Huh. Sure, I remember.'

'Well, it turns out they weren't all crappy old magazines.'

I watched him, beginning to twig. 'Go on . . .'

'The thought just occurred to me at the dog park last night, while I was watching him drop a deuce on a back issue of *Esquire*. So afterwards, when I got back to my apartment, I flipped through the box – and whaddya know? There they were, about halfway back. Tell you what: they got my bowels moving, too.'

'There *what* were . . . ?'

He opened the truck's glove compartment and lifted them gingerly into the light, each comic in its own clear plastic protective sleeve: *White Lightning #85* through *#88* – all four issues of the Black Bird storyline. They were somewhat yellowed by the decades, but otherwise in near-perfect condition. I stared in disbelief as he slid them onto my lap.

'Holy shit,' I said. What else was there to say?

'I had 'em the whole time. Didn't even know it.'

'This is incredible, Raúl. A complete bloody set? How much is that worth?'

'I dunno, dude. I mean, I looked up the first three issues online; they're not so rare. But with issue number four, I'd guess it's at least a hundred grand for the collected run. If you can find an asshole to buy 'em, that is.'

'Did you read them?'

'Skimmed 'em. With rubber gloves on.'

'And?'

He winced. 'It ain't pretty.'

I picked up the first issue and studied the cover. In the top left-hand corner was the Crusader Comics logo, the issue number – 85 – and a small, full-length portrait of the hero in his modified ancient-god garb. So far, so innocuous.

But the main image was where the trouble started: it was framed by White Lightning's beefy shoulder, blond mullet and chiselled jaw, which took up the bottom and left-hand edge of the page. Beyond, backed into a streetlit alley, spear in hand and ready to strike, was the Black Bird. Her eyes and gnashing teeth were vivid white, her afro spherical and substantial. She wore khaki safari hotpants and heavy beaded necklaces that obscured her naked breasts. Looming out of the dark to either side of her were two hungry lionesses.

Across the top of the cover ran the title, *White Lightning*; at the bottom, in another booming font, *Vs The Black Bird!* Slapped like a discount tag on the space to the right of the supervillain was a bright red circle containing the words: 'The Dazzler Faces His Darkest Foe!' And in the bottom right-hand corner, where the yellow glare of the streetlamp bled out into deep blue, was printed the tiny but damning dual signature: 'Wroblewski & Kann'.

The Black Bird may not have been *Birth of a Nation*, but it was pretty damned distasteful. I felt like I was handling Nazi crockery. *White Lightning #85* weighed in, by my estimate, at no more than thirty pages. Such a flimsy thing to have burned down a building, bankrupted a company and destroyed two men's careers. Bad, bad juju. I flipped it over: on the back cover was an advertisement for mail-order sea monkeys.

I sifted through the pile to the final, unpublished issue, *White Lightning #88*. The cover price was 15 cents – $92,499.85 shy of its current, grey-market value. The front page was fringed with lush greenery, and it showed White Lightning lashed to a baobab by pythons, apparently having pursued his adversary to her African jungle lair. He was surrounded by roaring lions, raging baboons and savage tribespeople led by the Black Bird herself, who spewed

167

patois bile in a speech bubble. The cover line asked: 'Can the Greek God Escape the African Queen?!' Little did its creators realise, the answer was no.

I passed the comics back to him without pulling them out of their plastic sleeves, and he returned the stack to its hiding place in the glove compartment. I wound down the driver's side window to let in some air. We sat in silence awhile, me smoking my e-cigarette, my partner sucking on one of Bart's peppermint Altoids.

'Can you imagine?' I said. 'Marty Kann. He kept them that whole time, squirrelled away in his garage. He must have been hiding them, I suppose.'

'From who, his wife?'

'Maybe his wife. Or his kid. From himself, even. Maybe he meant to get rid of them, but he forgot they were there? I don't know.'

Or maybe he didn't keep them in the garage at all. As I recalled, the cardboard container that Raúl had commandeered was one of Cleo's branded Habibi Estates packing boxes. It was entirely possible that she or one of her employees had failed to recognise the significance of the comics and simply heaped them in with the rest of the worthless magazines. But if Marty Kann had valued *The Black Bird*, then surely he would have left it to someone in his will, rather than abandon his radioactive creation to the random fate of an estate sale.

Raúl crunched the breath-mint between his teeth. 'So what do we do now?' he said. 'Sell 'em? That's a couple years' rent right there. For the store, I mean.'

'I don't know. We don't want to just advertise that we have them. Too risky.'

'You think we oughta tell Bart? Or Guzman? That Winslow kid starts work Saturday, y'know.'

'Honestly, I think this is one of those "need-to-know-basis" situations – and Bart doesn't need to know,' I said. 'As for

Guzman, we don't owe that guy anything. No, there's somebody else I want to talk to first.'

'Oh, yeah? Who?'

Rather than answer him directly, I took out my phone and started to dial.

21

There was a pall in the air above the Pacific Coast Highway as we approached Topanga Canyon. From what we could make out via the truck's ageing radio, the Overlook Fire had been 20 per cent contained by late Wednesday afternoon, only to break loose overnight and scurry over the ridge to the Valley side of the mountains. It smelled like a riot.

Topanga is a country town just minutes from civilisation, where the wild sage and manzanita tumble down the steep hillsides to the clustered cabins below. The neighbourhood may still have a Native American name, and no doubt there are plenty of feathered dreamcatchers adorning its bedroom windows. But if you ever find yourself in a sweat lodge around here, you can bet you'll be sharing it with a bunch of old white hippies doing sun salutations, not with a medicine man.

I drove through the middle of town, past the health-food merchants and the mind-body-spirit bookshops, and then up a wooded side road, further into the canyon. We reached our destination and turned into a dirt driveway, the overhanging oaks scraping along the sides of the truck. Finally we emerged into a large clearing of long grasses and wildflowers, shaded by the surrounding trees.

At the heart of the clearing sat an Airstream caravan, its buffed aluminium hull reflecting whatever sunlight filtered through the wildfire smoke that hung above the treeline. Beside it was a vintage Chevy pick-up, and beyond that someone had pitched a teepee. As I put the truck in park, I spotted a housecat prowling silently through the grass.

Scattered across the glade were strange metallic assemblages: car parts welded to look like creatures; oil barrels twisted into totems. Leaning against the outside of the caravan were several old mile-marker signs that seemed to have been stolen from the side of a road. One said 200 miles to Vegas, another 68 to Fresno.

Raúl and I had just started to stroll across the clearing to the Airstream, my partner with his messenger bag slung over his shoulder, when the air around us exploded with the sound of gunfire – PAP-PAP-*PCHOW*! – a close-range triple-burst that sent us both diving back towards the truck.

'What the fuck was *that*?' I said, as I cowered behind the cab.

Raúl laughed, half-giddy with terror. 'Holy *crap*, dude!'

Another burst clattered across the clearing – PAP-PAP-*PCHOW*! – and I covered my ears, fighting the urge to curl into the foetal position.

'Jesus!' My teeth jangled. 'Are they shooting at *us*?'

Raúl rose into a crouch to peer over the bonnet, and immediately dropped to the grass again as a third cacophonous burst rang out: PAP-PAP-*PCHOW*!

'Where's it bloody coming from?'

'Can't see.'

The final echo ricocheted off the trees and died away. I could hear Burgers whimpering from inside the cab. I turned to Raúl, who was squatting alongside me, breathing heavily and grinning. We waited, and in the silence I began to strategise an escape, until the breeze carried a new sound our way: a regular, repetitive squawk, like the cries of a dying bird being borne towards us.

At last, the source of the sound appeared around the side of the truck. It was an old BMX, spray-painted gold with silver handlebar tassels, ridden by a barefoot girl of little more than legal drinking age. She wore denim cut-offs and a crop-top, and she had long brown hair, stiff and textured as if soaked for hours in saltwater. She stopped when she saw us, and her bike's wheels ceased their squawking. I still wasn't sure whether we'd walked into the middle of a Joni Mitchell song, or an encounter with the Manson Family.

'Oh, hey!' the girl said, gaily. 'You guys here to see Marty?'

She led us past the Airstream to the far side of the clearing, where there stood an old steel shipping container and, in front of it, a stocky, bearded man holding an assault rifle longer than he was tall. I guessed Marty Kann Jr was thirty-something, though it was hard to tell because his face was half-obscured by his Orson Welles whiskers. He wore hiking boots, camo shorts, hi-spec ear-guards and a sleeveless check shirt, hanging open to display his shag-rug abs.

His arms were encased in tattoos and leather bangles, and a lit cigarette dangled from the corner of his mouth. He looked like a lumberjack. Or, to be strictly accurate, like a member of the Village People dressed as a lumberjack.

He held up a hand when he saw us and yelled: 'Just gimme ONE SECOND!'

The girl put her fingers in her ears, so Raúl and I copied her, as Marty Jr raised the weapon to his shoulder and fired one last burst – PAP-PAP-*PCHOW*! – towards the trees at the edge of the glade. I looked to see what he was shooting at: another road sign, resting against the base of an oak. It was riddled with bullet holes, but I could make out the lettering nonetheless: *San Luis Obispo 115, Los Angeles 319.*

Marty Jr shouldered the rifle and waved us over. He yanked off his ear-guards and let them sit around his neck. 'You Lucky?' he said, as we approached.

'That's right, Mr Kann. And this is Raúl.'

'Mr Kann's my dad,' he said. 'I'm Marty. Looks like you met Mona.'

The girl had spiralled off across the clearing on her bike again.

'Marty,' I replied. 'Thanks for making the time.'

'No problemo, man. I got all the time in the world.'

'I can see that.'

He bared his canines, wiped the sweat from his brow and flicked his spent cigarette into the dirt. Beneath an awning on the backside of the Airstream were a plastic patio chair and a kids' paddling pool, dead leaves floating on the shallow water. Marty Jr propped the gun against the chair.

'Hold on,' he said, and he strode over to the treeline to study his target. Apparently satisfied, he picked up the pockmarked road sign, hefted it back to the shipping container and disappeared inside. The rusted, rectangular hulk was speckled with moss. After much unidentified clanging and creaking, Marty Jr emerged without the sign and swaggered back towards us. He lit up again, and I almost asked him for a drag, but I restrained myself and sucked unhappily on my e-cigarette instead.

'So you're English, huh?' he said. 'Whereabouts in England you from?'

'Have you heard of Somerset?'

'Is that near London?'

'Not really.'

He put his hands on his hips. 'Man, I love London,' he said. 'Great fuckin' city. Whaddya call those eggs, with the sausage meat around 'em?'

'Scotch eggs?'

'Scotch eggs, that's *right*! I love that shit.'

'Cleo told me you lived in Reno.'

'Nah, man,' he replied. 'I travel. But this here is my crib. We were up in the desert by Reno for like a month, for Burning Man. Just got back last week.'

Raúl was admiring the assault rifle. 'Dude,' he said. 'That is a big frickin' gun.'

'Pretty rad, huh?' said Marty Jr. 'Bought it with my inheritance.'

Raúl nodded. 'What's with the road signs?'

He smoothed his beard reflexively. 'Yeah, so that's for my art.

We pick 'em up from all over. Every time we take a road trip. And then I shoot the shit out of 'em. I've got a solo show in Culver City this fall. You should come check it out.'

'But what does it mean?' said Raúl. 'The signs.'

Marty Jr sighed theatrically. 'Uhhh . . . like, *America*, I guess? But don't ask me, man. Ask my gallerist. She's the one writes the exhibition notes. Say, you boys care for a drink?'

We followed him into the Airstream's customised interior. At one end of the caravan a second girl lay face down on the king-size bed, asleep. In the pocket kitchen a cat sat on the counter, drinking from the dripping tap. Marty Jr grabbed it by the scruff of the neck and hurled it through the door onto the grass.

'Fuckin' cats, man,' he said. 'They were my mom's.'

At the other end of the narrow trailer was a red horseshoe banquette. The Formica table in front of it was covered in empty glasses and crushed cans of beer, some crammed with cigarette butts. Raúl and I squeezed onto the bench at Marty Jr's urging, while he rinsed some tumblers and produced a quart of tequila from a kitchen cabinet. He poured three large measures and came to the table.

'Down the hatch,' he said, raising his glass and sinking it. I followed suit, but I could see my partner would struggle with the daytime drinking. He took a sip and then pushed his tumbler aside, wincing as Marty Jr poured himself another.

'So, what can I do for you boys?' he said. 'The estate sale lady, Miss Habibi, she said you wanted to talk to me about something to do with my parents' place?'

Our chat and the clinking of glasses had woken the sleeping girl, who walked over, yawning, and parked herself on Marty Jr's lap. She was the dead spit of Mona, sun-kissed and freckled, sporting nothing but a green bikini.

'This is Lisa,' he said, winking. 'Twins.'

Raúl, who like me was trying not to stare, reached into his messenger bag and coolly removed the copy of *White Lightning #88: The Black Bird*.

'We came to ask you about this,' he said, placing it on the table in front of him. 'We found it among your father's effects.'

When he saw what it was, Marty Jr recoiled, barking: '*Fuck*, man!'

Lisa hiccuped in shock, and then observed Marty Jr anxiously as he tugged at his beard: 'Aw *shit*, Dad. You kept it. I didn't know he kept it.'

'I'm sorry, Marty,' I said. 'We didn't mean to upset you. We acquired this from your father's estate without understanding its significance. And when we found out what it was . . . Well, we weren't really sure what to do with it.'

He downed his second tequila and poured a third.

'Get fuckin' rid of it is my advice,' he said, belching. 'That thing is cursed.'

'Bad juju,' Raúl muttered.

'*Exactly!*' replied Marty Jr, and he jabbed the air with his smoking hand. 'Bad fuckin' juju, man.'

Raúl hastily brushed the cigarette ash from *The Black Bird*'s plastic sheath. Marty Jr bunched his fists against his temples, eyeing the comic book as if it were a crime-scene photo. Lisa rubbed his back, until at length he spoke again.

'You have anything from your past that keeps you up nights?' he said. 'That you're ashamed of? Something half of you wants to forget, but the other half – the half that hates itself – just won't let you . . . ?'

'I could tell you how I lost my virginity,' Raúl replied. 'Trust me: that would keep you *all* up at night.'

Lisa giggled obligingly, but Marty Jr appeared not to have heard the joke. 'That's what this comic book was like for my dad,' he went on. 'Tore him apart, but he couldn't let it go. I mean listen, he didn't open up about that stuff a lot. He was like one of those dudes never talks about what he saw in 'Nam. But when he drank, he spilled . . . I can't believe he kept it. Thought he tossed it out years ago.'

'I'm sorry,' I said again.

'Nah, man. It's cool,' he replied. 'I appreciate your coming by. Your intentions were pure. I get it. But this?' – he poked a finger at *The Black Bird* – 'I don't want any part of it.'

He tipped his third tequila down his throat. His eyes glazed over, and I could tell he was summoning a memory. 'He could be pretty hard to live with,' he said, licking his lips. 'My dad. Black moods. Never violent, just real introspective, know what I mean? My mom could handle it. But when she died . . . ?'

He drifted away into nostalgia for a moment, and then drifted back. 'You boys sell it if you want, I don't care. I don't need the money – not from that, anyhow. It'd be like, I dunno – profiting from my dad's sadness. Sell it, or fuckin' burn it.'

His voice cracked. He started to cry softly, and then he buried his face in Lisa's chest. Raúl and I shared an awkward glance as Marty Jr cupped one of the girl's half-naked breasts in his hand, cigarette still glowing between his fingers. The gesture seemed to soothe him, and he sat back up, sniffling.

'I apologise,' he said. 'You know my mom passed last year, too?'

I nodded. He reached out and put his palm flat on the comic, communing with his father's ghost. 'You wanna know the crazy thing? This was his best work. That's what he'd say: '72 was his peak. He never got close to that again, not after he started working in movies. I'm an artist too, man. I get it.

'I remember people used to write him, when I was a kid. People from New York, London, Japan. Fan letters: they loved *White Lightning*. My mom used to keep 'em. The letters. But they stopped writing after a while. Lost interest. I guess people grow up, they move on, they don't like comic books anymore.'

He removed his hand but went on staring morosely at *The Black Bird*. Raúl, sensing its presence was unwelcome, slid the comic off the table and into his bag. That broke the spell. Marty Jr took a deep breath, picked up the tequila bottle and offered to pour me another. I accepted, if only to help him feel less alone.

'I saw your old bedroom,' I said. 'The action figures, the posters. Seems like you were into comic books when you were younger, too.'

'Who, me? Nah, I never liked that superhero bullshit. That's all my dad's. Kinda rebelled against it, I guess. That's what kids do, right?'

He dropped his dying cigarette into a beer can, then he picked up Raúl's untouched tequila and necked it. He was slurring his words now.

'Dad left his comic-book collection to Freddy. The rest of 'em, I mean. You should talk to him if you're interested.'

'Freddy,' I replied. 'You mean Freddy Wroblewski?'

'Uh-huh.'

'He's still alive?'

Marty Jr's mouth curled into a sneer. 'Oh, *yeah*. He's alive.'

'Doesn't sound as if you like the guy very much,' said Raúl.

'Yeah, well.' He stroked his beard and rocked slowly in place. 'I don't have his number or anything, sorry. But you're smart guys; you can figure it out.'

Another thought occurred to him. 'Know what? If you boys wanna sell it, there's some people reached out after Dad croaked. Asking about the comic book. I got these emails from my lawyer, "To whom it may concern". I told 'em I thought Dad tossed the fuckin' thing out, but a couple of 'em were persistent. I said: "You're welcome to try the estate sale, but I am *not* about to go back through my dad's shit looking for it!" Guess I was probably kinda rude.'

Raúl and I shared a glance. 'Do you still have the emails?' Raúl said.

'Sure,' he replied.

He went to the bedroom, where I could hear him rummaging as I sipped my tequila. Raúl smiled at Lisa, now perched on the lip of the table in her bikini.

'You gonna take a swim?' he said.

She looked confused. 'Umm . . . No. Why?'

'Never mind,' he sighed.

Marty Jr returned with two crumpled sheets of A4, which he smoothed out on the Formica in front of us. On each page was a brief, printed email exchange. One of them was between Marty Jr's lawyer and Jeffrey Guzman, who had identified himself as the Executive Director of CRUSH. I passed it to Raúl, who saw Guzman's email signature and shrugged: *makes sense*. The other conversation also came from the lawyer, but whoever his second correspondent was, they hadn't signed their name.

'Do you have the full name for this person?' I said, reading the email address: TStark_@geronimail.com.

'Nope,' Marty Jr replied. 'Said they'd prefer to keep it anonymous, but "money was no object". Sounded like a fuckin' douchebag, you ask me.'

I agreed with him, but it also occurred to me that a discreet individual with deep pockets could be the perfect buyer. I folded the printout and stuffed it into the back pocket of my jeans.

'Mind if I take this?'

'Be my guest.'

Marty Jr saw us out. ' "Bart's Olde California",' he said, reading the lettering on the side of the truck. 'That your store? Sounds cool, man.'

'Thanks for the drink,' I replied, shaking his hand goodbye. 'And I meant to say: your parents had excellent taste. We found some great pieces at the sale.'

He smiled dreamily at that, and his eyes welled again. Raúl was staring up at the circle of darkening sky above the clearing.

'Aren't you worried about the fire?' he said.

Marty Jr laughed. 'It's not like I have a fuckin' house to burn down! Nah, man: this is Los Angeles — there's *always* smoke on the horizon. When the world ends, boys, Southern California is going first. May as well stick around to enjoy the view, am I right?'

As we climbed into the truck cab, Marty Jr was examining the road signs still piled against the side of the Airstream. I watched as he picked one out – *Boise 307* – and carried it back behind the caravan.

'Something bothering you, my liege?'

'Huh. Maybe. I'm not sure. I feel like I had something else to ask him.'

'Like what?'

'I don't know.'

I started the engine. Mona the bicycle girl was sitting in the long grass, watching a cat paw the air for mosquitoes.

'Our Craigslist guy,' I said. 'The one who has the cookie jar. Remind me when he said he wanted to meet.'

Raúl thought for a second. 'Friday morning,' he said. 'Tomorrow. But so what? He gave us a fake address.'

I was still pondering that as I pointed the truck back down the driveway towards the road, the snap, crackle and pop of high-powered gunfire receding behind us.

22

Before we left the store that morning, Raúl had pointed out that Topanga was just through the Santa Monica Mountains from Calabasas. So after leaving Marty Jr's place, we drove on up the winding pass to make another go of delivering the tanker desk to Whitney Blair. The sky grew darker the further north we ventured, smoke saddling the mountains, hellfire glowing inside it like the headlights of a big rig approaching through fog. The clouds doused the mid-afternoon sun, drenching the steep canyon walls in an eerie red twilight.

The crackle of radio static had long ago replaced KCRW, so we were starved of up-to-date traffic information, but after a couple of miles we rounded a bend and found ourselves in a line of cars being turned back by a police roadblock. A pair of LA County Sheriff's cruisers were parked sidelong in the carriageway with their lights spinning. A Fire Department helicopter passed low overhead, its shadow flashing across the asphalt faster than a rat across a kitchen floor.

Raúl groaned, and then insisted that I pull the truck over to the narrow shoulder, in spite of the symphony of honks from the vehicles stacking up behind us. He leapt out of the cab and strode towards one of the brown-shirted deputies patrolling the roadblock. I saw him try to open the exchange in a calm manner, reasonable man to reasonable man. The deputy stood coolly with his thumbs hooked into his belt while my partner's gesticulations became increasingly Mediterranean. I hoped he wouldn't earn himself a caution.

After I had watched several more cars cut their losses and turn around, Raúl seemed to control himself sufficiently to end the conversation with a curt handshake. He returned to the truck, fists clenched at his side, and climbed into the cab, muttering curses. Once he'd closed the door, his frustration finally spilled over. 'MOTHER*FUCKER*,' he bellowed, punching the dashboard. Burgers barked in sympathy.

'What's going on?' I said. 'The fire?'

'The frickin' fire. They closed the road all the way through to the Valley.' He slumped back in his seat. He knew as well as I did that driving the long way round to Calabasas would take us no less than two hours at that time of day.

'I guess we try again tomorrow,' I said.

'Time is of the essence, friend. I read in *US Weekly* that she had a powwow with Chad at Chipotle.'

'Who, Whitney?'

'Of course Whitney.'

'And who is Chad again? I forget.'

'Her ex-ex-boyfriend,' he replied. 'The one before Marcus.'

'And Chad is the one from the . . . ?'

'The sex tape, exactly.'

'So do you think they're, you know . . . ?'

'I frickin' *hope* not. She can do way better.'

'She could be dating you.'

'Precisely,' he said. 'I had a *plan*, dude: we'd deliver the desk, I'd make a couple jokes, persuade Whitney to come to my show . . .'

I scoffed at his stratagem. 'And what, she'd suddenly find you irresistible? Come on, Raúl. She's a TV star. Besides, the guy she was shagging in that porno – "Chad"? – he was ripped. And you're, well . . .'

'Go on. What? *What* am I, Sir Lucky? I'll have you know most of this is muscle,' he said, lifting his T-shirt and slapping his smooth belly. 'I was built this way. It's my optimum frickin' body shape.'

'Raúl, I didn't mean it like that,' I said. 'I just meant: maybe she has a type.'

'Types are bullshit. You make a woman laugh, anything can happen.'

I swung the truck around and we headed back to PCH. Raúl sulked all the way past Santa Monica. He texted Whitney to tell her we'd run into more trouble, and then sat staring sullenly at his Twitter feed. It wasn't like Raúl to sink into a bad mood for so long; I assumed he was nervous about the Lo-Ball gig. Only once we'd reached the 10 and were back within striking distance of Los Feliz did he speak up again.

'I know you're not gonna come, by the way,' he said.

'Huh?'

'To my show Saturday. I know you won't come. You'll think of a reason at the last minute, like you gotta do laundry, or go pick up your imaginary friend from the airport or something.'

'Hang on, hang on. When did I say I wasn't coming?'

He was gazing at the traffic now, Burgers in his lap. 'You didn't,' he replied. 'Not yet. But you didn't say you definitely are coming, either.'

'I'm sure I did,' I said, knowing full well that I had not.

'Nah. You didn't.'

'Raúl—'

'It's okay, dude. Don't worry about it. I've learned not to expect too much.'

'Excuse me, what?'

He took a deep breath, steeling himself to broach a subject. 'Y'know, when you told me about your old partner . . . Glyn, right? Anyhow, it kinda made sense.'

I didn't like where this was going. 'What made sense?' I said.

'Listen: you're a cool guy, Lucky. When I first met you, I thought you'd be a real stiff. With that frickin' accent, I thought: This dude is gonna be a total douche. And you are kind of a douche. But you're also cool. So I mean this in the nicest possible way, but it sounds like you let the guy down. Glyn, I mean.'

'What the hell do you mean by that?'

'Hey, it's just the impression I get, y'know. Hashtag-just-sayin'.'

My grip on the wheel tightened. 'You don't know what you're talking about, Raúl. Glyn and I were partners. We had an agreed set of principles. And he sold out – he sold us *both* out. He took the money, he took my fucking girlfriend, and now he's living like a Saudi prince while I drive this old hunk of junk around with you and your bloody dog in the passenger seat. So just because he and Bijou are on some kind of break, and he's a few weeks late with his latest shitty superhero screenplay, does not mean you need to start feeling sorry for him.'

'Oh, but I should feel sorry for *you*? With your frickin' "agreed set of principles"? C'mon, dude. You said it yourself: you quit. That was your choice. I dunno, maybe you just don't like to see your friends do well.'

'Unbelievable,' I said, so incensed that I almost wove the truck across the lane divider and straight into the Kia Sorento I'd just been overtaking. 'Has it never occurred to you that the reason I don't come to your gigs might be because I worry that you won't be funny? That you'll go down in fucking flames, and then I'll have to lie and tell you it was great?'

'Lucky,' he said calmly, 'I'm a stand-up comic. You think I've never bombed? Please. If I bomb, I know it. I embrace the bomb. I don't need you to spare my frickin' feelings. But I won't bomb. And you won't be there. So you can stop worrying about it.'

We drove the rest of the way back to the store in silence and barely exchanged a word for the remainder of the afternoon. The tension was sufficiently apparent that even Karen noticed, and asked me whether everything was okay. I told her we'd had difficulty with a delivery and she seemed to take the hint.

I sold a studded-leather Spanish Revival trunk to a photographer's assistant, and a vintage sombrero ashtray to a passing tourist. When closing time came, I didn't stick around or suggest an after-work drink. Instead, I walked briskly to Little Dom's on Hillhurst, took an empty booth and treated myself to a three-course dinner for one in the restaurant's anonymous half-dark.

While I munched on my arancini appetiser, I mused on the tragedy of Marty Kann: a master draftsman made to give up what he loved most, and all because he'd followed the plot-line of an unprincipled partner. It was a story sad enough for a folk ballad, if only it didn't involve superheroes. I wondered why he left all of his comic books to Freddy Wroblewski, except for *The Black Bird*. Maybe he just didn't want to give the guy the satisfaction of knowing he'd kept it. A final fuck-you-very-much.

I thought of his son, Marty Jr, maudlin and drunk by lunchtime, and of the things we pass unwittingly from one generation to the next. Of the Kluges, and of the last few Viscounts Wonersh: their ambition bred out of them by privilege; their privilege diminished by complacency.

It was as I drove home, stomach full of meatballs and Tuscan chianti, that I heard the muffled noise of a phone ringing. I tugged my handset from my pocket, but it was asleep – and anyway, would I really have the theme from *Quantum Leap* as my ringtone? I pulled the Bronco onto the forecourt of a carwash on Sunset, realising, in the same instant, that the ringing was coming from the glove compartment, and that I'd stashed Glyn's smartphone there the previous morning and forgotten about it. I reached over and opened the compartment.

The phone was nearly out of charge, but it bawled like a brass band nonetheless, with an incoming call from a blocked number. I almost didn't answer it. I almost switched it off, thinking I'd stick it in a jiffy bag and post it to Bijou in Brentwood, or c/o the Chagall. But my curiosity got the better of me.

'Hello?'

'Hello?' said the caller: a gruff whisper; a heavy accent. '*Hello!* Oh, thank God!'

'Who's this?' I said.

'It's Glyn. It's Glyn! Who's this?'

'Oh, shit,' I said, thinking: *Oh, shit*. 'Hi, Glyn. It's Lucius.'

'*Lucius?*'

'Yeah, I know. I have your phone. It's a long st—'

'Christ, they're coming. Lucius, mate. You have to get me out of here.'

'What? What do you mean?'

I heard muffled shouts and a frantic *thud-thud-thud* from behind him.

'I don't have much time,' he gasped. 'You have to talk to Bijou, get her to—'

'Glyn, calm down. Aren't you at your mum's?'

'What? *No!* Oh, Christ. Lucius . . . *Get away from me!* Lucius! Help, *LUCIUS*!'

There came a scuffle, a yell, some angry words in Spanish, the clatter of a phone being dropped to the floor – and then nothing. The handset still had a sliver of battery life, but the call had been cut off. I stared at the screen, waiting in vain for Glyn to call back, wondering what the hell I had just listened to – and whether I had imagined it. I was half-cut, after all. Eventually I laid the phone on the passenger seat, a soft dread slowly numbing my extremities. I kept half an eye on it as I steered myself towards home with uncommon caution.

When I got back to Angelino Heights, I plugged Glyn's phone into the wall and dropped Dennis Wilson's *Pacific Ocean Blue* onto the record player. I couldn't call Glyn back – the number had been blocked – but he'd said to talk to Bijou, so I dialled her number from my own phone. The call rang off. My cleaner had come during the day, so the cottage was orderly even if my thoughts were in disarray. I mixed myself a Dark & Stormy and stood out on the deck, watering my cacti, listening to the whisper of the nearby freeway and Wilson's craggy harmonies from the climax of 'River Song'. There was a skunk at large in the neighbourhood; its acrid musk curled through the streets, clung to the trees and collected like melancholy in the quiet back yards.

I believed Bijou and I had parted on good terms — at least by our usual standards — but unless they were playing an elaborate prank on me, she'd lied about Glyn being at his mum's in Port Talbot. Maybe she was a better actress than I thought. I sipped my drink, smoked my e-cigarette, and tried to posit where Glyn could possibly be without his car, his wife or his smartphone, and where Spanish-speaking men would physically restrain him from making a call.

I could only come up with two explanations: that he was in jail, or that he'd been kidnapped for ransom by a Mexican cartel. Glyn, by the way, is not the sort of guy who'd do well in jail. I called Bijou again and left a terse voicemail: 'Bijou, it's Lucky. Call me as soon as you get this. Bye.'

Ten minutes later, having received no response, I texted: *It's Lucky again. Do you have my number? Well, this is it. Call me re Glyn. Urgent.*

It occurred to me that she might be screening my calls, so I went back inside and dialled her number from Glyn's phone instead. It rang off again. By that point I'd given up expecting her to answer, but I called the landline in Brentwood just in case. It rang and rang and finally went dead. I supposed I'd probably woken up the kids. When I tried one final time, I got the busy tone.

I felt obliged to consult Bijou before going to the police. If this kidnapping was anything like the B-movie I'd begun to plot out on my mental index cards, then Glyn's captors would have told her not to talk to anyone — least of all the cops — unless she wanted his fingers to start showing up in the mailbox.

On the other hand, I couldn't just do nothing. Maybe Raúl had got to me after all, when he said I'd let Glyn down. And hey, I'm not stupid. I know you can look at what happened between Glyn and me and choose to read it that way. But he let me down, too. He let me down *more*.

I dug deep in my memory for a useful clue, and soon my spade hit pay-dirt: the call log on Glyn's smartphone, and the man I'd spoken to who sounded like a drug dealer. Perhaps he'd lead me halfway to whatever Glyn was mixed up in, cartel or otherwise. I didn't have a better idea, so I scrolled until I found the contact I was after: a string of late-evening calls to somebody named 'Gretchen'.

My thumbs left clammy smears on the screen. I needed something to occupy me, to keep the creeping angst at bay. How risky could a simple phone call be? I sank the rest of my drink and pressed call. This time, a woman's voice answered.

'Yes?'

'Oh. Er . . . Hi.'

'Hello,' the voice replied, patiently. I remembered then that the last time I'd bought my own drugs was from a bloke in an Oxford nightclub loo, and if I ever took coke during my Hollywood years, it was supplied by Bijou. Hard drugs are not my habit-former of choice. I was a cock at a dog-fight.

'Is this Gretchen?'

'It sure is.'

'Hi Gretchen, my name is, er . . . well, I got your number from a friend.'

'Oh, yeah? Who's your friend?'

'Glyn. Glyn Perkins.'

There was no telltale pause, no change in tone. If Gretchen was bluffing, she was good. 'Oh, yeah, sure,' she said. 'I know Glyn. Were you interested in a particular product?'

'Huh . . . I don't know, really.'

'You wanna come down, see what we've got?'

Her phone manner was alarmingly friendly for a drug dealer, so much so that I found myself agreeing to her suggestion: 'Er . . . okay?'

'If you can be in Downtown by ten o'clock, then you're welcome to swing by tonight. Otherwise it'd have to be another day.'

I looked at the carriage clock on the mantelpiece: it was nine-fifteen.

'I can be there in twenty minutes,' I said.

'That'll do it. You know it's cash only, right?'

'Well, yeah. I assumed as much.'

'Great. I don't suppose Glyn gave you the address?'

Gretchen told me the name of the street corner on which I was to meet her associate. As soon as I hung up, I began to think of reasons why I shouldn't go. But Dutch courage and dumb pride won out: this time, I would not let Glyn down. I would not give him something else to hold against me, the bastard.

23

The address Gretchen gave me was close to the river in what used to be known as the Warehouse District. My route obliged me to drive through Skid Row, that sorry, tented corridor of neglected souls that most Angelenos conspire to ignore, a shadow on the lung of LA. Until the creatives moved in and the coffee shops followed, the warehouses east of the Row were also part of its realm. Nowadays the graffiti is called street art, and the drug pushers are outnumbered by property developers.

By night, though, the neighbourhood reverts to its old self: underpopulated, sparely lit, a labyrinth of looming, right-angled shadows. Thinking it might somehow be safer if they didn't see my car, I parked one street over from the meeting spot and walked the rest of the way along the darkened block, my footsteps bouncing echoes between the blank walls.

As I drew close to the corner, I made out a pale, skinny dude in low-slung jeans and a white vest observing my approach. He had sunken eyes and a tribal neck tat that to my untrained eye suggested he'd served time. He was no oil painting – unless the painting was a Picasso. I came to a halt just out of arm's reach, wishing I'd borrowed Raúl's taser – wishing, in fact, that I'd forgiven Raúl and brought him along to stand in front of me.

'Yo,' the guy said, thrusting his chin out. 'You here to see Gretchen?'

'That's right.'

'C'mon.'

With reluctant steps and a thrumming heart, I followed the guy for half a block until we came to a thick metal door in the midst of the brick expanse, kept ajar by a crusty old trainer. He checked the street for people, then he kicked the shoe into the lighted interior and chased it inside, holding the heavy door open just long enough for me to squeeze through before it clanged shut behind me.

LA is a secret city. In London you can intuit from the outside of an unfamiliar pub whether you could drink in it without being roughed up by football fans or Irish Republicans. In New York you can spot a men's outfitters from across the street and know almost instantly whether you'd wear one of their shirts. But here, there's often no telling what tasteless horrors lurk beneath an alluring neon bar sign, nor what wonders hide in the plain sight of an unassuming strip mall.

Beyond the door was a warehouse space the size of two tennis courts, with harsh overhead lighting and scuffed concrete underfoot. I glanced around at the whitewashed walls, lined with shelves full of crates and industrial containers. It smelled like a fish market at four in the afternoon. A steel box occupied the back of the room, maybe twenty-five feet by ten across and another ten high, emitting a low, Tibetan-monk hum. The marijuana grow room, I guessed.

On a table in the far corner were a cash-box, a laptop and a display rack holding several pamphlets that proved too much effort to read from a distance while partially inebriated. A middle-aged woman with wire-rimmed specs rose from her chair behind the table and ambled towards me. She wore sandals and a flowy patterned blouse, her grey hair in braids and the kind of smile a school principal keeps handy for the first dad to arrive at the PTA meeting.

'Hey there,' she said. 'I'm Gretchen.'

'Gretchen, hi. We spoke on the phone.'

I reached out my hand to shake and she clasped it between both palms. To my unease, the skinny guy had donned a butcher's apron and was knotting the cord around his waist. 'I don't think I caught your name,' Gretchen said.

'It's Lucky.'

'Lucky, great to meet you.'

The skinny guy snickered to himself and muttered something disparaging.

'Tobe!' Gretchen snapped, which sent him scuttling into the steel box through a side door. 'Don't mind my nephew,' she said, and she smiled again as she turned back to me. 'So, did Glyn tell you how this works?'

'Er . . . not exactly, no.'

'No problem,' she said, and she beckoned me over to the table. 'So, you have to become a member. It's very simple: fifty dollars per person per year, and you need one referral. But you can get that from Glyn later. Tonight, since you came all this way so late, I'll give you a free pass. You're welcome to check out the produce, see what you might like to try, make a purchase if you want. Like I said on the phone, it's cash only. And we close up at ten, so you have, oooh' – she checked her watch – 'fifteen minutes. But I'll give you twenty if you behave!'

She sat back behind the table, laced her fingers in front of her and beamed up at me, apparently unperturbed by my conspicuous bafflement. I picked up one of the pamphlets from the display rack and peered at it. 'Battling the Mutants,' it said, with a sub-title: 'How GM Foods Are Killing Our Future.'

I looked around the room, taking in the contents of the shelves more carefully this time. In one of the crates were twist-tied plastic bags filled with what I'd first assumed were pills, but now realised were almonds. I saw a row of glass jars, and inside them an amber-hued substance labelled 'Bolivian honey' – not exactly the Bolivian export I'd been expecting. On the shelf closest to me were cardboard containers holding several dozen eggs, some with feathers still clinging to them, others smeared with what seemed to be chicken faeces.

'I'm terribly sorry, Gretchen,' I said, 'but what is this place?'

'What do you mean?' she replied, her brow furrowing.

'I mean, what exactly are you selling here? I thought . . .'

'You thought what?'

'Well, I kind of thought you guys were drug dealers.'

Her frown deepened momentarily, and then dissipated as she broke into a braying laugh. The laugh was long and loud enough that skinny Tobe, her nephew, emerged from the steel box to see what was going on. She waved him back inside as she caught her breath. 'Oh, that's very funny,' she said, dabbing her eyes. 'Especially since we're the *opposite* of drug dealers.'

'How's that?'

'I don't understand. Did Glyn not explain?'

It was slowly dawning on me, in my semi-drunken state, that these may not be dangerous people, after all. 'To be honest, Gretchen,' I replied, 'I just got your number from his phone. It's all a little bit complicated.'

'Oh.' Now it was her turn to look baffled. 'Well, look,' she said, after a pause. 'We sell raw food.'

'Raw food?'

'Raw food. Raw, unprocessed, unpasteurised, natural food.'

'That's it?'

'That's it.'

'Huh. But, hang on. What about the cloak and dagger stuff? Your nephew, I spoke to him by phone a couple of days ago and he accused me of being a cop!'

'Oh, Tobe. I'm sorry about that, he didn't mention it. Cards on the table, Lucky? Some of what we sell here is not, strictly speaking, "legal".'

Gretchen accompanied the word 'legal' with air quotes, universal sign language of the self-important. 'We used to have a place in Silver Lake,' she went on, 'but it was raided by the FDA and California Food and Ag. We're really just getting started up again. That's why the shelves are still sorta bare.'

My eyes drifted back to the excrement-encrusted eggs.

'But why would the FDA raid a grocery store?' I said.

'I *know*, right? Good question! The government calls us "food radicals", because we refuse to abide by its so-called "safety" standards.'

There she went with the air quotes again.

'Why would you do that?' I said.

She rolled her eyes as if I'd just told her I voted for Romney. 'Oh Lord, where do I *start*? You know how many chemicals there are in supermarket food? You know how much high-fructose corn syrup the average American consumes every year, and what it's doing *to their BODIES*? How much white flour and refined sugar? How many hydrogenated oils? Do you know the effect that fertilisers and pesticides are having on ecosystems? On our *children*? I could explain to you just how dangerous GMOs are, but we'd probably be here all night. You can take that pamphlet with you, read it when you get home. It'll give you nightmares.'

I stuffed the pamphlet back into the rack – I was going to have nightmares anyway. 'I think I get the picture,' I said. 'Explains the smell, at least.'

Gretchen breathed in deep through her nose. 'Wonderful, isn't it?' she said. 'I am sorry to disappoint you, though. Were you hoping to buy pot, or something stronger? I'm sure Tobe would let you share a blunt if you ask him nicely. He always smokes one after closing time. It's organic.'

'Naturally,' I replied. 'Thanks, but I was really just trying to find Glyn. He's gone AWOL. I saw your number in his phone and I thought . . . I don't know what I thought. I thought maybe you were his drug dealer, like I said.'

She took off her glasses, pursed her lips and looked at the ceiling. 'You know, now that you mention it, I'm pretty sure we haven't seen Glyn in at least a couple weeks,' she said. 'He's missing? Well, that's no good.'

'Was he a regular customer?'

'For a while, yes.'

'I didn't know Glyn was into this stuff,' I said, looking around the room again, seeing crates of grapefruit, onions, squash. When Glyn and I were friends he'd happily scarf frozen pizzas, sliced cheese, microwave meals, instant noodles, processed meats. I remember him once returning to our apartment, triumphant because he'd finally found a place in Los Angeles that served a decent meat pie.

'Oh yes, he was more than a dabbler,' Gretchen insisted. 'He was originally referred to us by that director friend of his. Perhaps you know him. Dash?'

'Dash Smith is a customer? Jesus.'

'We get all sorts,' she said. 'Celebrities, foodies, hippies, sick people. People who are just looking for something *different*.'

'Did Glyn ever talk about . . . I don't know. About what *he* was looking for?'

She took the question seriously, savouring it for several moments like a mouthful of Wagyu.

'He's a writer, isn't he?' she said at last. 'That film about the cowboy?'

'*Marshal Eagle*.'

'That's the one. I never saw it; was it good?'

'I hear the sequel's better.'

'Hmm. I think he told me he was working on a new film, but he was finding it hard to think straight – to focus, you get my meaning? He needed something pure to cleanse his senses. You know what they say: healthy body, healthy mind.'

I was at a loss. Glyn was at a hotel, only he wasn't. He was at his mum's in Wales, only he wasn't. He'd been kidnapped by the cartels, only the cartels turned out to be Bolivian honey importers. His ambition had been satisfied in spades, only something was still eating at him. And now, somehow, somewhere, it seemed he was in jeopardy. If Bijou wouldn't answer my calls, then it was time to inform the police and let the professionals find him. If only I'd told Abby that right from the start, I could have stayed well away from the whole damned situation.

'Are you alright?' Gretchen looked closely at me, her face flushed with matronly concern. I didn't have much cash, but I felt sufficiently guilty for putting her out that I fished the last few notes from my wallet and counted them.

'What'll twenty-four dollars get me?'

She rose from her chair again. 'Come take a look in the cooler,' she said, and she guided me over to the steel box, gesturing for me to go in ahead of her.

I pulled open the door and stepped inside. The grow room turned out to be a walk-in refrigerator: not quite refrigerated enough, I feared, for the produce it contained. The dank food odour grew denser as I stood staring at the racks of raw cheeses, yoghurts, milks and meats. There were paper wraps of butter, tubs of ice cream, ranks of suspect juices, beef cuts and whole raw chickens with a whiff of the fields where they were reared. A mason jar of murky liquid was labelled 'raw cow colostrum'. At the back of the narrow room, Tobe was decanting milk into glass bottles from a perspiring plastic barrel.

'That's camel's milk,' Gretchen said, straight-faced, and then prodded a piece of greying meat: 'That's bison spleen – a little out of your comfort zone?'

She plucked a glass quart bottle from a crate and proffered it to me. 'Try this. On the house – call it a new-member incentive. Make you feel better, I promise.'

I took the bottle from her; it was cool and fresh in my palm and I felt like pressing it to my forehead. 'What is it?' I said.

'Just straight-up raw cow's milk. From an Amish farm in Pennsylvania. Here . . .' She took the bottle, upended it once to clear the cream, twisted off the plastic cap and then handed it back to me. 'If you like it, it's fifteen dollars a gallon – and I bet you will.'

I examined the spermy, off-white goo around the rim. 'Is it safe?'

'Safer than whatever you've been squeezing through your small intestine most of your life. Lucky, I'll tell ya: it's like drinking from the teat. Clears up your skin in days, clears your mind just as quick. Cures allergies, depression – even cancer!'

'Okay, okay,' I said. 'Let's not get carried away, Gretchen.'

She grinned. 'Go on, try it. It's delicious.'

I was sceptical, of course: it's my default setting. But I also believed that I, as much as anyone, understood the quest for something raw and authentic, a product untainted by the demands of soulless mass consumerism. I lowered my nose to the bottle and sniffed, and all at once I pictured my father, dipping a cup deep into a milking bucket on the estate farm at Tinderley and thrusting it into my clumsy hands. I remembered him urging me to drink while the farmhand looked on, ruddy-faced and chortling. I must have been six years old.

I sipped a spoonful and let it sit on my tongue a few seconds before swallowing. It was rich, mulchy and moreish. Sweet, but with the promise of sourness to come.

24

I looked from one grim-faced flatfoot to the other in disbelief.

'A *restraining* order?'

Officer Schooley, fastidious about his work, slid his little notebook back into his breast pocket and buttoned it securely. Officer Park, fastidious about his physique, tensed and untensed his biceps. At least his wraparound sunglasses made sense on the morning shift. We stood throwing nine a.m. shadows across the pavement outside the store, where I hoped Karen would be out of earshot. Both officers stood closer to me than I considered polite. I guess that's in the training manual.

'Mrs Perkins reported you to Western Division. Says you've been calling her repeatedly,' Schooley said, hands on hips. 'That you turned up at her home unannounced and after dark, when you knew that her husband was away. That you talked to her children without her permission. A judge might consider that harassment, Mr Kluge.'

'Officers, this is nonsense,' I replied. 'I've known Bijou – Mrs Perkins – for a long time. We used to date, and I can tell you right now: she is fucking crazy.'

'Mr Kluge, please.' Schooley winced for effect. 'Watch your language.'

'Okay, okay. I apologise. But she's still crazy.'

The gangly cop sighed, feigning endless patience. 'Well, see, Mr Kluge. The way she tells it is: the two of you broke up several years back, and then, when she started dating her husband, you had some sort of a nervous breakdown?'

A torrent of acid curses rose in my throat and I swallowed them down with difficulty. 'That is *not* how it happened,' I replied through gritted teeth.

'Seems like a nice lady,' said Park. The one thing Bijou absolutely does not seem like is a *nice lady*. Officer Park was never going to make detective.

'Look. Officer Schooley, Officer Park. If Bijou is threatening to take out a restraining order against me, then so be it. Frankly, I couldn't be happier to stay the hell away from her. But none of that is important right now. What's important is that Glyn – *Mr Perkins* – has gone missing. He is being held somewhere against his will. And the reason I called Bijou last night, the reason I turned up on her doorstep the night before – which, believe me, I would not have done otherwise – is that I was trying to find out where he is and what the hell is going on. You know all this! It's why I called you in the bloody first place!'

'But y'see, Mr Kluge, this is exactly what I'm talking about,' said Schooley, exasperated. 'We just came from Mrs Perkins, and she told us that her husband is out of town. Said she spoke to him only yesterday and he's absolutely fine.'

'She's *lying*! That woman is about as trustworthy as week-old seafood.'

'She's the next of kin, sir, and there is nothing whatsoever to indicate that she's not telling the truth. We can't file a Missing Persons report on the strength of your claims. You haven't seen Mr Perkins in years, by your own admission.'

'But that's not—'

'Mr Kluge. Please. Work with me here. Don't you think you've wasted enough police time this week already?'

I threw my hands up. I thought I saw Park's thumb edging along his belt towards his cuffs, as if daring me to do something worthy of arrest. Instead, I produced my e-cigarette and took out my anger on my tonsils. I could sense the stares of the breakfast crowd outside Sasquatch Pete's.

'You know what? You're right,' I said. 'You're totally right! I was just trying to help out an old friend. But I see now that I should've kept out of it altogether.'

Nodding sagely, Schooley said, 'Have you thought of talking to someone about all this?'

'"Talking to someone"? Like who? I'm talking to you, aren't I?'

'No, I meant . . . like a therapist, say.'

That was the final straw. As I yanked open the door and made to go in, Park, who plainly hadn't listened to a word, piped up: '"Glyn Perkins". What is that, anyway? Irish?'

'It's Welsh,' I replied, my voice rising. 'It's FUCKING WELSH!'

I stomped inside and slammed the door behind me, punctuating the pitiable chimes of 'The Star-Spangled Banner'. Karen was vacuuming. Raúl was sitting on the counter, watching Schooley and Park climb back into their police cruiser while he picked at a tub of chopped chili pineapple.

'Morning, Sir Lucky. What did the Keystone Cops want?'

'Nothing,' I replied. 'Doesn't matter.'

'Y'know we were due to meet the Craigslist guy today, right?'

'Shit. Of course. When?'

'Like, now.'

Raúl had low expectations of our latest jaunt to Mid-City, but he insisted we bring the Moose Skowron bat and the taser with us just in case. I was taking the turns a little faster than usual, so he kept a steady hand on Burgers's pet crate to keep it from sliding up and down the bench seat.

'You're aware that this is pointless, right?' he said. 'We already know it's a fake address.'

'You keep saying that, Raúl. But why would this person give us a fake address? They want to sell the cookie jar, don't they? Just because they don't live there, doesn't mean they can't *meet* us there.'

199

'What if they're on to us? Could be they saw through my fake name. "Ralph". Nobody's called *Ralph*. Idiot.'

I found a vacant spot to stash the truck a little way down Colfax from Hal Green's place, hoping that if the perp were to turn up they wouldn't be spooked by the Bart's Olde California logo. From there we had a view along the street to number 826, where we could see, even at a distance, that the concrete parking square out front was now occupied by a tumbledown RV.

'Hey,' said Raúl. 'You think . . . ?'

'I don't know,' I replied. 'Could be.'

'Take this,' he said, handing me the taser, then Burgers's leash: '. . . and this.'

He slipped out of the truck with the Dodgers bat under his arm. I coaxed Burgers from the crate and clipped on his leash, then together we pursued Raúl towards the apartment building. A layer of morning cloud was creeping in from the west, which left the street's faded pastel facades looking even more glum than usual. The pavements were streaked with sprinkler run-off, and palm-tree detritus lay in heaps against the storm drains at the kerb.

As we drew closer, I got a better look at the RV. The old vehicle squatted thickly on its axles like Fat Elvis taking a dump, with flabby tyres and bumper stickers wallpapered across its backside. There were surfboards lashed to the roof. When we got to within about fifty yards, Raúl froze.

'Holy *crapola*,' he whispered, grabbing my arm. 'I recognise that RV. Isn't that the "Keep Venice Weird" dude's rig?'

'Huh?'

'From outside Scooter's place, remember?'

'Are you sure?'

He took another look. 'I think so,' he said. 'Mother*fucker*.'

Silently, using makeshift military hand signals, he directed me to come at the RV from one side with Burgers, while he would circle around to attack from the other flank. I watched as he jogged off stealthily past the parked cars with the bat in both hands, and then, with some trepidation, I approached the target.

There are plenty of shabby RVs on the streets of LA, but as I snuck up behind this one I definitely noticed some familiar traits: the rusted exhaust pipe hanging loose from the underside, tied in place with an oily bungee; the bumper stickers, a swill of liberal, libertarian and lame stoner humour.

I tugged Burgers's leash to bring him to heel and poked my head around the side of the vehicle. Sure enough, the same old acid casualty with the straggly grey-blond mane was reclining in his deckchair on the concrete outside Hal Green's home, in a moth-eaten T-shirt, LA Kings cap, board shorts and busted flip-flops. There was an old Discman in his lap, a can of Pabst in his hand and a pair of huge headphones over his ears, and he was nodding along to a beat with his eyes closed.

I moved out from behind my hiding place, clutching the taser, and glanced over to the RV's open side door. There, perching smugly on the step, was the Ringmaster cookie jar. Before I had time to grok the implications of its presence, Raúl came into view around the front of the RV. He noticed me pointing, looked and saw the jar. His eyes widened, his grip tightened, and then he raised the Dodgers bat above his shoulder and swung it straight and true at the vehicle's passenger-side window, hollering: '*YO!*'

The plexiglass imploded with a loud crunch. The sound was sufficient to break the bum's reverie, and he sprang off the deckchair faster than a fly dodging a swat. The headphone cord dragged the Discman to the ground; it cracked open and sent the CD inside rolling across the concrete to my feet, where it finally spun to a halt: Alanis Morissette. The bum saw Raúl first and swivelled away from him, but he pulled up short as soon as he ran into me, the bulldog and the taser. He dropped into a crouch and took up a kung-fu stance.

'Don't come any closer, assholes!' he shouted, dancing back

and forth between us, the headphones still clamped to his ears. 'I gotta fuckin' *black belt* in this shit!'

I couldn't tell whether he was being truthful, or whether he'd seen just enough Bruce Lee movies to fake it with conviction. I brandished the taser and pressed the trigger so he could see the warning crackle. But as he peered closer at me, his expression slipped from anger into recognition.

'Hey,' he said, tugging off the headphones. 'I know you!'

'You sure do, pal,' said Raúl, the Dodgers bat raised again. 'You stole our property. Now, we can do this the easy way, or we can do it the hard way.'

His recognition turned to puzzlement. '*What?* I didn't steal shit, asshole.'

'That's our frickin' cookie jar,' said Raúl, pointing with the bat. 'You like using that kung-fu crap on defenceless old men?'

Bemused, the bum lowered his fists. 'The *fuck* are you talkin' about, man?'

While he was distracted by my partner, I took the opportunity to snatch up the ransomed Ringmaster from its roost on the step of the RV. I gave it a swift once-over: the hairline crack on the base was there, but it had widened, rendering the cookie jar structurally unsound and in need of repair. Meanwhile, a sizeable sliver of glaze had flaked off the fat figurine's buttocks. Somewhere between the back of our truck and the bum's RV, the Ringmaster had shed about half his value.

'This!' I said. 'You stole this from our store, right?'

'The gnome?' He screwed up his weather-worn features. 'Man, I picked that ugly piece of shit outta the trash.'

'Bullshit. Whose trash?'

'What? You *know* – your friend!'

I was as puzzled as he was. 'You're talking about Bart? The man you attacked?'

'Who the fuck is *Bart?* Nah, man. That Google motherfucker.'

'Wait,' said Raúl. 'You mean Scooter?'

'Right! *Scooter*. Stupid fuckin' name.'

'In Venice?' I said.

'Of course in Venice. What are you, a fuckin' *retard*? It was in his goddam recycling! Shoulda been in the regular trash. Like I told ya, guy doesn't think about the community – you ask me, I did a fuckin' public service removin' it.'

Raúl let the Dodgers bat dangle limp at his side. 'You took it from Scooter Benjamin's trash,' he murmured. 'You're sure?'

'What I just *said*, ain't it?'

'When was this?'

'I don't know! Few days ago. What the *fuck*, man.'

'Well, it wasn't his to throw in the trash,' I said. 'It's the property of Bart's Olde California. And it's a cookie jar, by the way, not a bloody gnome.'

The man took off his Kings cap and scratched the livid-pink bald patch beneath it. 'Well, that explains it,' he said. 'I was wonderin' why the head was broken. So, you wanna give me my hundred dollars?'

'Bite me,' said Raúl. 'C'mon, Sir Lucky. We're leaving.'

'Hey, fuck *you*, man,' the bum said. 'I know my rights.'

'Fuck you, too,' Raúl glowered. 'You want us to call the cops?'

The bum narrowed his eyes, muttering profanities under his breath as my partner began to stride away towards the truck.

'Why'd you give us this address?' I said. 'On Craiglist.'

The old derelict turned and gazed at Hal the actor's dingbat apartment block. 'Used to have a girlfriend lived here,' he said, suddenly wistful. 'Moved to Santa Fe in '97. I didn't treat her right, I guess.'

'Huh. Guess not.'

He was a guy with stories to tell, if only he could remember them. I suppose the booze and drugs had obscured the details, like flip-flops half-buried in the sand. Burgers was straining at the

203

leash to follow his master, so I shrugged a goodbye and walked away with the Ringmaster under my arm. As I caught up with Raúl, the bum's empty beer can landed with a clatter on the pavement in front of us. I looked back at the RV, where the guy started yelling. 'You broke my goddam window, assholes! This is fuckin' exploitation of the working classes!'

Raúl took a practice swing and yelled back at him: 'I don't see you WORKING, motherfucker!'

Beaten, the bum flipped us the bird, scooped up his deckchair and scuttled back into his vehicle. After a pause, the RV started up and sputtered away.

Raúl and I returned to the truck, where Raúl tossed the bat into the cab and clambered in after it. I opened the back and hopped up into the cube. Marty Kann's tanker desk was still strapped in place, ready for delivery. There were some old packing boxes lying around in there, too, replete with Styrofoam peanuts. I found one that was a suitable size for the Ringmaster and stuffed him into it, then I carried it back around to the cab. Raúl was festering in the passenger seat – two parts angry, one part disconsolate, with a dash of bitter. Burgers nuzzled his belly in a bid to cheer him up. I climbed in and slid the box onto the bench between us.

'Is it definitely the same cookie jar?' Raúl said.

'Has to be,' I replied.

'I don't get it. You think Scooter stole it?'

'He's a multimillionaire. Why would he steal a cookie jar worth a few grand, chuck it in the recycling, and then spend another few grand at the store the next day? Doesn't make a lot of sense.'

'So you think the dude was lying?'

'I didn't say that.'

Raúl cracked open the box and stared at the portly statuette, who was grinning up at us and twirling his moustaches. It was one of Cleo's packing boxes, with the Habibi Estates logo printed on the side. While my partner sat there, sombrely contemplating the new information, I watched an idea dawn on him by degrees, as if accompanied by 'Thus Spake Zarathustra'.

'Hold on,' he said. 'Do you still have that email from Marty Jr?'

'Huh?'

'The email. From the guy who wanted to buy *The Black Bird*.'

I patted myself down and found the folded A4 printout, still crumpled in the back pocket of my jeans. 'Here.'

I handed it to my partner, who unfolded the page, scanned Marty Jr's exchange with the anonymous buyer, and nodded.

'Didn't you say Cleo has a mailing list of people who were at the Kann sale?'

'Yeah,' I replied. 'Why? Where are you going with this?'

'Ask her if this email address is on the list.'

'What, now?'

He nodded urgently. 'Of course now.'

I took out my phone and wrote Cleo a text: *Hey, cd u check if an email address is on Habibi Estates mailing list? TStark_@geroni mail.com. Ta.*

We didn't have to wait long for a response: *Yep. Subscribed last week x.*

'Well?' said Raúl, when he heard my phone ping. I passed him the handset.

'Dude,' he said, 'you didn't even put a frickin' kiss on your text.'

'She says they signed up to the mailing list last week,' I said.

'Right before the Kann sale,' he replied, smiling now.

'I suppose so. Why? What am I missing?'

'"*T. Stark*". Like Tony Stark.'

'Who's Tony Stark?'

'You know, Iron Man.'

'For God's sake, Raúl. If this is another bloody superhero reference, then no: clearly I do not know.'

'Oh *c'mon*, dude! Stark Industries? Robert Downey Jr? Tony Stark is like, this genius tech billionaire, builds a cool flying suit, becomes a superhero. Iron Man.'

'Fine. But what does that have to do with . . . ? Wait a second. Did you say he's a *tech* genius?'

25

The grey marine layer grew thicker as we approached the coast. A stiff crosswind cut through the hot, glutinous air and sought to nudge the truck from the 10's middle lane. Earthquake weather. *Les Mis* was in the tape deck, and my partner hummed loudly along to 'Do You Hear the People Sing?', as if stiffening his resolve for a revolutionary act.

'Listen, Raúl,' I said. 'About yesterday . . .'

'Don't worry about it,' he replied.

'No, you were right about some things. Not everything. But some things.'

'You don't have to explain yourself to me, Your Lordship.'

'I'll come to your show tomorrow, alright? I promise.'

'You're still on the guest list, dude. Do whatever feels right.'

I circled until I found a parking spot on Benjamin's street. His poured-concrete carbuncle was flanked by a stucco fourplex on one side and a clapboard bungalow on the other. If Venice has planning regulations, nobody's enforcing them. I told Raúl to leave the Dodgers bat in the truck this time; I didn't think we were going to need it. He left the taser, too – but he brought Burgers.

The front door to the house was ajar, and as we stepped through it I could hear yelling from deeper inside. In the front room off the hallway, a handful of nerdy, beardless bottom-feeders in hoodies and plaid sat at their laptops around a trestle table arrayed with hard drives, coffee cups and half-eaten sugary snacks. There was a beat-up couch and a busy pinboard; a watercooler and a coffee machine; a giant flatscreen and a games console. On the couch was an open cardboard box full of Bacon Ninja T-shirts. The bottom-feeders all looked up warily when we walked in, as if we'd caught them watching cat videos on company time. I thought I recognised a couple of them from the Ultimate Frisbee game.

'Where's the boss?' I said to the room.

One pointed behind him, towards a teak sliding door set into the wall between two framed, signed Warriors jerseys. As he did so, the yelling increased in volume and pitch, then the door slid open abruptly and another underling stumbled out, pink-cheeked and curly-haired, his eyes swollen with tears. He shuffled to his workstation, pursued by Benjamin's loud instruction: 'Get your SHIT *together*, Randall, 'fore I snap your fuckin' *dick* off!'

Raúl, Burgers and I followed the sound through the sliding door into Benjamin's private office. It was a spotlit grey cell. A long Persian rug unscrolled across the polished wooden floor from the doorway to the Scandinavian desk at the far end. The two leather chairs in front of the desk were low and slouch-inducing, a conspicuous power-play by the man in the swivelling throne behind it.

On the wall to our left were an Ed Ruscha print and the neon we'd sold him several days earlier: 'Burgers Fries Shakes'. In the corner a life-sized, fibreglass Bacon Ninja wielded a frying pan as if it were a katana. Two rectangular alcoves set into the wall on our right were neatly lined with vintage action figures. It had all started to make sense: Benjamin was a compulsive collector.

He sat with his back to the room, gazing through a widescreen window at his landscaped zen garden: combed red sand, smooth pebbles in artful heaps, a tiny jungle of succulents. All he needed was a cat in his lap to stroke.

Raúl slid the door shut behind us and cleared his throat. Benjamin spun around in the chair, scowling, but he broke into a baffled grin when he saw who it was. He wore a navy Stanford sweater with the sleeves rolled to his elbows, inordinately keen to advertise the college he'd dropped out of. I could smell his sickly, dorm-room deodorant wafting towards us.

'Oh hey, Gupta,' he said. 'What are you guys doing here?'

'Is that in the Steve Jobs playbook?' I said, jerking a thumb back towards the front room and the unfortunate man-boy he'd just bollocked.

'Oh, you heard that?' he replied. 'Randall's used to it. It's motivational.'

He scooped a handful of M&Ms from a bowl on the desk, tossed one into the air and caught it in his mouth. 'It's Lucky, right? You guys wanna sit down?'

My partner and the dog at his heel shared the same unimpressed expression, like the rhythm section in a rock-band portrait. 'Not really,' said Raúl.

'Uh, is everything okay?' said Benjamin, apparently sensing the temperature in the room. The antique neon hummed softly into the silence.

'Scooter,' I said at length. 'Remember you told me you were always in the market for cool shit, and that money was no object? You remember that?'

He crunched another M&M. 'Did I say that? I guess I could have. Why?'

'Well, we have something we think you might be interested in.'

He leaned back in his chair, the overhead light throwing his cleft chin into relief. We'd caught him off guard, and I thought I saw curiosity warring with caution behind his confident gaze.

'Oh, yeah? Awesome. What is it?'

'It's going to cost you,' I replied.

'*Okaaay* . . . Sounds cool. I'm interested. How much?'

'A confession.'

He laughed, stopped, and then sat forward again, slow. 'A *confession*? To what?'

'You stole our cookie jar,' said Raúl. 'And you beat up our boss.'

'*What?*' Benjamin gaped, eyes shuttling from my partner's face to mine. 'What are you talking about? Hold on: you're punking me, right?'

He palmed the last of the chocolates into his mouth.

'Deny it all you want, Scooter,' I said. 'But the cookie jar was found in your recycling bin. We have it bagged and I'll bet my shirt your prints are all over it.'

Benjamin toyed with his computer mouse. He was blushing harder than a bachelorette with a handful of strippagram. 'I don't . . . C'mon, what the *hell*, guys? You barge in here, accuse me of— I don't have *time* for this, okay? I have a lunch meeting. I can't just . . .'

He stood up, then he sat down again.

'Sorry to ruin your appetite, but here's what I think happened,' I said. 'You like superheroes; that much we know. You collect all this merch, and I guess you collect comics, too. Money is no object – your words – and you wanted to get your hands on *The Black Bird*, whatever it took. So when you heard Marty Kann was dead, you emailed Marty Jr to see if he'd left a copy behind. He told you to get stuffed – but he also said to try the estate sale.'

Raúl reached into his messenger bag and produced the printed email. 'Tony Stark,' he said, stepping forward to slap it down on the desk. 'Nice alias.'

Benjamin still had a hand at his mouth, maybe to keep the truth from dribbling out. With the other hand, he slid the paper towards him and stared at it.

I went on: 'When you didn't find it in the estate sale, you thought maybe Bart's Olde California had got to it first. Maybe you saw our truck at the Kann house. Either way, you came to the store that night to . . . what, pilfer it? But Bart interrupted you, so you walloped him and made off with the first box you saw. Unlucky for you, it turned out to be the Ringmaster cookie jar. Which is worth a cool six grand, by the way – or it was, until you tossed it out.'

'Then you came back to the store the next day,' said Raúl. 'To try again.'

Benjamin clenched his jaw and pushed the email printout to the edge of the desk. I'd bitten down deep enough to hit his hard, peanut centre: the ruthlessness that had turned Bacon Ninja into a few million bucks. I wondered whether he was capable of violence if it meant getting his way. Burgers thought so: his back was up, and he was breathing hard through his narrow, overbred pipes.

'Guys, seriously. I don't know what you're talking about,' Benjamin said, turning his cool blue eyes back to his computer screen, feigning frat-boy disregard. 'Now I'm busy and I think you should leave.'

Raúl retrieved the email and returned it to his bag. 'If that's how you wanna play it,' he said. 'I guess we can assume you're not interested in *The Black Bird*?'

Our client's acquisitive nature finally got the better of him. 'Do you even fucking *have* it . . . ?' he said sharply, trailing off as he realised that he'd revealed himself. Raúl and I shared a glance: *Gotcha.*

He took a deep breath, thumbed his eyes and laid his palms flat on the desk, staring from his left hand to his right as if one of them hid an ace. Then he spilled like a blocked toilet: 'Shitshitshit. Okay, look. It wasn't my fault, you guys. I'll pay you back for the cookie jar. With interest. I had no idea it was valuable. But whatever happened to your boss had nothing to do with me. I *swear.*'

'Keep talking,' said Raúl.

'Okay, okay. You're right. I emailed Kann's son. He told me about the estate sale. But while I was waiting in the line outside the house Sunday morning, I saw you guys leaving with a whole darned truckful of stuff. You must have some kinda arrangement with that lady who ran the sale? That's good business, I guess.'

'It pays the bills,' I said. 'Almost. So you were there.'

'Yeah. I was sorta incognito.'

'Incognito?'

'I wore a disguise. Nothing dumb. Just dark glasses and a fedora. So no one would recognise me. Look, do you guys have the comic book or not . . . ?'

'Get on with it,' said Raúl.

'Okay. Alright. So I saw you guys leaving, and then there was no trace of *The Black Bird* in the house. I looked all over. Most of the other people there didn't even know whose place it was; they were just buying lamps or plates or whatever. If anybody had the comic book, I figured it had to be you guys. So I looked up your store, thought I'd come by after closing so I could catch your boss alone, y'know?'

'Mother*fucker*,' said Raúl. I was glad he didn't have the taser with him.

'No, no! Not like *that*,' Benjamin replied, flapping his hands frantically. 'I just wanted to talk to him in private. You guys do know about *The Black Bird*, right? You know that it's an extremely sensitive item. I wanted to see if we could work out a deal, sorta like off the books, know what I mean?'

'Why do you even want that piece of crap in the first place?' said Raúl.

'Piece of crap? It's a piece of *history*, brah! It killed Crusader Comics! Don't you think that's pretty dope? I do . . . But if people found out I bought something like that? Well, let's just say the optics would be awful.'

'If *who* found out?' I said.

'My enemies! I'm a public figure. They'd tear me apart on Twitter. You don't understand, there are people out there who want to destroy me.'

'Oh, *yeah*,' said Raúl. 'The lawsuit. You screwed over your college buddy, right? The guy who co-created Bacon Ninja?'

'Hey, I did not screw over *anybody*,' said Benjamin, standing suddenly. He had a temper shorter than a spent match. 'That shitbird had nothing to do with Bacon Ninja. NOTHING!

Guy spends two months eating take-out pizza on my goddam dorm-room couch and thinks he's a *partner*? "Creative input" my ass. He can take his fucking lawsuit and sh—'

'Okay, Scooter,' I said. 'Simmer down. So you came to the store . . . ?'

'Right.' He regained his composure, raked a hand through his hair and remembered. 'Right. The place was closed already when I got there, so I went around back. And there was your truck. The back of it was . . . It was wide open. There was no one around, and the boxes I saw you taking from Marty Kann's place? They were just sitting there! So, y'know, I opened one of 'em, to see – but it was just a bunch of Styrofoam. So I was about to open the next one – to *see*, that's all – but that's when I heard somebody coming . . .'

'Bart,' said Raúl.

'I guess. I don't know. I panicked. I knew how it would look if I was just there going through your shit.'

'It would look like you were stealing,' I said.

'Precisely,' he replied. 'I don't know what I was thinking. I just picked up the box and ran. I didn't mean to take anything. *Really*. It was instinctual, I guess. Didn't even open it until I got home. And it was just that cookie jar. So.'

'Wait,' said Raúl. 'So you're saying that you stole the Ring-master, but you didn't whack Bart?'

'Well, yeah. That's right.'

'And you expect us to believe that?'

He flailed again, a mime in a swarm of imagined bees. 'It's the truth! I didn't even know the guy got assaulted until you just told me! Guys, listen: I felt so bad about it, I came back the next day and spent ten *thousand* dollars! I didn't even *like* that cowboy table I bought. I gave it to my *mom*! I'll pay for the cookie jar, okay? I'll pay *double* if you want! I'm *sorry*!'

'So when you came back to the store the next day, it wasn't because you were still looking for *The Black Bird*.'

'NO! *No.* No, I was just . . . I'm saying – unless you *have* it . . . ?'

I looked at Raúl. He reached back into his bag and revealed our winning hand: *White Lightning #88*. Benjamin's eyes ballooned.

'My God,' he whispered. 'It's *real* . . .'

He circled the desk to see the comic up close, but Raúl held on to it and Burgers's low, automotive growl kept the preppy scumbag at bay.

'Hey, Scooter,' I said, and I clicked my fingers to recapture his attention. 'Tell me: what do you think your colleagues, your mum and the cops are all going to think when we tell them you knocked out a seventy-year-old man and stole a valuable antique while you were trying to get your hands on a racist comic book?'

I'd landed a kidney punch. Benjamin gripped the edge of the desk to steady himself and started quietly hyperventilating. I smoked my e-cigarette as I watched him squirm. 'Guys,' he said, thrusting out his free hand in supplication. '*Guys.* You can't go to the cops. I did not hurt your boss. I fucking *pinkie* swear it. You can't tell anyone about this. Please! My reputation. My *business*! I'm a good person. I have investors! This could *destroy* Bacon Ninja! Please, guys!'

He'd sunk halfway to his knees. He might have been right: having finished off one business several decades ago, the comic book still wielded sufficient power to cripple another. It would have given me no small satisfaction to wipe his stupid game from the face of the Earth and rescue thousands from its tyrannical distractions. But I had a different plan.

'There aren't any "good" people, Scooter,' I said. 'You're young; you'll learn. But I think we can all come out of this okay – even Bacon Ninja.'

'Anything,' he pleaded. 'I'll do *anything*.'

'First thing you can do is get up off the bloody floor.'

He scrambled back to his feet, still clinging for dear life to the desk.

'Now, Raúl here has all four of the offending comic books in his possession . . .'

'*White Lightning* issues 85 through 88,' Raúl said. 'The complete Black Bird storyline.'

I continued: 'According to our calculations, the market value of the full set is approximately one hundred thousand dollars. We think that's a fair price.'

'Wait,' said Benjamin. '*What?*'

'Raúl tells me that when Bacon Ninja first introduced . . . What was it, Raúl?'

'Ads and in-app purchases,' said Raúl.

'Right. When you first introduced "ads and in-app purchases", you were earning a hundred grand per day. Must be even more than that by now.'

'Guys,' Benjamin chuckled nervously. 'That's a gross figure. And I have significant outgoings. We've only had one funding round.'

'Like I said, Scooter: that's market value for *White Lightning vs The Black Bird*. And besides, I watched you drop ten large the other day as coolly as you'd drop a quarter into a parking meter.'

'But I actually already *have* the first three issues. I just wanted the last—'

'Put a sock in it, Scooter. I'm not finished. That Ringmaster cookie jar is a 1940 original, worth six thousand bucks. And Bart's going to have a significant deductible to cover for his medical care after your little run-in.'

'For Chrissakes, guys. I didn't touch him. I've never even *met* the guy!'

'I'll tell you what, Scooter: you write out a cheque for a hundred and ten thousand dollars to Bart's Olde California, and Raúl and I will be perfectly happy to pretend we believe you. We'll give you the comic books, and then we can all go our separate ways and never speak of this again. How do you like *those* optics?'

'But . . . You mean now? A hundred and ten thousand, right *now*?'

'Before you decide, Scooter, I think you ought to weigh that one-ten against what you think Bacon Ninja is worth, and the bail amount a judge might set for aggravated robbery and assault charges – not to mention whatever your fancy lawyers bill per hour. You should probably factor in some public-relations costs, too. All in all, I think you'll conclude that it's a bargain.'

Benjamin sat back against the lip of the desk, his cheeks pallid and his brow slick. He wasn't a man accustomed to losing. Hell, I'm not a man accustomed to winning. This was fresh territory for us both.

'Okay, shit,' he said at last. '*RANDALL!*'

Almost immediately, the door behind us slid open and the curly-haired bottom-feeder stepped shyly across the threshold. 'Yuh?' he said.

'Do we have a chequebook?' said Benjamin.

'Whuh?'

'You know. A fucking *chequebook*, for writing *cheques*. Old-timey MONEY SHIT, Randall! That's supposed to be YOUR motherfuckin' department!'

'Uh, yuh . . .'

Randall scuttled to Benjamin's desk and tugged at a basement drawer, lifting out a leather-bound chequebook and a fountain pen. He had a face like a spaniel returning a tennis ball. Benjamin sat back in his chair. 'Thank you,' he said, as Randall smoothed open the chequebook at the latest page.

'Okay, Randall, I got it. Now get the fuck outta here. This is private.'

'Uhuh,' Randall said, and then scurried back to the outer office, sliding the door closed behind him.

'Randall's our CFO,' said Benjamin, by way of explanation. He took a moment to collect himself, then he scrawled the amount, swearing under his breath as he signed. He tore the slip quickly, like a Band-Aid, and held it out to me. I scanned the particulars before folding it into my breast pocket. Bart's cashflow problems were behind him, for now.

'The comics?' said Benjamin, resigned.

'Of course,' I replied. 'Raúl?'

Casually, Raúl tossed the comics to the floor in front of the desk. They landed flat on the rug with a slap, the precious final issue atop the stack. Burgers seized his moment, sidled over to the pile and squatted over *The Black Bird*, squinting in concentration. Benjamin, dazed, took a moment to register what exactly was happening before he leapt up and raced around the desk.

'Wait,' he said, horrified. 'What the fuck is he . . . Oh my *God*!'

Burgers had deposited a twist of hot turd in the middle of the comic's front cover. Satisfied, and several ounces lighter, the dog trotted across the densely patterned rug to the door, with the two of us close behind him, leaving Benjamin on his knees trying to salvage his prized acquisition.

I come from the world's oldest money, and here I was grabbing a share of the newest. The future belongs to men like Benjamin; his despotic self-belief would be dented for just a few short hours or days. But we retained the power to shame him if the mood should take us, and that was triumph enough. Raúl grabbed a handful of Bacon Ninja T-shirts from the box on the couch in the front room, observed yet unobstructed by Randall and his colleagues, and we left the house as we'd entered it: accompanied by the muffled yells of an angry young rich guy.

Raúl sprang for a celebratory lunch at a mariscos shack by the side of Lincoln Boulevard, the fumy four-lane strip that joins Venice to Santa Monica. I ordered a horchata and a tub of shrimp ceviche. We ate fast, standing on the pavement, tossing chunks of tostada and tomato salsa to the hungry dog, who had an empty stomach to fill. Engine oil rose off the asphalt in the muggy midday. My partner peered intently at the lengthening line for the order window.

'What is it?'

'Thought I saw Calista Flockhart,' he said. 'But it's not her.'

He impaled a prawn on his disposable fork, then paused as it dripped with citrus. 'You believe him?' he said.

'Who, Scooter?'

'Yeah. Maybe he didn't whack Bart.'

'Of course he did. Guy's about as plausible as a telenovela.'

He shrugged. 'I guess he did.'

'I'm sorry,' I replied. 'I know you thought you'd made a friend. You want to go to Calabasas? Deliver that desk once and for all?'

'Why not? I'm feeling lucky.'

'That's what she said.'

'Hey, you're funny. You oughta be a comedian.'

PART THREE

THE HERO'S JOURNEY

26

We took the 10 to the 405 to the 101. As we closed in on Calabasas, it became all too clear that the Overlook Fire had refocused
its energies on the Valley side of the Santa Monicas. Ahead of us
hung dark smoke-clouds as heavy as a Bergman movie. High
above them a fire-fighting plane turned lazily inland. News chop-
pers buzzed to and fro. I took the Hidden Hills exit and steered
us against the flow, up into the old town, where half the vehicles
on the road had flashing emergency lights, and the other half were
laden with children, pets and possessions.

The first roadblock was a mile shy of our destination, two
sheriffs' cruisers parked nose-to-tail across a T-junction, with
deputies redirecting traffic back towards the freeway. But this time
Raúl was prepared: consulting his smartphone, he navigated us
determinedly down leafy side streets, along residential rat-runs
and through an open-air premium-outlet mall, taking a zigzag
route around the cops and fire crews, up the slope towards
Whitney Blair. With one last roadblock to bypass, we bounced
across the empty car park of a three-star motel and out the back
exit, sneaking into an unmanned gap in the law-enforcement
perimeter and onto the deserted streets directly in the path of the
blaze.

'Whitney was hanging at Jamba Juice with the Jenner sisters
Wednesday,' Raúl said. 'She put it on Instagram.'

'Any sign of the ex-boyfriend?'

'Marcus? Nah.'

'What about the other one?'

'Chad? *People* magazine says he's dating an underwear model.'

'So he and Whitney aren't an item?'

'Guess not.'

'So she might be in the market for a rebound, after all?'

'Dude, just get us there.'

As we raced down the hedge-lined drive that led to Jacaranda Groves, the view ahead grew dim and gauzy. A Forest Service jeep popped from the gloaming and sped past in the opposite direction. The estate's cast-iron gates had been flung open and the Jobsworth's guard post abandoned. I had already suggested we turn back, but my partner would brook no dissent, and just this once I felt obliged to follow his lead. Besides, this was our fourth attempt to deliver the desk to Calabasas; I did not intend to make a fifth.

The truck loped along the wide, landscaped lanes towards Whitney Blair's home, past the empty driveways of the community's depopulated McMansions. The homes were mostly new builds in old styles, with columned porticoes and colonial shutters. Minor celebrities, music execs, TV producers, entertainment lawyers, cosmetic surgeons: their manicured lawns and four-car garages were now mere kibble for the approaching inferno that tore through the hillsides above them like Vikings through a monastery.

We could see Whitney's sculptural form stippled by the heat haze as we approached; she was on the driveway outside her ranch-style bungalow, vainly attempting to cram an old armchair into the boot of her Mini Cooper. The back seats of the little car were already jammed with designer suitcases. I stopped the truck at the kerb; Raúl leapt out and sprinted towards her.

Opening the driver's side door was like opening a lit oven; I could feel the warmth of the far-off flames on my face. The fire might still have been a half-mile upslope, but thick black battlements of smoke towered over the subdivision. The distant ridge was smothered in darkness, its outline discernible only by a bright, flaming corona. Above that was the only hope for Jacaranda Groves and the neighbourhoods downslope: swollen grey cumulonimbi, almost fit to burst.

Raúl and Whitney were conversing feverishly. She had on a vest, trainers, running shorts and a rolled bandana as a hairband. There's a certain genre of celebrity who seems always to have just left the gym. She made sweat look like baby oil. I tried to forget that I'd seen her naked, but the effort was futile.

'Everyone's been evacuated,' said Raúl, turning to me. 'They say Jacaranda Groves is maybe in the way of the fire.'

'Well, does she want the desk or doesn't she?'

'Forget the frickin' *desk*, dude – we gotta help her get her shit outta here!'

'Please,' Whitney pleaded, her immaculately proportioned features dimpled in distress. 'Is there like space in your truck for some of my stuff?'

I looked back up the slope into the smoke. If the wind moved fast enough, we'd all be toast. I could taste the bitter charcoal on my tongue. But I knew Raúl wouldn't leave without helping. Maybe if her house burned down, I reflected, we could sell the tanker desk to somebody else.

'Okay,' I said. 'But we have to make it quick. Ten minutes max. We'll only take stuff you can't replace. No bloody flatscreens or running machines. Just heirlooms and personal items. Whatever has the most sentimental value. Alright?'

'For sure,' she said, clasping her hands at her chest. 'Omigod, *thank* you.'

'Thank Raúl,' I replied. 'But do it later.'

The bungalow's interior comprised fewer rooms than its square-footage seemed to demand, with large, sparse reception spaces for which its owner had plainly failed to find a function. Still in her twenties and apparently living alone, she'd yet to acquire enough stuff to adequately fill the house – which at least made our task easier. It's confounding to me that a young person with so much disposable income would choose the dismal calm of suburban privilege over a Downtown loft apartment.

Yet somehow, perhaps by accident, Whitney had taste. Among the predictable Crate & Barrel furnishings were pieces that would make fine additions to the Bart's Olde California inventory: a Danny Ho Fong wicker lounge chair; a pole lamp designed by Gino Sarfatti for Arteluce. We salvaged those along with her Kentucky grandmother's jewellery, a carpet bought on a vacation in Dubai, some signed Christina Aguilera CDs and a limited-edition Slim Aarons print, scooping each item up and hustling it out to the truck.

Whitney pointed to the potted yucca beside her suede couch. 'Can you lift that?' she said. 'It was a gift from my ex-boyfriend.'

'Marcus?' said Raúl, as he lugged the heavy pot towards the front door.

'Chad,' she replied, following him.

As they left the room I thought I heard a dog whining somewhere, but I dismissed it as the noise of a tumble dryer finishing a cycle. In what looked like a nascent study, I noticed an empty space between two tall bookshelves that I guessed had been cleared to make way for the tanker desk.

The shelves were full of books: one contained the feminist canon and some assorted cultural theory; another self-help, spiritual claptrap and a copy of the Bible; a third was replete with nineteenth-century novels: the English, the French, the Russians — their spines sufficiently creased to suggest actual reading had occurred. I always judge books by their covers, and a person by their books. Maybe Raúl was right, and the object of his desire had a richer inner life than I'd given her credit for. Or maybe she'd just bought them all second-hand.

I might've been distracted just long enough to be burned alive, had my partner not appeared in the room behind me and clapped his hands. 'Hey,' he said. 'That's ten minutes, my liege. We're outta here.'

I made a stack of what I considered the most valuable titles. Outside, the heat of the fire was intensifying. Just past the tree-line, I could see sparks dancing among the dry brown pines. Further up the slope, fifty-foot trees were ablaze, and hot curling embers had begun to fall silently on the driveway like snow. My sense of danger was perversely diminished by the comforting, log-fire crackle of burning timber.

As Raúl yanked the back of the truck closed, another big rig raced past the driveway and stopped a few houses down. A hot-shot crew of a dozen or more men emerged in yellow overalls and helmets, carrying shovels and backpacks, and started to make their way across the lawn in formation, towards the fire's front-line. They were followed by a sheriff's cruiser, which came to an abrupt halt beside us. The deputy wound his window down, face pink and perspiring.

'You folks need to get your asses the hell outta here stat,' he said. 'There's homes already burnin' up that hill.'

'Don't worry, Deputy, we're leaving,' I replied.

'Well, giddy up, else you'll be kindlin'! Do you need some assistance, ma'am?'

Whitney was coming out of the house. 'It's Dustin, my dog,' she said, hurrying down the driveway, her eyes watering, her bandana now tied over her nose and mouth. 'He's scared and I can't get him out of the laundry room!'

'I'll go,' Raúl said, and he jogged back towards the bungalow.

'Sir,' the deputy yelled at him. 'SIR! Y'all need to leave *right now*!'

Raúl turned as he reached the open front door and yelled: 'Start the engine, Sir Lucky: I GOT THIS!'

He disappeared inside just as one of the tall trees in the copse behind the house burst into flames, and then another. Smoke settled in my lungs, familiar but unwelcome. The deputy sped away in search of more-willing evacuees. Whitney seemed not to know what to do with herself.

'Get in your car and go, Whitney,' I said. 'We'll be right behind you.'

'But. Dustin—'

'Raúl'll fetch him, don't worry. But you really have to go.'

'Where?' she said.

'You remember how to get to our store? Los Feliz? We'll meet you there.'

She nodded, climbed into the Mini and stuffed her key clumsily into the ignition. But she didn't turn it. 'I can't leave him,' she cried. 'I just *can't*!'

Which was when Raúl finally staggered from the house, the hillside aflame at his back, smoke billowing around his stocky frame, and over his shoulder a whimpering Alsatian the size of a pony – the only big dog in Los Angeles.

27

Forests burn, freeways collapse, reservoirs run dry, yet still the brave people of the Southland fill their gas tanks and water their lawns as if the end will never come. And so, ninety minutes later and still stinking of smoke, we sat at a table outside Sasquatch Pete's café, polishing off a spread of jackfruit tacos and buffalo cauliflower wings. The French bulldog and the German shepherd lay side by side on the pavement, each chewing a vegan treat.

'Your dog's like so cute,' said Whitney. 'What's his name?'

'Burgers,' Raúl replied.

'That's funny.'

'Thank you.'

Whitney waved off a bothersome insect and smiled at Raúl, who smiled back, rapt. Sitting across from her made us both look like brutes.

'Aren't you writing a book, Whitney?' I said. 'How's that going?'

She sighed and stared into her shake. 'Okay, I guess? I mean, I keep getting distracted by like bullshit, y'know? Like, I was on this reality show, and it got cancelled last year. *Beyond the Hills: The Valley*. Did you see it?'

'Raúl did.'

'Oh, seriously? Rad. So I have this little, like, window of celebrity but it's closing fast, y'know? So I gotta choose my next move soon, and it's gotta be the right move. Like, for me. And I just thought, I mean, a book would totally help me explain my shit to people. The *real* Whitney, y'know?'

'Sounds outstanding,' said Raúl.

'Sounds like you're running for President,' I said.

'It's like my take on being a woman celebrity today, with essays about fame and feminism and culture and relationships and stuff? Kinda like a Didion-meets-Friedan-meets-Kardashian sorta thing?'

I felt my kale shake go down the wrong way. 'You read Joan Didion?'

'OMG, I *loooove* Joan Didion, don't you? Didn't her house in Malibu burn down once? What is that quote? Like, "The city on fire is LA's vision of itself"? Something like that. Anyways, my manager's totally gonna hire one of those ghost-writers to help me out. But I wanted to do the first draft myself. So that it's really, like, *me*? Because, like, sometimes I feel like people just see me as, like, a caricature, y'know?'

'Totally,' I nodded, though the sarcasm escaped her. 'I hope your manuscript isn't still at the house.'

'I saved my laptop,' she smiled sadly. 'I mean maybe it's a good thing, the fire? Like, I *so* need to get out of town to write, anyway. Somewhere with no cellphones or photographers or people tweeting shitty things at me. I heard about this one, like, *super*-private writers' retreat? It's in the Mexican *desert*. You sign like a waiver and they won't let you leave until you're done with your project. It's like being in, like, a convent or something. Mexico! Can you *believe* that?'

'You got a place to stay tonight?' said Raúl, ever the optimist.

'Oh, *yeah*. My friend Chad says I can stay at his place in Hollywood.'

My partner's pained look was for the ages.

'What would you like us to do with your things?' I said.

'Chad says I can keep my stuff in his garage. Would you take it there? I'll pay.'

'Don't worry, Whitney,' I replied. 'This one's on the house.'

She smiled again. Every parade of her perfect teeth induced a dopamine hit. I wondered whether that sort of power was a blessing or a curse.

'What about the tanker desk? You still want it?'

'Hmm. I dunno. I mean, like, yes. Omigod. For *sure*. But I guess I gotta see about my house first.'

'You never know,' said Raúl. 'Maybe those hotshot guys stopped the fire.'

'Do you think I could like take another look at it, maybe? The desk?'

We settled the bill and strolled around to the store car park. I opened the truck to reveal the tanker desk, which still faced out from the back of the cube, confident in heft and crisp in composition. Raúl, acting the gent, unfolded Bart's retractable stairs so that Whitney could step up into the truckbed without effort.

The next half-second seemed to happen in super-slo-mo. Whitney put her foot on the first step, and her modest weight was sufficient to unbalance the truck's shonky suspension. The entire cube tilted backwards ever so slightly, which sent the desk trundling towards her on the old castors Marty Kann had fitted. It moved no more than a few inches before its progress was sharply arrested by the too-loose straps Raúl had used to lash it in place.

But its momentum spat out the slim, unlocked pencil drawer — precisely far enough to catch Whitney square on the bridge of her million-dollar nose with a dull, steel *thunk*. She arced back off the step and straight into Raúl's arms, out cold. The truck righted itself and the pencil drawer slid coolly home. My partner held Whitney's unconscious form as we stared at each other in shock — and then the exact same thought occurred to us both at once:

'Bad juju.'

It started to rain.

28

The rain was an English rain. It came down in cool, fleshy droplets, forming trapezoidal puddles on the crooked pavements and turning the cycle lanes along Sunset into streambeds. Thunder rolled back and forth across the firmament, as if an upstairs neighbour were vacuuming their floors.

Angelenos do not drive well in weather, so it took me a while to hack through traffic, but I found Bart just where Karen said he would be: with his rod poised over the water on the sloping west bank of the LA River in Frogtown.

The river was clad in concrete during the '30s, by the US Corps of Engineers, when the city authorities got it into their heads that floods would be the greatest existential threat to a young Los Angeles. The section that runs past Downtown, beneath the Fourth and Sixth Street bridges, is just a trickling creek across a vast expanse of drainage canal. You'd probably recognise it from *Point Blank*. But upstream are sections deep enough to fish, where wildfowl roam among the reeds and rushes, mere yards from the petroleum buzz of the 5 freeway.

Bart wore a roomy plastic poncho and a wide-brimmed bush hat and appeared to be unfazed by the rainfall, which by then had slowed to a thick drizzle.

'Thelma!' he cried out, as I crab-walked down the gentle grade to where he perched on a rolled blanket. 'Where's Louise?'

'He's at the hospital,' I said.

'The *hospital*? Is he okay?'

'Yeah, he had to take a friend to the ER. Should you be out in the rain, Bart? What about your rheumatism?'

'Ach, of course I should! Brings the carp to the surface.'

I stood over him, watching the bright-orange bobber at the end of his line as it trembled on the water, troubled by nothing but currents. His eyes were still shrouded in dark bruises, but the swelling had decreased, and the Band-Aid across his nose was fresher and smaller than the last time I'd seen him.

'You caught anything?'

'Give me a chance, brother. I've only been here three hours.'

'It's good to see you up and about.'

'You got something for me?' he said.

I reached into my waxed jacket and pulled out a flat package wrapped in aluminium foil. He beamed as I peeled it half-open and handed it to him.

'There's a lady with a cart at Sunset and Echo Park,' I said. 'Does the best blue-corn Oaxacan quesadillas in the Tri-Hipster Area. That one's potato chorizo.'

He was already eating it. 'It's a tour-de-force,' he replied, his mouth full. 'But you didn't come all this way in the rain to bring me a snack, did you?'

'No,' I confessed.

'So . . . ?'

On my way from the store, I'd thought seriously about how much I ought to tell Bart, and decided he would have to know some of why we'd ended up with a cheque for $110k from the CEO of Bacon Ninja. So I crouched beside him and told him about *The Black Bird*, how we'd acquired it unwittingly from Cleo's sale and then sold it to a wealthy collector. But I left out the parts about Guzman and The Villain's Lair, and about Scooter filching the cookie jar. Finally, I broke it to him that he had probably not been attacked after all — at least, not by a human assailant — and explained exactly what had just happened to Whitney Blair.

Bart grappled silently with the new information, chewing his final mouthful of quesadilla, then he frowned and said: 'She's not going to *sue*, is she?'

'I should bloody well hope not,' I replied. 'We helped her out of a spot. If she does, then at least now we can afford a lawyer.'

He chuckled and shook his head. 'Stupid, stupid. The desk! What an old fool I am . . .' He paused. 'But *wait*, what about the box that was stolen? The cookie jar? And what about that foul odour in the parking lot before I was knocked out?'

I puffed my cheeks, affecting ignorance. 'Dunno. A crackhead, maybe?'

Bart turned back to the river, where his hook still dangled contemplatively without a catch. Rainwater collected in the brim of his hat. My jeans were damp and my haunches were seizing up, so I stood and shook out my limbs.

'You know, Lucky,' he said. 'All this . . . It's got me to thinking about my legacy. See, Karen has been begging me to retire for a while. And now? Well, perhaps it is time for me to slow down. Work three days, not six. But I've always worried about giving up the store. I thought if I left, soon enough somebody'd turn the place into a craft-beer bar, or a goddamned American Apparel . . .'

He stood up as well, unfolding stiffly like a rusted deckchair, and he put out a hand to prod me in the chest. 'But *you*, Lucky – you're a fellow who respects the past. I'd like you to think about becoming more than an employee of Bart's Olde California. I'd like you to think about being my partner. And, if you're interested, to take over one day. Now, what do you say to that?'

He held my gaze, hopeful but not insistent. One of his weary eyes was still half-crimson with burst capillaries. I've never liked making big decisions quickly. Actually, I've never liked making big decisions, full stop.

'Huh,' I said, to buy myself another second or two of thinking time. 'I don't know what to say, Bart. Honestly, I suppose . . .

You know what? I always thought that I'd end up going home one of these days.'

'What, you mean this isn't home? How long have you lived in Los Angeles?'

I had to work it out before giving him an answer; that's how long it had been. I stared at the river and thought of the trout stream that winds through the estate at Tinderley, whispering over stones and under oaks, past the rope-swing and Mater's favourite picnic spot. It's so long since I paddled in it with my brother and sister, corduroys rolled to my knees, that the memories now seem no more reliable than a dream. I should call my parents, I thought.

'Thirteen years,' I replied. 'Almost.'

'Lucky thirteen,' said Bart, smirking at his own witticism. 'Well?'

'I'll give it serious consideration,' I said, and then: 'What about Raúl?'

'What about him?'

'Do you think he'd want a stake in the business, too?'

'Dear God, no. Raúl has bigger fish to fry. He's going to be a star.'

'Ha. Yeah, right.'

Bart began to reel in his line. The carp of Southern California would live to see another day. 'You don't believe it?' he said. 'Don't you think his act is superb?'

I shrugged. 'I've never seen him.'

'You've *never* seen him do stand-up? Lucky, I'm disappointed! How long have you two been working together?'

'Okay, okay. I just never got around to it.'

'You must. He's very skilled. Doesn't he have a show—?'

'Tomorrow, yes – I know.'

'And did you know that he has more than eleven thousand Twitter followers?'

'Bart, don't start pretending like you get how Twitter works.'

'In point of fact, the Olde California Twitter account has three hundred and seventeen followers, as of this week. Which you would know, if you weren't such a stick-in-the-mud about social media and whatnot.'

He collapsed his telescopic rod and stuffed it into a canvas shoulder bag, which he picked up along with the blanket he'd been sitting on.

'So wait,' I said. 'You really believe Raúl's going to be successful?'

'Why do you think he's always late getting to the store?'

'Because he doesn't have a car. Or an alarm clock.'

'No,' said Bart. 'It's because he gets up at seven a.m. and works on his act for two hours every morning, because he read somewhere that that's what Jerry Seinfeld does. Some nights he's been up past midnight performing, too.'

'Well, I guess I knew that. The performing part, I mean.'

'He has a great career ahead of him. You watch.'

So Raúl was the next Seinfeld. Who knew? Everyone but me, apparently. It's easy to believe that you're the hero of your own life: that every woman you meet is your next rom-com co-star, and that everyone else is secretly planning your surprise birthday party. But finding out that the real talent is the guy standing next to you? Been there, done that. Maybe I've been the sidekick all along.

I was still processing this idea as Bart began to walk creakily up the concrete riverbank. He stopped after a couple of steps and squinted into the drizzle.

'Who is that young man?' he said.

I looked in the same direction and saw Winslow waiting on the path at the top of the bank, beneath a large umbrella. The kid was wearing the same specs and gilet as when I'd last seen him, and he carried a satchel over his shoulder.

'Nice brolly,' I said, as I reached the path.

'Could use one yourself,' he muttered. My hair was matted, my jeans wet through, my toes swimming in damp socks.

'Go ahead, kid: laugh it up,' I said. 'What are you doing here?'

'Lady at the antique store said this is where you'd be.'

Bart had made it to the top of the bank, too. He looked from me to Winslow, anticipating an introduction. 'Winslow, this is Mr Abernathy,' I said. 'Bart, this is Winslow. If it's all the same to you, he'll be doing some work experience at the store the next few weekends.'

'I see,' Bart replied. 'How wonderful. "Winslow", did you say?'

'That's right. His dad teaches art history.'

'Fascinating. How do you do, Winslow?'

They shook hands, and then Bart's face froze.

'What is that smell?' he said, suddenly uneasy.

The kid looked confused. I sniffed the air and smelled it too: a sweet, sickly scent like rotting fruit, or crackheads, or college dorms – or Scooter Benjamin.

'Lucky, *that's* the smell!' said Bart, and he gripped me by the arm as if he might lose his balance.

I turned to Winslow. 'Are you wearing cologne, kid? What do you smell of?'

'Uh . . . Africa,' said Winslow.

Bart and I glanced at one another, confused. '*Africa?*' I replied.

Winslow rummaged in his satchel and came up clutching a black spray-can, which he twisted to display the label.

'Axe Africa,' he said. 'You know – the antiperspirant.'

It took a minute or two to reassure Bart that Axe was an extremely common brand of body spray. He apologised to Winslow for his strange behaviour, then we watched as he trundled off home towards Atwater Village.

Winslow was jonesing to tell me something, and he did not appear to have transportation, so I offered him a ride back to his parents' place.

'It's your friend, Perkins,' he said at last, as I flipped on the wipers and peeled the Bronco away from the kerb. 'I got information regarding his whereabouts.'

'You mean Glyn?'

'Yeah. You told us he'd gone AWOL, remember? So I did some investigating.'

'What do you mean, "investigating"?'

'I staked out his house.'

'You did *what*?'

'I staked out his house for a couple nights. Watched his wife. The spouse is always the prime suspect, know what I'm saying?'

'What is this, the Famous Five?'

'You mean the Fantastic Four?'

'No, I mean the Famous F— Forget it. So wait, you're saying you conducted surveillance on Bijou? You have got to give the amateur-detective thing a rest, kid. Were you wearing your bloody Batman suit again?'

'Saw you, actually. With Mrs Perkins. Looked pretty cosy for a minute there.'

I almost jumped a red light. 'You've been *spying* on me?'

'Nah, man,' he replied, calmly. 'I been spying on *her*.'

'Jesus Christ. How did you even get their address?'

'Pfft. Google.'

'How did you get to Brentwood? You're too young to drive, aren't you?'

'You never heard of Uber?'

'And your parents just let you stay out as late as you want?'

'I'm a free-range kid.'

'You realise the Brentwood neighbourhood watch would have you locked up for life if they caught you snooping around. Does Guzman know about this?'

'Jeff? Nah.'

'Jesus Christ,' I said again, softer now as my fury subsided. Winslow sat silently watching the road with his satchel in his lap. I could hardly condone his behaviour – but, then again, if he really had been surveilling Bijou . . .

'So what's this "information" that you think you've gleaned, anyway?'

He grinned and reached into the satchel, fished out a spiral-bound A4 notebook and leafed through it until he found the page he was looking for.

'So,' he said. 'First night, she put her kids to bed and walked her dog. Then you showed up. All that, I guess you know already. But last night, there was this other guy came by, and they had a real interesting conversation.'

'Oh, yeah? Who was the guy?'

'Suit. Drove a sporty Mercedes. I drew his picture. Check it out.'

'Hang on,' I said. We were on Riverside Drive, so I pulled into the next car park I could find, which turned out to be a gas-station forecourt.

I grabbed the notebook and stared at the drawing. It was a pencil portrait in comic-book style, of a forty-something man with a hungry face, hooded eyes and a shaved bald head. The background was shaded with dark, angry cross-hatching. He looked a lot like a scheming supervillain.

'You drew this? Huh. It's good.'

'I know,' Winslow replied. 'You got any clue who it is?'

'It's Glyn's agent,' I said, handing him back the notebook. 'His name is Todd Carver. He's a piece of work.'

The kid turned to another page. This one was filled with neatly handwritten script. 'Taped 'em on my phone,' he explained. 'Didn't catch all of what was said, but I transcribed what I could. They started out talking smack about some dude named "Lucky". That's you, right?'

He handed me the notebook again.

'How the hell did you get close enough to record this?'

'Hid in the bushes. They were in the yard out back, by the pool.'

'Winslow, I am seriously worried about you.'

He grinned again and pushed his specs back up his nose. I started to read.

EXT. TERRACE — NIGHT.

MAN paces. MRS PERKINS sits at the table,
drinking.

                    MAN
       Why's that dickwad suddenly interested in
       Glyn's wellbeing, anyway? Never seemed to
                give a crap before.

                 MRS PERKINS
       Claimed he was doing a favor for Abby Musker.
                  Fucking asshole.

                    MAN
       Fucking Abby. Shit. And you told him Glyn was
              in England, like I said?

                 MRS PERKINS
       Wales. I told him I called Glyn's mom. Said
         Glyn was there working on ME3.

                    MAN
             You think he believed you?

                 MRS PERKINS
            I was pretty persuasive.

                    MAN
       I'll bet you were. You did good, Bijou.

                 MRS PERKINS
         It's lucky I called you first.

MAN

I know, right? I'm sorry you had to find out like this, but Glyn agreed we ought to keep it purely between us. You see why we can't have this getting out there, don't you?

MRS PERKINS
I know, I know.

MAN

Because if people in this town find out Glyn has a problem, he'll be radioactive. And that's no good for him, it's no good for me, and it's sure as shit no good for you and your family.

MRS PERKINS finishes her drink and sighs. MAN squats beside her and takes her hand.

MAN (CONT'D)

It's gonna be fine, Bijou. Trust me on this. I've used Doctor Evelyn before, and he is the best in the business. Completely discreet. He really got Chris's head together after his last turkey. Glyn is going to thank us both, I promise you that. You have to think about your future.

Her cellphone rings. She checks the caller ID.

MRS PERKINS
Fuck. It's him.

MAN
Who, Glyn? Again?

```
                MRS PERKINS
    Lucky. It's fucking Lucky. Fuck. Shit.
        Motherfucker. What do I do?


                    MAN
                Ignore it!


                MRS PERKINS
            Fucking asshole.
```

Her guard dog growls and approaches the
bushes where BATMAN is hiding. BATMAN melts
silently into the night.

The transcript came to an end.

'"Guard dog"?' I said. 'Doesn't she have a chihuahua?'

Winslow shrugged. 'I don't like dogs,' he replied.

The windows of the car were steamed up, and so were his specs. I puffed once or twice on my e-cigarette, pondering. Outside, the rain still pitter-pattered on the bodywork as the windscreen wipers went to and fro.

'Sounds to me like they put the guy in rehab,' Winslow said, sliding the notebook back into his satchel. 'Drugs or liquor, you think?'

He was a smart kid, but he had plenty yet to learn – and besides, I'd finally begun to piece everything together, like an Ikea bookcase bought second-hand.

'If you got rid of all the drug dependants in this town, Winslow, then the only movies getting made would be Pixar movies. And being an alcoholic screenwriter makes you *colourful*, not "radioactive".'

I put the Bronco back in gear and pulled out onto Riverside. 'If you ask me,' I said, 'Glyn's problem is a whole lot worse than that.'

29

There's a long word for that piney, ripe, redolent scent that the ground gives off after the first rainfall following a dry spell – but I'll leave it to you to look it up. Suffice it to say the air was full of it as I set out from home just after dawn. Chattering squirrels chased each other along the fence-tops. The path from my cottage to the car was plastered with soggy, blood-orange hibiscus petals.

I steered the Bronco south on the 5 and made it to San Ysidro by eight-thirty a.m. I had 'Ohio' turned up loud on the stereo, Neil Young's angry tenor cutting a groove through the early-morning traffic. At the border, weekenders funnelled into line ahead of me, their boots full of beach gear, surfboards strapped to their roofs, but it didn't take long to get across. As you drive out of the US, the guards wave you by like a float in the Rose Parade; it's getting back in that's the problem.

I had nothing out of the ordinary on me besides my American passport and a folded scrap of notepaper, on which I'd scribbled a name, some basic directions and a highly approximate map. The previous evening, I'd arrived home after dropping Winslow at his parents' place in West Adams, opened a Stone IPA and called Abby Musker. Had she ever heard Todd talk about a Dr Evelyn? The name rang a bell, she said, but she couldn't be sure why.

'Is he a dermatologist?' she said, and then: 'Have you googled him?'

I hadn't, so I did. My search for 'Dr Evelyn' returned a handful of Los Angeles-area family physicians and a character from a

Cold War conspiracy movie. But at the foot of the first page of results I found the link I'd been looking for: *The Hollywood Reporter*'s annual list of the Top 25 Writers' Retreats. I skimmed the rankings until I came to number seven, a place called The Colony.

They call him 'The Script Doctor'. For the height of discretion and isolation, there's no better regarded destination than Dr Chester Evelyn's The Colony: the most remote and extreme writers' retreat in California – *Baja* California, to be precise. This is where screenwriters straining to break a story or wrestling with a troublesome third act go to overcome their writer's block in absolute seclusion. Former 'patients' swear by Evelyn's therapeutic methods, which are confidential – and by his strict guest policies, which are whispered about over power brunches at the Polo Lounge. Industry sources say guests at The Colony must sign a waiver permitting Evelyn and his staff to detain them until their chosen project is complete, medical emergencies and family bereavements notwithstanding. Cash, cellphones and internet access are verboten – and the nearest town is too far to walk to through the punishing Baja desert. There's no escaping it: you have to finish that draft! One A-list writer-director tells *THR*: 'Dr Evelyn is the real thing. When he first treated me, I was struggling to complete a commission while working on my passion project. I finished both scripts in under a month at The Colony – and my next three movies all grossed over $150m!'

I hung a right after the border and skirted the top edge of Tijuana until I hit the beach, then I turned south again, motoring down the coast as the waves rolled in rhythmically off the postcard-blue Pacific. Past the cheap surf motels and the gated vacation communities, the taco shacks and the margarita bars. Ninety minutes later I reached Ensenada, checked my directions and nosed back inland.

The interior was an expanse of dry rolling scrub, littered with grey rocks. Fields broiled to stubble by the summer heat. Low brown mountains sweltering on the far horizon. Barely a trace of humanity, besides a single, infinitely receding overhead power line and some stringy fences to marshal the wildlife.

The landscape was so monotonous that I drifted into a reverie: brooding on the past; contemplating the future. I was passing my turn before I noticed it was there, so I flipped a bitch fifty yards up and swung the jeep back around to meet the dirt road that led off into the bush. The Bronco's ground clearance meant it bounced along the potholed track without effort.

After a mile or more I came to a free-standing wooden arch, capped with a hand-carved sign that read: 'Rancho La Colonia'. Beyond that, in a wide dip ringed by hills, was a tall, white adobe wall, several hundred yards across and at least as deep, like the ramparts of an ancient village, or a medium-security prison. Over the wall I could see sloping roofs of red clay tile. There looked to be a gap on the near side – the only visible way in – so that's where I aimed the jeep.

The gates clanked open automatically on my approach, closing behind me again as I drove through the wall into a small, cobbled square with a dribbling fountain at its centre. Parked along the left-hand side were half a dozen identical Chrysler minivans with dust-caked wheel arches, and a single black Porsche Cayenne with a personalised California plate: 'D0C 3VLN'. Not a soul in sight.

I stopped in one of the visitor bays and killed the engine. The silence was deeper than Shakespeare. The shadows were shortening beneath the still-rising sun. As I stepped out of the jeep, my Chucks squeaked on the hot cobbles and the scent of eucalyptus mentholated the motionless, late-morning air.

I strolled to the end of the square, where there stood a broad, two-storey estancia with a textured ochre facade, scant windows and a long, covered porch, under which a trio of saddled horses were tied up and drinking from a trough. I took off my Wayfarers, waved the bugs away from my face and stepped through the open oak door.

The lobby was cool and dim, with terracotta floor squares, a chesterfield suite and a tall clear vase of cut flowers displayed on a Duncan Phyfe-style mahogany drum table. A pretty señorita sat tapping a Mac keyboard at the reception, flanked by two inscrutable Mexican orderlies with matching white uniforms. Were they there to keep people out, or in? I suspect they cultivated the ambiguity.

On the wall behind them, looming over the receptionist, was a large portrait of a trim, middle-aged white man in shirtsleeves, mom jeans and a mauve cravat, standing hands-on-hips in a sunlit meadow grazed by buffalo. He had deep-green eyes that glinted in the sun, sculpted silver hair and a televangelist smile. Dr Evelyn, I presumed. I rapped my knuckles gently on the desk. The señorita looked me up and down with a thin smile, and I wondered whether I ought to have switched my threadbare flannel shirt for something smarter.

'Welcome to The Colony,' she said, betraying just a hint of an accent.

'Thanks,' I replied. 'I'm here to see Glyn Perkins.'

'Are you his registered visitor?'

I glanced at the orderlies on either side of me. One was absent-mindedly chewing gum. The other was watching our conversation out of the corner of his eye. I couldn't quite decide whether he looked menacing or bored.

'Yup,' I replied.

'Name?'

'Todd Carver.'

She turned back to her computer and punched in the necessary details, then she checked her wristwatch. I think I was holding my breath.

'Thank you, Mr Carver. We'll let Glyn know you're here. Visitors are permitted during rec hour, which starts at noon. You're forty-five minutes early. Would you like to wait at the patio bar? Miguel will show you the way.'

I followed the gum-chewing orderly along a corridor to a cloistered courtyard with a shaded patio at one end, where there nestled a bar and an arrangement of cast-iron café tables and chairs. I could see the tops of trees over the tiled roof on the far side of the cloister; it seemed that most of the compound was off-limits to visitors. The barman did his best impression of being glad to see me. So far, I was his only customer. I figured it was almost brunch-time.

'I'll have a Michelada, thanks.'

'I'm sorry, sir. We don't serve alcohol.'

'Huh. Okay. Root beer?'

He shook his head ruefully.

'Mineral water?'

'Coming right up.'

'Can I get a slice of lime in that?'

I sat at the farthest table, nursing my sparkling water, and thought about the last time I'd seen my old partner.

It was in the brief, unhappy period after I broke up with Glyn, and before Bijou broke up with me. Bijou and I had been drinking and arguing, though I did most of the drinking and she most of the arguing. That particular fight probably began because I had yet to put any serious effort into unpacking my belongings, most of which were still in a heap in the middle of her spare room, which she liked to use for yoga because the sliding closet doors were also floor-length mirrors.

We'd reached a lull in negotiations, and I was glowering on her couch with a lit cigarette, getting worked up watching some old Cagney flick on TCM, when all of a sudden Glyn was standing there in the sitting room, clean-shaven, clear-eyed and wearing his customary pressed Oxford shirt.

Bijou flicked off the TV and the two of them started yakking at me: about how they were alarmed by my behaviour, bothered by my drinking, concerned about my state of mind. It was as I was demanding Bijou hand me back the remote that it occurred to me this little get-together had somehow been prearranged behind my back, which was when I really flew off the handle. I started yelling at Glyn to fuck off – yelling at them both to fuck off, in fact, though of course we were in Bijou's apartment.

In the event, it was me who fucked off first, slamming the door and locking myself out without any shoes on, shortly after I'd flicked my glowing cigarette stub at Glyn, seen it land on the V of bare flesh at the top of his chest and drop down into his shirt, and then watched him frantically slapping at his flabby stomach to put it out, until I tossed most of my G&T down his front.

Afterwards, I sat in my socks in the laundromat opposite Bijou's Fairfax apartment building, watching the entrance and waiting for Glyn to emerge. I seem to recall waiting at least an hour; I dread to think what happened between the two of them in that time. When he finally came out, he was wearing my *Sticky Fingers* T-shirt and holding his own ruined outfit in a Trader Joe's carrier bag.

I watched as he glanced around anxiously, in case I'd been lurking in the shadows to do him an injury. Eventually he sighed, dropped his head and walked away with his eyes on the pavement.

As the rec hour approached, a couple more visitors trickled into the cloister and claimed tables of their own: an older woman, expertly put together and extravagantly perfumed, whom I took to be somebody's wife; and a twitchy young guy with sweat patches and a man-bag, whom I took to be somebody's personal assistant. I could hear what sounded like chanting from nearby, several low voices repeating the same barely audible incantation over and over.

246

Not long after the chanting ceased, there was a shuffle in the corridor outside and three men entered the cloister, each wearing a loose grey smock, light linen trousers and leather flip-flops. Two of them made straight for the other visitors, and as the milf kissed one and the twitchy guy produced a sheaf of documents for the other, I congratulated myself on the accuracy of my preconceptions.

The third man hung back, glancing anxiously around the patio bar. If not for his close-cropped ginger hair, I might not have recognised him. He had a weight-trainer's physique and a cheer-leader's complexion. The smock was draped over his hard, prominent pecs like a drop cloth over a piano, and at the centre of his tanned, unlined, unbespectacled face was a nose as straight and narrow as a former gangbanger who'd found God. I raised my hand and said his name: 'Glyn?'

The man squinted in my direction, frowned – and then his features popped with recognition. He smiled briefly, warily, flash-ing a ramrod row of glistening white teeth. As he crossed the patio and sat down opposite me, he glanced right and left and right again, as if preparing to cross a busy road.

'Lucius,' he said. 'Is that you? Christ, this is a surprise.'

'Of all the gin joints,' I replied.

He stared at me, blinking, taking in whatever ravages time had wrought. I didn't know whether to snicker or scowl at his unfamil-iar features, but I certainly felt something other than the bitterness and rancour for which I'd prepared myself. I'd often scripted the fight we'd have if I ever saw Glyn again, but now those scenes just seemed a little pointless, like something a smart producer would cut from the second or third draft. It was almost as if we were glad to see each other.

'They told me Todd was here,' he said.

'That's because I told them I was Todd.'

'I see,' he replied, nodding. 'Good, that's good. Blow me down, Lucius. How long has it been?'

'Long time. You look different.'

'You too.'

'Yeah, but. Glyn. You look *really* different.'

He seemed edgy, preoccupied. 'Oh, you mean the nose? Yeah. That was Bijou's idea. Said it would improve my self-esteem.'

'Right, the nose. That must be it.'

This was not the Glyn that I remembered, the humble Glyn who'd eat microwave meals and get sucker-punched in pubs. This was the Glyn of Bijou, of Brentwood, of Bryony the Pilates instructor. A Glyn familiar with therapists, nutritionists and personal trainers. When they say Hollywood changes you, sometimes they mean it literally. At least his Welsh brogue was still intact.

'What are you doing here, mate?' he said.

'You tell me,' I replied. 'What is this place, a monastery or an asylum?'

Paranoid, he peered over his shoulder to make sure no one was paying us too much attention, then he leaned in and said in a whisper: 'Todd sent me down here to cure my writer's block. I couldn't make the breakthrough on the *Marshal Eagle 3* script. I kept trying things to get my head right . . . I tried *a lot* of things.'

'Dream therapy, raw foods . . .'

'That's right. How'd you know?'

'I've been looking for you, Glyn. Abby came to see me. She was worried you'd gone AWOL. I told her I'd find out where you'd got to. Didn't think it would involve leaving the country – but screw it, I don't have any other weekend plans. How long have you been locked up in this loony bin, anyway?'

'Five weeks,' he said glumly.

'Five *weeks*?'

'Maybe six. I've lost track. Todd signed me up for three months, or until I finish the script. The studio pushed back production because of scheduling or some bollocks, but I'm still completely buggered. First draft ought to have been done ages ago. I made it to page sixty and I'd been staring out the bloody window ever since.'

'How did you get here? Did Todd drive you?'

'They pick you up from LA in a minivan.'

I summoned the address that Abby had found folded into his book at the Chagall. 'Let me guess: corner of Melrose and Robertson, opposite Cecconi's.'

'Exactly. You're only allowed to bring one small bag. Change of clothes, laptop, toothbrush, research materials. That's it. No distractions.'

'So why did you call? The other night, I mean.'

He glanced around again, in case of eavesdropping orderlies. 'I have to get out of here, Lucius,' he said. 'There's only one phone at the ranch, in the office above reception. You're allowed to call your one approved contact, so I told Todd to come get me, but he wasn't having it. Said I had to push through. I snuck back up there after hours to call Bijou, but Todd'd got to her already. She said she thought it was good for me.' He grimaced. 'We've been having some problems . . .'

'I know,' I said. 'I saw her.'

'You did? Christ. How is she?'

'After *I* turned up on the doorstep? How do you think?'

'Bloody hell,' he said. 'You two.'

'She told me you were at the Chagall. Lent me your room-key. That's where I found your phone.'

'Right, okay. Hmph. Well, my number's the only other one I can remember by heart, apart from my mam's. I was there in the office, Bijou hung up on me, so I just dialled it, because why not, eh? And you picked it up. Kismet, I suppose. But then the lads here caught me on the phone. You probably heard the rest. I was properly in the doghouse for a day.'

'Huh. So who's this Dr Evelyn character, anyway? Sounds like a quack.'

He winced. 'Lucius, keep your voice down, eh?'

'Fine,' I said, doing as instructed. 'Well?'

'Todd thinks he's a bloody genius,' Glyn explained, under his breath. 'They say he started out as an actor. Wrote some episodes of *Bonanza*. Back in the day, rumour is United Artists was all set to produce one of his screenplays – but then, you know, *Heaven's Gate*. He went and studied psychology or psychiatry or psycho-therapy, one of those. Travelled in India. Started this place in '88. There were some Oscar winners written here, supposedly.'

'And what are his methods, exactly?'

'Ach, I shouldn't really say,' he said, and stared at his hands; then: 'It's all supposed to be confidential. There's a diet cleanse and a mindfulness programme. Brainstorm Therapy. Anxiety and Tension Control. Story Jamming.'

'"Story Jamming"?'

'Don't ask. Mostly it's about the isolation. The silence. You'd be amazed how many distractions there are back in the real world, Lucius. I couldn't hear myself think at home. The kids, Bijou, the studio, the news, bloody Facebook.'

'So what, it doesn't work?'

'It does work,' he said. 'I've been writing like mad, man – just the *wrong words*. I scrapped the *ME3* script the second day I was here, started again and wrote sixty pages before the end of the week. Then I got blocked again, scrapped that, wrote another sixty. Then I set *ME3* aside altogether, wrote an entire family drama about the miners' strike off the top of my head in nine bloody days.'

'Huh. Title?'

'*Black Country*.'

'Is it any good?'

'Who cares if it's good? It's bloody kitchen sink. No one's ever going to *make* it, are they? The studio's going to start asking questions again soon. If I don't deliver *ME3* by the end of this month . . .'

He tailed off momentarily, gave a long, heartfelt sigh, and went on: 'Maybe they've already decided to fire me. I've probably breached my contract. You have to understand, this is all privileged information. We're talking about a billion-dollar franchise. If I get thrown off it, I'm poison. I'm *radioactive*, Lucius.'

For all the success of his efforts at self-improvement, I got the distinct impression Glyn was miserable. 'Okay,' I said, 'so let's get the hell out of here.'

'I don't think you get it, mate. I can't just *leave*. I'm not being funny, but I signed a bloody waiver. We're not in the Land of the Free anymore.'

His eyes were wide and fearful. He seemed serious. I had no idea about the legal or financial ramifications of skipping out on his stay at The Colony, but there were practical, logistical ones to consider, too. For instance: would we have to go through the orderlies to get out of the front door?

'We'll tell them your mum died,' I suggested.

'What if they check? No, listen – you came in a car, right?'

'Yeah, of course.'

'Is it fast?'

'It's forty years old, Glyn. It's fast-*ish*.'

'Christ on a bike. You and your bloody vintage cars. Okay, I suppose it'll have to do. There's a tree by the wall in the meditation garden, on the east side of the ranch. I'm pretty sure I can climb it.'

'You serious? Those walls are bloody high, Glyn.'

'I do a lot of squats. I can take the drop. Just meet me round there at the end of the rec hour. One, on the dot.'

'What about your stuff?'

'They have my wallet and passport locked up in the safe,' he said, breathless now with the anticipation of freedom. 'But all I need is my laptop. I can cancel all my cards. I left my phone in LA, but you knew that.'

'Wait, they have your *passport*? How the fuck are we supposed to get you back across the border? Hide you under a blanket?'

251

He tapped the side of his new nose and dropped his voice to a whisper once more. 'I took US citizenship last year. They have my *British* passport. I smuggled my American one in the lining of a Moleskine notebook.'

A shadow fell across the table. Glyn went deathly quiet. It was the barman.

'Sir,' he said. 'You can't smoke here.'

'What, you mean this?' I replied. 'But it's not even a real cigarette.'

'You can't smoke here, sir.'

I stuffed it back in my pocket. 'Fine,' I said.

'Thank you, sir.'

He disappeared, taking my empty water glass with him.

'An e-cigarette, eh?' said Glyn, smiling wryly. 'So you finally quit smoking?'

'Don't be a smart alec,' I replied. 'It doesn't suit you.'

Breaking Glyn out meant defying Todd and Bijou, and it's fair to say my resolve was strengthened by the thought of the looks on their faces when they learned I was responsible. I timed my departure as Glyn had requested, trying my best to play it cool as I strolled back through the lobby. The PA and the milf were leaving at the same time, he in a Hyundai and she in a Lexus. I drove out of the cobbled car park behind them, peeling away from the convoy as soon as we were through the gates. A rutted track circled the back of the ranch and led off into the wilderness, though I suspect it was frequented only by horses.

At one p.m. precisely, I brought the Bronco alongside the east wall of the compound and let the engine idle. Nobody had followed me, that I could see. I guessed the walls were fifteen feet high, maybe twenty. After a minute or so, I spotted movement ahead: two hands appeared over the lip of the rampart, then two hairy forearms, and then Glyn was straddling the top of the wall like a bear asleep in a tree, still wearing his smock and linen trousers. I rolled forward until I was almost underneath him and leapt from the car to offer encouragement. He was dangling a small rucksack from one hand and he shouted, as he dropped it: '*Laptop!*'

I lurched to catch it, but too late, and the bag landed with a thud on the brittle brown grass at the base of the wall. I scooped it up, hoping he could salvage the contents of the hard drive, even if the computer itself was done for. He grunted as he eased himself down the outside of the wall until he was clinging to it by the tips of his fingers. As he hesitated, one of his leather flip-flops fluttered from his foot to the ground. 'Come on, Glyn,' I said, exasperated, and he let go.

The drop was more than ten feet – and Glyn's no featherweight, so he came down hard. He crumpled and rolled backwards as he hit the dirt, swearing loudly and clutching his ankle. 'Buggery bastard bollocks,' he cried. 'Proper sprained it!' I dragged him to his feet, helped him hobble to the Bronco, jumped into the driver's seat and tossed the dusty rucksack across his lap. I checked the mirrors, checked my blind spots: nothing behind me; nothing ahead. Story of my life.

30

I floored it as far as the coast road, overtaking the twitchy PA in his Hyundai on the way. If anybody was following us, they never caught up. By the time we got halfway back to the border it was deep into lunch hour, so I pulled over at a cheap restaurant on the seaward side of the highway.

Glyn ordered six fish tacos and an Arnold Palmer, but when he saw my margarita arrive, he ordered one of those, too. We sat beneath an umbrella on plastic chairs with a view of the ocean and a clay pot full of free toothpicks, and I watched him stuff his face like Cool Hand Luke trying to win a jailhouse bet.

'Take it easy,' I said. 'We're not in a rush anymore.'

He tapped his chest until a belch came. 'Sorry,' he replied. 'The food at The Colony is calorie-controlled. Feels like I haven't eaten in weeks.'

'Calorie-controlled?'

'There's sirloin steak on the dinner menu, but it's the size of a bloody postage stamp. Besides, Bijou always has me on some sort of diet.'

'Well, looks like it's working.'

I suppose I'd paid him a compliment, and he didn't seem to know quite how to take it. It felt unnatural to me, too. I drank a mouthful of margarita and changed the subject. 'Bijou thinks you're having an affair,' I said.

He sighed. 'She told you that?'

'Are you?'

'Christ, no. I've just been . . . *distracted*. I moved to the Chagall because we were arguing, and I had to focus. On the script. But I'm only writing it for *her*, for the boys. That's the whole point! Why would I bloody cheat? My wife is beautiful, we've two fantastic kids—'

'Still a demon in the sack too, I bet.'

He studiously ignored that, and started to eat another taco.

'I met your eldest,' I said.

'Really? Dylan?'

'Said his middle name was Lucius.'

'That was my idea.' He nodded. 'Bijou was against it, but I put my foot down.'

'Huh. Thanks.'

'He has three middle names,' Glyn said. 'So don't go getting a big head.'

'Too late,' I replied.

He was munching his last taco. He gazed at me as he chewed. 'You know, Lucius, Bijou is a wonderful woman. But she's not forgiving. She really knows how to hold a grudge. I suppose she's like you in that way.'

Here we go, I thought. 'See, Glyn: here's what I don't get about this writer's block of yours. It's a superhero movie. A sequel, at that. How hard can it be?'

Glyn pushed his empty plate away and cleared his throat. 'Ah,' he said. 'That old chestnut. Not being funny, Lucius, but I take pride in my work. You wanted to make art; I wanted to make movies. But just because something makes a profit, doesn't mean it's a worthless piece of shit.'

'Don't see you winning any Oscars,' I replied, downing the last of my drink. 'You wrote the first two easily enough, right? What's so difficult about this one?'

'Well, I wrote *Marshal Eagle* from our outline, yours and mine.'

'You did? Never saw it.'

'You never . . . ?' He sighed again. 'I suppose that makes sense. Christ, you're an obstinate prick.'

255

'And the second one?'

He turned his face to the ocean. A school of surfers sat on the flat water a few hundred yards out, waiting for a break. '*ME2* just seemed to flow, you know? I suppose I was riding the success. It felt liberating then . . . But now? Now it feels like a burden.'

'How's that?'

He blinked. 'I have a wife, two kids, an elderly mother and a billion-dollar franchise, Lucius. "With great power comes great responsibility."'

'Voltaire?'

'*Spider-Man.*'

'Huh. Abby said it made three hundred million.'

He shook his head. 'A billion and change, mate: three hundred domestic for *Marshal Eagle*, almost four for *ME2*, plus global box office. For some reason they bloody love it in China. That's part of the problem. I have to write two scenes set in Hong Kong and a part for a Chinese pop singer who can't act for toffee! Remember I used to tell you we'd do one for them, one for us?' He slapped the table for emphasis, his face full of feeling. 'You remember that?'

'Of course I do.'

'Well, now I've done three for them. And that's not counting my passes on *Deadbolt 2* and *3*, or the punch-up I did for *Axeman: Fires of Hell.*'

Glyn and I were each other's only link to our transatlantic past, and we'd long ago come unmoored. I'd always assumed that I was the ship – but maybe I was the shore, after all. 'So why don't you write a project of your own?' I said. 'Make an indie. Do a Kickstarter campaign. What about that miners'-strike thing?'

'*Black Country?* What, and remortgage the house? Pay for the craft service myself? Take it to Sundance and open it in seven bloody theatres? I think you've overestimated my financial clout, Lucius. This isn't the '90s. They're not handing out million-dollar paycheques for bloody spec scripts. I am an indentured servant of the studio. My car is a lease. I'm mortgaged up the bloody backside. Bijou pays the daycare fees with the money from the boutique!'

He snatched up his margarita and drained it in about four seconds, spilling plenty of it on his smock. 'That reminds me,' he said. 'I don't have any cash on me, so you're paying for lunch.'

It was almost five p.m. by the time we got back to the border at Tijuana, and the wait for the crossing looked to be at least an hour. Cars sat bumper to bumper across a dozen lanes, edging patiently towards America in the dog-day afternoon. Not for the first time, I kicked myself for never having updated the Bronco's a/c. Glyn was still hungry, so I gave him twenty bucks to fill up from the food carts that trundled among the gridlocked vehicles. Within several minutes he'd accumulated a bowl of Tostilocos, two lengths of grilled sweetcorn, a bag of churros and a six-inch plastic Jesus, which he set on the dashboard in front of us. I fanned myself with the road atlas.

'So, you work in antiques now?' he said, nibbling at his corn. 'That vintage furniture store in Los Feliz?'

'How did you know?'

'Abby,' he said. 'She lets me know when she hears from you. I've thought about popping in once or twice. Restrained myself.'

'Huh.'

'I almost envy you, you know. No stress. No burdens.'

'Don't patronise me, Glyn.'

'You happy?'

'What kind of question is that?'

'Pretty simple one, I reckon.'

'Are you?'

'I should be, shouldn't I?'

The margarita had gone straight to his head. Glyn never could hold his drink, which, given his Welsh heritage, made him something of a genetic anomaly. He eyed me, clumsily excavating yellow scraps of sweetcorn from his fancy dentalwork with one of the toothpicks from the restaurant. 'Maybe you'd have handled it better than I have,' he said. 'Success. You Kluges come from money.'

'We left it behind a long time ago,' I replied.

'I'm not being funny,' he said, wagging the toothpick at me. 'But for all your posturing, for all those so-called "artistic principles" of yours, I'm pretty convinced you never really cared about superheroes one way or the other. No, no, no: I've thought this over a lot, Lucius, and I think all that bollocks about how much you hate superheroes is just an excuse. Maybe you've used it so many times now, you've started to believe it.

'But I think what really bothered you was that some hack director might come along and bugger up one of your precious bloody screenplays, or some critic would shred it and nobody would see it – or *everybody* would see it. You love making things, same as me. But the thought of them getting out into the world? It terrifies you. You tell yourself you made this noble choice to be a failure, but really you were just too scared to succeed. You bottled it. That's what I think.'

'Whatever you say, Glyn.'

'It's what Bijou thinks, too.'

'Huh. Why am I not surprised?'

A gap opened up ahead. I started the engine and pulled the Bronco forward another ten feet. Glyn looked near-hysterical, as if he might teeter into laughter or tears. His eyes were dinner-plates.

'I'm bloody serious. Maybe you were *right* to be scared! Maybe you had the right bloody idea! Fat lot of good it did me, eh? I'm about to fail spectacularly – only now, everyone's watching. Everyone's bloody watching!'

He began to moan and massage his temples. 'Ah, Christ! Lucius, I dunno what's *wrong* with me,' he said. 'Do you think I might be having some sort of slow-acting nervous breakdown? Same as you?'

'FUCK!' I shouted suddenly, involuntarily — a sulphurous burp of rage — and I thumped the steering wheel with the heel of my palm. 'Fuck you, Glyn! I did NOT have a *fucking* nervous BREAK-DOWN! Fucking *arsehole*. Shit. FUCK! Why does everyone keep *saying* that? Where did this BULLSHIT *come from?*'

If you'd been idling in the next lane at that particular moment and happened to glance to your right, you would have seen me, cursing loudly and repeatedly as I assaulted the wheel, and Glyn in his grey smock, moaning and gurning, and you would have understandably assumed that we'd escaped not from a writers' retreat, but from a mental institution.

After a minute or so, the madness abated and we both just sat there breathing heavily, until Glyn said: 'So . . . did you ever go to a therapist about it?'

That was enough for me. I cut the engine again and exited the Bronco, anxious to inhale new air. Glyn pursued me, trotting around the jeep until we came face to face. I had to fight back the tears that had welled unexpectedly, inexplicably. He gripped my shoulders and I made to shove him away, but there was no fight in me. It was too damn hot.

'Wait,' he said. 'Lucius, I'm sorry. I'm sorry. Just listen. Listen to me for a second: I don't care that you wanted to quit the writing, okay? It bothered me at the time, sure — and maybe you could have been a bit more bloody *graceful* about it . . . But I don't care about losing my *partner*. Alright? I care that I lost my *friend*. I'm only saying. I don't feel guilty — about my career, about Bijou — I don't feel guilty. But I am *sorry*. You should have been a better friend, Lucius. We both should. Don't you think, eh . . . ?'

I realised then that we were following the script Glyn had written for this confrontation. He likes a happy resolution; I've always preferred to leave things ambiguous, or on a down note. I looked at the sky. I looked at the ground. I looked at the car. I looked at Glyn, looking at me. I looked at the time.

'Damn,' I said.

'What is it?' Glyn replied.

'My friend Raúl has a show tonight,' I said. 'I'm going to be late.'

It took us until six p.m. to get across the border, and then I headed for LA like a small-town girl chasing a dream. Some combination of the heat, the margaritas, the churros and the yelling had given us both headaches, so we were silent as far as Oceanside. Glyn had dozed off in the passenger seat, but when I couldn't find anything I liked on the radio, I poked him awake again. He shuddered into consciousness, taking a moment to remember where he was, and why.

'Tell me more about the script,' I said.

'What? The miners'-strike thing?'

'No, *Marshal Eagle 3*. What's the sticking point? What's so terrifying about page sixty-one?'

'Ach, you'll think it's stupid,' he replied, still bleary. 'I don't need another of your declinist lectures, Lucius.'

'Try me.'

He thumbed his eyes. I guessed his contact lenses were giving him gyp.

'Alright, then,' he said. 'If you insist. I have a bad-guy problem.'

'A bad-guy problem?'

'We used up all the iconic *Marshal Eagle* supervillains in the first two movies. Packed 'em in, to be honest: Shaman, Prairie Dog, The Barkeep. And Pathogen, and Flintlock. Originally we planned to have Rattlesnake be the main villain in *ME3*, but now the studio wants to keep him in the bag for the *Peacemaker* spin-off.'

'The Peacemaker?'

'He was in *ME2*. Went down a storm. He's a biker-gang fella – kind of an antihero, but he becomes Eagle's ally. Did you not even watch the trailer . . . ?'

I shrugged. Glyn sighed.

'Never mind. The point is, now we're left with the lesser-known villains from the Thunder catalogue. So Boxcutter and Carbomb are already in *Deadbolt 3*. Oh, and of course we're saving up The Wraith to be the big bad in *The Ultras*. I was first choice to write that – but now who knows, eh?'

' "Ultras"? You're really losing me here, Glyn.'

'*The Ultras*,' he said, growing impatient. He counted names off on his fingers: 'Marshal Eagle, Deadbolt, Axeman, The Peacemaker, Hummingbird and Rock-Face. And Hummingbird is sort of a love interest for Marshal Eagle in *ME3*. Should have mentioned that.'

'Okay. But what's your *specific* bad-guy problem? Come on, don't be shy.'

'Alright, alright. So now the baddie in *ME3* is this boyo named Carrion Crow. You heard of him?'

'What do you think?'

'No, of course you haven't. Well, look, he's got this wonderful origin story. I'm doing that as a long pre-credits sequence, you know? It's really bittersweet ... Don't sneer, Lucius. I'm serious.'

'Okay, I'm listening.'

'Well, the studio *always* wants to raise the stakes. Flood Manhattan. Flatten Paris. Burn Tokyo. End-of-the-world stuff. So that it plays in China. This time I wanted to tell a human story, about Carrion Crow. But I can't seem to get from an intimate Act One to an apocalyptic Act Three. You see?'

'Huh. Yeah, I guess. So tell me this origin story, then.'

'You're not really interested though, are you?'

'Well, what else are we going to talk about?'

The sun was setting on our left, its last pastel beams glinting on the cars ahead. I flicked on my headlights. Glyn composed himself, collecting his thoughts as if for a studio pitch. And then he began.

31

We made it to the Lo-Ball on La Brea with minutes to spare. The theatre was at the back of the venue, behind a rowdy cocktail bar. The girl at the box office said it was a sell-out, but she found my name on the guest list with the promised plus one, so Glyn and I snuck into the stuffy auditorium and, by the glow of my phone, found the last two unoccupied seats up beside the control booth.

The stage was small and had a flat wooden backdrop wallpapered to look like bare bricks. The seating was on a steep rake, with about enough space for 150 people. It was too dark to make out many faces, but the room was full and the crowd fidgety. I felt pretty sure the big man a few rows from the front, ruining the show for the poor small folks behind him, was Sasquatch Pete.

The emcee was onstage, holding a scrap of notepaper where he'd scribbled some prototype jokes. His schtick elicited little more than low chuckles, and he seemed in a rush to get through the material. The pockets of dead air swelled my anxiety; I was fatigued by the mere thought that my partner might bomb, and that I would be forced to endure it. I needed the loo, but it was too late: the seatbelt light was switched on and the plane was lifting off. I heard the emcee yell his name – 'Raúl *Gupta*!' – followed by a surprisingly fervent round of applause.

Raúl appeared from the wings in full, unbridled hipster: combed moustache, buffed trainers, snug logo T, Ray-Bans dangling from his crew-neck collar. He was carrying Burgers, whom he deposited on the bar stool beside the mic stand as if the dog were a ventriloquist's dummy. People were already chortling. I glanced over at Glyn, who wore a tiny frown, puzzled but not resistant to the prospect of being amused. Raúl plucked the mic from the stand and paused for a moment, soaking up the atmosphere, letting the laughter ripple and sway.

'So, my dogsitter cancelled at the last minute,' he said, and paused again for the audience to hoot. Burgers just sat there, sphinx-like. My nerves began to dissipate. Raúl's delivery was unhurried, his calm in the spotlight was compelling.

'This is Burgers. He's a French bulldog. Yes, ladies – he's adorable. I noticed. But you oughta be aware this dog is half poop. Okay? Twenty-five per cent fur, twenty per cent saliva, five per cent eyeballs – fifty per cent faeces.'

That was the icebreaker. Now Raúl began to roam the stage.

'So I totalled my car a while back,' he said. 'That was a bummer. But you should see the other guy. It was a cyclist. No, I'm kidding. I'm kidding. It was a single-vehicle collision. Nothing injured but my pride. And my phone wasn't damaged, so, y'know, I finished writing my text afterwards.

'But since then I've been taking a lot of Ubers. I love Uber. It's like *Uber*, but for taxicabs. Y'know, one thing I love about Uber: they can always use the carpool lane. Tell me, is there anything more dispiriting than an empty carpool lane at rush hour? Empty carpool lane, then five regular lanes, bumper-to-bumper – which means every single one of those drivers is alone. A-*lone*. LA, man . . .'

He sighed extravagantly, riding the crowd's amusement as it swelled and then subsided. 'Have you ever noticed, like, one in every three Uber drivers here is an actor? Lotta actors driving Ubers. Lotta actors driving Ubers. I mean, who's left waiting the tables at Dan Tana's? Couple weeks ago – I shit you not – my Uber driver tells me he had a speaking role in *Fast Times at Ridgemont High*. I looked him up on IMDb. It was true!

'*Fast Times*. That was a good movie, huh? Who else is in that movie? Sean Penn, right? Forest Whitaker. Forest Whitaker! The guy won an Oscar. Penn, he won two! Sean Penn has *two* Oscars, and he married Madonna. Meanwhile, his co-star? He's driving me to Target to buy Oreos and a new shower curtain. It's okay, though. No, it's okay – I rated him five stars.

'I think that's why actors love Uber. Spend a year making a web series, all you get is three hundred YouTube views and some constructive criticism from your college roommate. But drive a guy from here to Santa Monica in under thirty minutes? BOOM. Five-star review. "Best. Ride. Ever."'

You could boil an egg by his comic timing.

'Anyway, thanks for coming. I'm Raúl Gupta. You can probably tell by the name that I'm originally from the Valley . . .'

I remembered the first time I'd heard Glyn guffaw, across a crowded Oxford playhouse during some third-rate student Stoppard; back then, I couldn't tell whether it was the quality of the play or the crappiness of the production that he found so hilarious. He started laughing now as if his life depended on it, laughing like a pantomime villain, laughing as if he hadn't laughed in a really long time. I didn't laugh so much – but I'm a tough crowd.

'My parents still live up there, in Encino,' Raúl was saying. 'Nice neighbourhood. They chose it for the schools. Naturally, Dr Gupta couldn't be happier that his oldest son is pursuing a career in comedy . . . My mother is second-generation Mexican and, let's be real, she's getting kinda worried about the fourth generation – in that there isn't one. Working on it, Mom!'

When Raúl finished his set, Glyn and I retired to the bar, where I spotted Hal Green sipping a Coke alone in a corner booth and almost took pity on him. But we were quickly accosted by Abby Musker, who emerged from the throng dragging Raúl behind her. She yanked Glyn into a hug.

'Abby,' Glyn said. 'What are you doing here?'

'Lucky texted me,' she said. 'I wanted to see you. What's with the outfit?'

Glyn was still wearing his grey smock and sandals. He looked like an extra from *Ben-Hur*. Abby didn't wait for an answer.

'But what about this guy, huh?' she said, gesturing at Raúl, who had Burgers under his arm. 'So *funny*! You guys caught his set?'

'Yeah,' said Glyn. 'Good job, mate. You were spectacular.'

'Aw, thanks,' Raúl replied. 'It's Glyn, right?'

'Hang on.' I looked from Abby to Raúl. 'Do you guys know each other?'

'We just met,' said Abby. 'But I want Raúl to try out in the writers' room for Seth's new sitcom. He's got such a fresh voice. I loved that bit about "Why doesn't Will Smith do raps for his movies anymore"; didn't that just *kill* you?'

'You're going to rep Raúl? Who the hell is *Seth*?'

'Well, sure I am,' she said. 'Can you believe he didn't have representation already? I cannot wait to hear your podcast, Raúl. I'm going to download it now for the drive home.'

I turned to Raúl. 'You have a *podcast*?'

'This guy.' Raúl hooked a thumb at me. 'Never listens, does he?'

Glyn and Abby both had a good snigger at my expense. I may have deserved it. Abby said the drinks were on her and led Glyn off to the bar. She was probably trying to sign him, too. Well, better her than Todd. I nodded at Raúl.

'So – you think you're funny, huh?'

'I have my moments,' he grinned.

Raúl was soon surrounded by a small flock of admirers, and Abby made it her business to shepherd them. She kept a steadying hand on Glyn, too, as if he were a loose manuscript whose pages might blow apart in a passing breeze. I watched them – my friends – through the bottom of an Old Fashioned glass, and tried the best I could not to begrudge them their future successes. I almost managed it.

You want to know the truth? Or part of it, anyway. I was bred to think of myself as special. Honourable, lucky, clever. I grew up convinced of my own capacity for brilliance. Would you believe, it was only when Glyn and I were getting to work on our treatment for *Marshal Eagle* that it finally occurred to me: I was just another hack. And I couldn't hack being just another hack.

At last I put Glyn in a taxi to the Chagall and advised him not to go home to Bijou until he'd fortified himself with eight hours' sleep and a pancake breakfast. He thanked me for my help with the script, not that he'd really needed it. He just needed a sounding board. A straight man. Maybe that's all I was ever good for.

'How am I going to look her in the eye?'

'Don't ask me, Glyn. You're the one she married. Remember?'

'Bloody hell, Lucius,' he said, standing in the car's open door, his rucksack slung over his shoulder. 'I just realised: I don't even have your number.'

'You sure you want it?'

'Of course! You should come to the house for dinner.'

'I don't know. Bijou—'

'Ach, she'll get over it.'

But would I?

'Tell you what,' I said. 'Why don't you come find me at the shop sometime? You know where it is.'

He smiled resignedly and clapped me on the shoulder. 'Okay, mate,' he said, as he backed into the car. 'Okay.'

I'd planned to slope off quietly while nobody was paying attention, but as I waited outside for the valet to bring me the Bronco, Cleo materialised beside me.

'Hey, Lucky. You ghosting?'

She'd worn a dress and pumps and some more of that sandalwood perfume, but all I wanted at that moment was to drive home, pour myself a nightcap and listen to some early Tom Waits. I felt as if I'd fixed a few old, broken things, and I needed to sleep on them before I started in on screwing up something new. Besides, I still hadn't figured out if or how I should tell her that she was probably owed her standard 30 per cent share of the $110k from *The Black Bird*.

'Yeah,' I said. 'Been a long day.'

'Raúl's pretty great, huh?'

'So he tells me.'

'You sure I can't talk you into one more drink?'

'I'm sorry, Cleo. Today really was . . . I'll tell you all about it sometime.'

'Will it take long?'

It was another warm night in Hollywood. The lights from the bar and the billboards and the passing traffic kept our shadows dancing in circles on the pavement. The jeep swerved to the kerb in front of us. I folded five bucks, palmed them to the valet, looked Cleo in the eye and said: 'Do you like Tom Waits?'

32

The dead lady's place was in an old part of Pasadena, an Italian-ate villa set back from the street behind a lawn the size of a golf course. I say *an old part of Pasadena*, but around here 'old' means last week. Where I come from, the very idea of America is still nouveau. Nobody wrote their great nineteenth-century novel in LA.

I followed the Habibi Estates signs up the looping driveway to the front door, where Cleo stood flanked by hydrangeas, awaiting the truck's approach. She looked as composed as she does every Sunday, in jeans and a tan blazer, her dark hair plump and loose, her folded arms cradling her tablet computer.

Pretty impressive, given that she'd crept out of my house somewhere in the small hours, and apparently found time since then to go home, sleep and scrub up before an early commute to supervise final preparations for the sale. I dragged my feet across the gravel towards her, grinning sheepishly. It was days since I'd even considered shaving, and I needed at least two more espresso shots to get me straight. I probably looked like Nick Nolte in a high wind.

'Hey, Sleeping Beauty,' said Cleo, handing me the tablet with a smirk.

I replied by clearing my throat. I had big hopes for this estate, and the inventory was impressive: silver by Schulz & Fischer of San Francisco, a selection of antique snuff boxes and a Hollywood Regency bar cart.

'Is Raúl coming?'

'I gave him the day off,' I said. 'Winslow is taking up the slack.'

I pointed back towards the truck, where Winslow was clambering down from the cab. He waved at Cleo, who waved back. I returned the tablet.

'Looks promising,' I said. 'So, you doing anything later? Like, for dinner?'

I owed her an evening out, plus that $33k commission I still hadn't mentioned.

'Think you can keep your eyes open this time?' she replied.

The last thing I remembered from the previous night was pouring my third Scotch and listening to 'Closing Time' as Cleo stood browsing my bookshelves for clues. I'd awoken on the sofa a little after dawn, my lap smelling of stale, spilled booze, to an empty cottage and two clean tumblers drying on a dish-towel by the kitchen sink.

'Maybe let's make it an *early* dinner?' I said.

In the end, I couldn't get a table at Jones on Santa Monica until eight-thirty p.m., but that suited me fine because I had another, prior appointment to keep beforehand. It was close to dusk as I slalomed the Bronco along Mulholland with a Habibi Estates packing box on the passenger seat and the *All Things Must Pass* reissue on the stereo, already wearing my date outfit: a fitted check shirt, short enough to leave untucked over my jeans and Chuck Taylors.

I still remembered the address, and I recognised the stocky totems on either side of the entrance as I turned down the slope into Frank Waggoner's empty driveway. Silence greeted the engine's last sputter; it's quiet in them Hills. A young Asian guy answered the door and offered to carry the box that was under my arm. But I held on to it as I followed him through the hall and down the spiral stairs into the redwood vastness of the living room, where the old man sat in an armchair by the hearth, cooled by the a/c but warmed by a crackling fire.

A large, ugly piece of fan art hung over the mantelpiece. It was a group portrait, a pastiche of Leonardo's *The Last Supper*, with Waggoner himself as Christ, surrounded by his superhero creations. Among them I counted Marshal Eagle, Deadbolt, Axeman and a handful of others in costumes of varying absurdity, whom I took to be the remaining members of the Ultras.

His joints creaked and snapped as he rose to greet me, but Waggoner still looked spry: slim, white-haired and dark-eyed, in a pale, anonymous polyester sweater and slacks. He still had that livid birthmark, too, edging from the confines of his collar like a gang tattoo threatening to sabotage a job interview.

'Mr Kluge. Well, this is a surprise. I was thinking: it must be almost ten years since we last saw each other.'

I shook his hand and held his gaze. 'And I'm very grateful that you agreed to see me at such short notice,' I said. 'Particularly given my behaviour last time.'

'Not at all, not at all. Water under the bridge. Besides, you've piqued my curiosity.' He gestured to the oxblood leather sofa. 'Sit down, sit down. Can I have Atsuo fix you a drink?'

'Thank you, but no. I can't stay long.'

'So I recall,' he replied, his black eyes glinting. He waved his assistant away. 'I'm told you have something for me from Martin's effects?'

'Sort of,' I said, sitting and placing the packing box on the coffee table between us. 'I'm afraid it's damaged, but not irreparably. I must admit I was surprised to learn you were the executor.'

Beyond the glass concertina doors at the back of the room, the sunset cast a salmon glow over the deck.

'You work in antiques now, I understand,' said Waggoner.

'That's right. It's a good fit for me – temperamentally speaking.'

'The quiet life,' he said, nodding. 'Well, shall we . . . ?'

He slid the packing box towards him, opened it and plunged his hands into the well of Styrofoam peanuts, frowning and

270

feeling for the object within. At length, he lifted it out carefully and set it on the table in front of him: the Ringmaster cookie jar. He looked it up and down, puzzled.

'It's a cookie jar,' I said.

'I see.'

'It's the Ringmaster, from *Dumbo*. The Disney movie. He was the bad guy.'

A spark of recognition flared in Waggoner's features, the small, frail glow of childhood nostalgia. 'Yes,' he said. 'Of course. I *do* remember. Gosh, do you know, I think I saw that movie in the theatre.'

'In 1941?'

'No,' he replied, tracing his fingertips over the glaze. 'No, it must have been a rerelease. The *Ringmaster*, you say? What a wonderful name for a villain.'

'I'm sure you're wondering why I brought you a cookie jar, Mr Waggoner. The truth is, I needed a reason to come and talk with you about my friend, Glyn.'

Waggoner leaned back and looked at me, a shade warier than before. I began to regret having declined his offer of a drink.

'Glyn Perkins?' he replied. 'Talented fellow.'

'Yes, he is. I don't know how much the studio keeps you up to date, but Glyn has been running a little behind on the script for *Marshal Eagle 3*.'

'Oh?'

'He's a perfectionist, you understand. I'm sure it's going to come together very nicely, but he had some difficulty incorporating the bad guy, Carrion Crow?'

'Ah,' said Waggoner. He crossed his spindly legs and sank deeper into the armchair, still visibly confused as to where I was driving the conversation. I hardly knew where it was headed myself – all I had to guide me was a hunch.

I pressed on: 'Glyn was telling me about the character, that he starts out as a Marine officer in Vietnam? He's updating it to

Afghanistan for the movie, but anyway. This guy, Carrion Crow –
only he's not Carrion Crow just yet – he's been brutalised by the
things he's seen in combat. And one day, he just snaps. Leads his
platoon into a village in VC territory and orders a massacre. They
level the whole place, execute women and children, torch their
homes.

'It's a scandal. A war crime. And afterwards, wracked with
guilt, one of the soldiers frags the officer in his foxhole – burns
him alive like they did those villagers. But the guy survives, with
horrific burns over half his body. He ends up as a subject in a
military experiment, where they pump him full of some sort of
crazy, superhuman serum that makes him more powerful than
ever . . .'

Waggoner held up a hand to stop me. His expression was grim,
his pallor grey, aside from the deep-purple blot below his jawline.

'I know the origins of Carrion Crow,' he said. 'I co-created him.
Are you telling me a story, or are you asking me a question?'

I hadn't felt quite this sober in forever. After Glyn had told me
the story of Carrion Crow, something about it niggled at me, an
itch beneath the skin. The scandal. The fire. The scars. It all
sounded somehow . . . familiar.

'That mark on your neck,' I said, trying not to stare at it. 'I
always assumed it was a birthmark. Maybe everyone else did, too.
But it's a burn, isn't it? You got it in the Crusader Comics fire in
'72. After you created the Black Bird with Marty Kann . . . You're
Freddy. Freddy Wroblewksi.'

He stared at me steadily. After a few seconds of weighted
silence, I lost my nerve and looked away to the smouldering
hickory logs in the hearth. When I glanced back again, Waggoner
was gazing at the fire, too. His face was a death mask, its deep
faultlines cast in bronze.

'Martin had a dark side, like many great talents,' he said at last.
'We were arguing that night – about the Black Bird, yes. He was
drunk, desperate to assign the blame elsewhere. He poured our

best bourbon over a stack of the latest issue and set it alight. But the fire blazed out of control. I tried to put it out . . .'

'Wait. Marty started the fire? I thought it was a fire-bombing.'

'Well, that's what we told the authorities,' Waggoner snapped. 'We had so much to contend with already. Crusader was ruined. Martin was devastated enough, without my subjecting him to a court case. I suppose it hardly matters now. Now that he's gone, I mean.'

'I was told there were protests. The Black Panthers?'

'Pah,' he scoffed. 'San Francisco in the '70s. People would have held a sit-in if the city changed the ferry timetable. Of course there were a handful of students with placards, a disapproving item in the *Chronicle*. But Black Panthers? A convenient boogeyman. The paranoid group-think of the comics community, I'm afraid. The truth is always more banal than the legend.

'Still, those placards were enough to unsettle Martin. He was a very sensitive character. Held me responsible for the whole affair – even though he was the one who drew the darned thing. Shame is a corollary of success, Lucius. But people deal with shame in different ways. I think regret is a wasted emotion. But Martin found it difficult ever to put things behind him.'

'You changed your name. Why didn't he?'

He pursed his lips. 'Martyrdom, I suppose. I preferred not to have the taint of that episode pursue me when I founded Thunder Comics. Although, of course, in a way I've been tainted ever since . . .'

He unpicked the second button on his shirt and tugged his collar loose to reveal the burn. It was clear the damning mark spread across his chest, perhaps further.

'I always did my best to help Martin,' he said. '*The Black Bird*'s notoriety gave it some value. I sold one of my copies at auction to help him out of financial straits. I found him work as a production illustrator on *Deadbolt* when he was in the doldrums again. The movie business does not reward human frailty. But God knows I did what I could, even when his bitterness got the better of him.'

History is written by the victors, I thought to myself.

'You stayed friends all this time?'

'I like to think so. Martin may have felt differently.'

'How come no one ever looked into your past?'

'I suppose they could have,' he replied. 'It wouldn't be so difficult to uncover, as you have amply demonstrated. But I have found that most people in this city are not as interested in the past as you appear to be, Lucius.'

'Huh. I bet *Deadline Hollywood* would be interested.'

He stiffened, gripped the arms of his chair and said, icily: 'I thought you said you wished to talk about your friend, not mine.'

'That's right. I trust you've been happy with Glyn's work on *Marshal Eagle*?'

'Very.'

'This delay with the script. It could leave him in hot water with the studio. I wondered, for old times' sake, whether you might put in a good word for him.'

I was never any good at making deals; that's what agents are for. But nothing is more precious in Hollywood than an idea, and now I had a controlling stake in a crucial intellectual property: the truth about the Black Bird.

'I have no influence over the studio's decision-making.'

'The way I was always given to understand it, Mr Waggoner, you're like the Queen of England: they don't bother you with the details, but if your signature's on it, then it's the law. Like I said, Glyn's just working out his ending. He'll get it done. But maybe you could remind the studio that you believe he's been vital to the success of the franchise. They value your opinion, surely?'

He tipped his head and smiled faintly. I took that as a yes.

'Do you know, Lucius: I don't think we ever finished our conversation about superheroes. People often ask me why there are so many comic-book movies now, and I'm still looking for an adequate answer. Besides the money, of course.'

'Can't help you there, I'm afraid.'

'Hmm. I did hear one compelling theory, which is that people want superheroes because there are no *real* heroes anymore. None of our politicians come up to snuff. Our business leaders, celebrities. They're small fry. They don't inspire. Where are the astronauts? The knights in shining armour? What does a hero even look like nowadays?'

If he was waiting for me to provide an answer, he'd be waiting a long time.

'Are you any more interested in superheroes than when we last met, Lucius?'

'Heroes are boring,' I replied, rising to leave.

I geed the Bronco back up the steep driveway and out onto Mulholland, swinging the headlight beams into the half-dark. From the Hills the city was a swarm of fireflies, each luminescent backside a life, still glowing. That view always puts me in mind of something Polanski once said: 'Los Angeles is the most beautiful city in the world – provided it's seen at night and from a distance.'

I had bought myself a pack of American Spirits, the first in months, and I readied a fresh smoke between my teeth as I descended towards Hollywood. Punched the jeep's cigarette lighter and waited for it to pop. Yeah, I know what you're thinking.

But a man can only give up so much.

ACKNOWLEDGEMENTS

My thanks to Jonathan Stewart, for screenwriting stories and studio notes. To Eric Berg, for advice on selling antiques and surviving bad juju. To Neil Burkey and Jon Digby, for motivational email chains and writerly camaraderie. To Honor Fraser, for a spot to spend some writing days away from it all. To Trevor Kann, who loaned me his last name and looked out for misplaced Britishisms. To Professor Ian Campbell Ross, who taught me 'Detective Fiction' and 'The Hero'. To Larry Ryan, for Red and Taco.

To everyone at Lutyens & Rubinstein and William Heinemann, for all they do – seen and unseen – on this author's behalf. But especially to my indomitable agent, Jane Finigan, for her patience and encouragement from across the pond, and to my editor, the estimable Jason Arthur, who trained another flabby first draft to be trim and beach-ready.

Lastly, to my daughter Peggy – who, like this book, was born in Los Angeles. If you weren't such a good sleeper, I'd still be writing it.